He stepped rapidly backward to retreat down the stairs. Too rapidly.

He felt something grab his shirt from behind. Something metal and sharp snagged at his shirtsleeve, slid icily along his side. A ripping, tearing sound as he lost his balance. He slammed back against the plasterboard.

Poking out from the wall, from between two cans of dried house paint, were the long, gleaming blades of the garden shears.

If he wasn't careful, his new home was going to kill him.

University Ghost Story

by

Nick DiMartino

Cover and Illustrations

by

Charles Nitti

ROSEBRIAR PUBLISHING
Lynnwood, Washington

This is a work of fiction. The characters in this book do not represent real people. Although real buildings, streets, restaurants and establishments appear in the story, their description and the incidents occuring in them are entirely fiction. Any resemblance to actual events or persons, living or dead, is entirely coincidental.

University Ghost Story
Copyright © 1997 by Nick DiMartino

Cover and illustrations © 1997 by Charles Nitti

Rosebriar Publishing
820 195th Place S.W.
Lynnwood, Washington 98036
(425) 776-3865

ISBN 0-9653918-1-7

Library of Congress cataloguing-in-publication data is available.

for

MIKE EGAN

wherever you are

Thanks to

Jolene Lennon, Robert Carlberg, Diane Mapes,
Jena and Kent Schliiter, Sherry Laing, Geoff Wright,
Antoinette Wills, Molly McGee, Roger Kim, Jill Tamane, Terri Tyler,
Judith Chandler, Stephanie Wolfe, Courtney Hudak,
Debbie Kilgren, Ruth and Paul Lewing, Pauline Twitchell,
Ken Collard, Jo Brodahl, Lois Holt, Rebecca Cooper,
Tasha Croydon, Nancy M. Robinson, D. J. Schreffler, Liz Fugate,
Anita Smith, Glenda Pearson, Audrey Morrill, Naomi Ruden,
Robin Williams, Jody Aliesan, Gabriel Mendoza,
Aaron Rabin, Chuck Nitti, Mark Mouser, Jonathan Day,
Mark Todd, and all the others

UNIVERSITY
GHOST STORY

CHAPTER ONE

Wednesday, December 11

1
"Nothing to Be Afraid Of"

Dr Veronica Glass was determined to find a place on the covered side of the parking garage. It was already getting crowded, even at that early hour on the last teaching day of Autumn Quarter. And yet — there was a slot magically reserved just for her, conveniently close to the escalator. She swerved into it with swift, efficient grace. At last something had gone right in her morning!

She turned off the engine and gathered her belongings from the seat beside her, then swung open the door of the white Volvo and climbed out. She was a tall, handsome woman in her early forties with straight black hair gone gray at the temples and cut short. She looked well-tailored, professional. She was wrapped up warmly in a black wool coat with a tasteful paisley scarf around her throat.

Juggling her briefcase with an armful of books, she was locking the door when she noticed a large mound of garbage by the front wheel of the car parked next to her. The unsightly lump was only partially visible beyond the fender. She went closer to make sure that none of the mess was going to dirty her car. It smelled like something spoiled. She nudged it with the end of her shoe, causing the pile to shift slightly. Due to the unnatural lighting in the underground lot, the unpleasant lump almost resembled a human body.

Though all the safety lights were blazing, though it was seven o'clock in the morning, the four cement levels of the parking lot felt isolated and vulnerable. In an hour cars would be nosing and swerving from every direction. At that particular moment, not another car was in sight.

The parking levels descended in staggered sections down the campus hillside, four feeble slabs of light in the December blackness.

1

Each level was supported by cement pillars with low ceilings and gray, anonymous walls. In spite of the best intentions, the lights cast unsettling shadows. Footsteps had an unpredictable echo. It was the place on the University of Washington campus that Dr Veronica Glass liked the least.

She was already in a bad mood, irritable, with mounting end-of-the-quarter stress. She had stayed up far too late the night before grading term papers, and still had far too many to go. She hadn't had time to finish her morning coffee. She was grumpy and tired. She certainly had no time to waste.

She had driven to campus early to continue working her way through the mound of term papers crowding her already-overburdened desk. Her office was on the third floor of Padelford Hall. The building's tiers of Arts and Sciences offices clung to the irregular cliff along the tree-lined eastern boundary of the university.

Tucked away underneath Padelford was the parking garage where Veronica currently found herself facing that unsightly pile of trash which so disturbingly resembled a corpse.

She stared at the lump against the wall, hesitating. She turned away to leave, then turned back toward the heap of rubbish. Better to know what it might be, to prove to herself that it was nothing more than urban debris.

It moved, with a slight rustling.

Veronica froze, not daring to make a sound, not alerting it to her presence, utterly alone with it in the hollow cement depths.

The heap of garbage shifted sluggishly.

Alive! It was alive. She couldn't ignore it. She couldn't walk away from a possibly injured person. She had some responsibilities as a fellow human being. She took a step toward the human shape. She tried to be ready for any sudden movement, to be braced for any possibility, but she was still caught off-guard when the heap of rags scrambled onto its feet.

A lanky young man in a torn green parka stared at her in panic. He wore a grimy thermal undershirt, with a hole the size of a silver dollar above his heart. His arms defensively clutched to his chest a bulging old grocery sack. The wrinkled brown bag was stuffed full of sheets of paper.

"Sorry sorry sorry," he said. "I was just sleeping. I won't hurt you. Don't be afraid. No offense. Not dangerous. Not dangerous at all. I'm not one of those psychos." He said the last word too loudly.

She took an abrupt step backward, and bumped into her car. She tried to breathe evenly, to harden the features of her face. "You have

Padelford Hall Parking Garage

no business being here," she said, trying to keep her voice firm and steady.

"No business at all," he said quickly. "Oh, I agree. I agree completely. No business. You're right. You're very right. You're absolutely right."

At first glance she took the gangly derelict to be in his late teens. He had boyish cheeks and a gaping slash of a mouth. Not until she saw the lines around his bulging eyes did she realize that he might just as easily be approaching thirty.

"Sorry to disturb you," he said. "I'm going. I'm harmless. But first let me give you this. Do you like poems? Honestly, yes or no, poems? You *do* like poems, don't you?" He smiled disarmingly. "I mean, everyone likes poems, when it comes right down to it. But how about you? I mean, doesn't a beautiful poem get you right here?" He pounded on his chest, then suddenly shoved a dirty piece of paper in her direction. She flinched away, out of reach. "No, go ahead, take it."

"No, thank you. Stay away from me."

"It's just a poem. You can have it."

"I've got all the poems I need."

"But you don't have *this* poem."

"No, thank you. And don't come one step closer."

"You do like poems, don't you?" He looked at her sadly, as though possibly his worst fear might be true, that maybe she was one of those dangerous, psychotic people who didn't like poems. "I mean, please, it's my poem. Most of it is perfectly clear. Except for maybe the fine print down at the bottom. Really, I think you might like it. You'll understand it. Here."

She reacted suddenly, instinctively. Taking a step backward away from the homeless man, she moved too quickly and tripped.

The parking garage lurched sideways. The cement floor slipped out from under her and struck her from behind. She was suddenly, horribly prone on the cold cement beside her car's front fender, her legs splayed out in front of her, gasping in shock, sucking at air she couldn't quite drag into her lungs.

The dirty young man crouched down beside the car, blocking her escape. He reached into his back pocket and produced a folded piece of paper and a pen.

His back propped against a hubcap, the sheet of paper spread across his knees, he huddled over and began furiously printing out a lengthy and complicated communication. His teeth were clenched, his spine tensely hunched, his eyes squinting with concentration,

4

scowling at the wall as though trying to decipher words in the concrete. His thinking was interspersed with bouts of sudden scribbling.

He glanced up and noticed her. "I hope you're not hurt. You fell over so fast I couldn't catch you."

He jotted down a last few words, sighed with relief, and looked up at her again. "Don't be afraid of me," he said with a smile. "You've got enough trouble being afraid of yourself."

Veronica rose cautiously to her feet, considering how to get past him. "I'm not afraid of you," she said, with as much conviction as she could muster.

"Nothing to be afraid of," he said.

Before she realized what he was doing, he took a step forward and gave her a light, brief touch on the hand, so gentle and unexpected that for a moment she actually forgot to jerk away from him. She didn't realize he'd given her the poem. It seemed to stick to her fingers, and a moment later it was crushed into the bottom of her overcoat pocket.

Scooping up her fallen books and briefcase, she backed away from him.

"Forgive yourself," he called after her. "Just live the best life you can. It's all you can do." He smiled. "It's all *I* do."

2
Mistletoe and Mountain

In her eagerness to get away from the homeless man as quickly as she could, Veronica veared away from the escalator, her usual route to her office, and hurried toward the north end of the parking garage, out into the struggling light of morning.

She failed to see anyone else approaching until she was confronted by a pair of wrinkled lips. The lips planted a big, unexpected kiss on her cheek.

She jerked away, about to scream, ready to hurl her books at whatever was attacking her.

A big, ribbon-wrapped sprig of mistletoe was thrust before her eyes, silver bell tingling triumphantly.

"Merry Christmas, Merry Christmas!" It was that irritating old French professor whose name eluded her at the moment, the one who was constantly indulging his "charming" Old World accent. The horny sixtyish import to the Romance Languages Department dangled the mistletoe above her as though it were an authorized excuse for rudeness. "The most beautiful woman in the English Department, but oh, she would be so much prettier if she could smile. Merry Christmas!" He scurried away from her like a gleeful child. "Merry Christmas!"

Grumbling, she continued up the cinder trail to the street.

"I see you're letting romance into your life," said an amused voice behind her.

Clarice Jackson, English Department secretary, came huffing and puffing toward her, striding like an African queen up the sidewalk. Her long red overcoat blew open at her sides. Though many years had passed since she'd been in shape, the handsome woman carried herself as though the extra pounds didn't show.

"Mistletoe!" said Veronica in contempt.

"I was a witness," said Clarice, solemnly raising her hand as though taking an oath before a judge. "That man sexually harrassed her, Your Honor." She took a second look at Veronica. "He really upset you."

"Oh, it wasn't him." She hesitated, then decided to tell. "It was — well, there was a homeless man down in the parking garage who just scared me."

"You've got to be kidding. Did he attack you?"

"No," she said lamely. "He was harmless. He was writing a poem, actually. I totally over-reacted, tripped and fell. He just startled the wits out of me."

"You should call Campus Police from your office."

"No, thanks. He's long gone by now, anyway. Besides, if my graduate students worked on their papers as hard as this guy worked on his poem, they'd all win Pulitzer Prizes."

"Well, if you're sure he's harmless," said Clarice. "So, how do I look? I've been walking to work every morning for a month now. It's cold and boring and I hate it, but I've lost five pounds."

With grim, firm strides, the two women made their way up the steep, winding sidewalk. On their right towered the cement blockpile of McMahon Hall dormitory.

"Started your Christmas shopping yet?" said Clarice.

"Please, not this early in the morning! We are getting far too close to my least favorite day of the year."

"My, my, my." Clarice took another look at her. "You make bah-humbug sound enthusiastic."

An attractive blonde girl across the street gave a cry.

"Professor Glass!" She waved an arm, and lunged between two slow-moving cars. "Professor Glass, I've got to talk to you."

Veronica smiled as pleasantly as she could at that hour of the morning as the sorority girl rushed up to her. "You missed your appointment yesterday, Bethany."

"That's just it!" cried Bethany White in dismay. "Everything's so out of control in my life. Do you realize the paper for your class is due on the exact same day as my feature article for *The Daily*, not to mention the Theta Chi dance? I mean, I'm swamped! Please, Professor Glass, I've got to have another weekend to finish my paper. That's all I need." She shook her healthy mane of blonde hair and smiled like a beautiful, trusting child. "Just the weekend. I'm really doing my best. Please."

"Bethany, the course requirements have been clear for over two months," said Veronica. "Your paper is due on the same day as everyone else's paper."

"But, couldn't you just give me a chance—"

"Bethany, you know my office hours. I have to be fair to everyone else. I expect your paper."

The unhappy sorority girl started to say something, faltered, and dropped away behind them as they continued up the hill.

"My!" said Clarice. "Integrity. I didn't think anyone suffered from that anymore. I just hope you won't get a rebuke from the Board of Regents. The English Department could get cut from the budget. You know whose daughter she is."

Veronica didn't seem to hear her. Instead she stopped dead in her tracks, staring out toward the water, peering through the winter-stripped branches of the trees, out over the parking garage. "Look at the mountain. Isn't it gorgeous?"

The silhouette of Mount Rainier rose up into a dawn-lit blur of clouds over Lake Washington. A belt of bright headlights on the floating bridge flickered across the shimmering water.

"I've got to think more about mountains. Mountains are worth thinking about. I can't let myself mope over Christmas and mistletoe and sorority girls with scheduling problems."

"Mountains, huh?" said Clarice. She squinted at the view, and shrugged. "A mountain is a mountain. Personally, I can look a lot longer at a nice-looking man. Whatever works for you, honey. If mountains are your thing, take a good look at that one, because it's a real beauty and you've got a long day ahead."

Clarice escorted her to the top of the hill. Morning traffic was slowly orbiting Stevens Way in its stop-and-start loop around campus. They dodged a jogging squadron of shouting R.O.T.C. students with rifles, and turned up the cement walkway into Padelford Hall.

"Isn't this a bit early, even for you?" Clarice paused before the door of the English Department office. "Two hours before your first lecture?"

"Two hours to lock myself into my office, chain myself to my desk, and grade papers," said Veronica grimly.

Clarice winked. "Remember that mountain."

3
Last Lecture

"—so, as we've seen this quarter, it's no surprise that the Victorian era became the Golden Age of the British ghost story," said Veronica to her class of forty damp, rumpled students. She paced back and forth across the cramped front of the lecture room on the third floor of Thomson Hall, her ivory cashmere sweater and wool slacks still relatively chalk-free. "The greatest Victorian thinkers found themselves on the edge of the ultimate scientific breakthrough of the human race. The final solution to the mystery of death. And although no final answer—"

Before she could reach the conclusion of her last lecture of the quarter, Bethany White's arm shot up, swaying back and forth urgently in the air. Veronica ignored it. She would finish her lecture first.

She spoke on, looking over the girl's head, out through the third floor windows into the rain. It had been drizzling for the last hour. Through the sparkling drip from the evergreen branches she could see the bright windows of Padelford Hall on the other side of the parking lot. She spoke to the lights in the far windows. She spoke to the rain. She spoke to the girl in the back row, the one student who possibly cared. She blurred her vision on Bethany's waving, intrusive arm. There was no doubt in her mind what question the sorority girl was so anxious to ask. Quarter after quarter, some things never changed.

"Can you tell us what will be on the test?" blurted out Bethany, unable to wait.

Veronica sighed. For Bethany, like most of her students, the official grade on the transcript was the thing that counted. One of the great disillusionments of her teaching career was that most of her students would never really care about the subject of her passion.

"Yes, I was just getting to that, Bethany," she said. "The final exam will be an essay question." She stepped over the sprawling legs of the young man in the front row. He was pretending not to notice that he was in her way. "Mr Wates, would you kindly pull in your legs? It's better for your posture, and better for my pacing."

The class laughed.

Tyler Wates grinned at her, beaming his most charming smile. "Sorry, Professor Glass!" He patted down his baseball cap securely backwards on his head, and reluctantly drew in his legs. The silver cross he wore on a chain around his neck flashed as it slid over his chest.

She ignored him. She had to. The troublesome young man was her tenant, as well as her student.

"To answer the question on your final exam," she continued, "you'll have to draw on everything you've learned this quarter. A truly frightening thought."

More laughter from her students.

"That includes a working knowledge of Spiritualism, the Society for Psychical Research, and so on. I expect an intelligent analysis of the question, which will be something like this." Pens suddenly hovered anxiously over paper, gripped in tense fingerholds. "The editor of your Norton textbook—" The buzz of terrified penpoints. "—calls M. R. James and Henry James the two masters of the ghost story."

She paused, giving their furious scribbling time to catch up. Her glance inadvertently darted toward the young man in the front row. Tyler was staring at her again. She quickly looked away, and continued pacing from one end of the classroom to the other. "But what about Edith Wharton?" Pens hissed over paper in a flurry of renewed anxiety. "Wharton added an American tragic vision to the ghost story genre. True or false. Discuss."

"Professor Glass, could you repeat that?" wailed Bethany White in desperation. "Slowly, please."

"Certainly," said Veronica. "But what about Edith Wharton?" And so on, slowly, through to the end. She was waiting for the class to finish writing when she noticed the upturned face of thirteen-year-old Angela Harrow in the back row.

Angela was in her second year of the Early Entrance Program. She was shy and brilliant, wide-eyed with freckles, rosy cheeked, with long chestnut hair tumbling down over her shoulders. She shared little with anyone, being seven years younger than most of her fellow students. She sat alone in the back, and seldom spoke. But she had nerve enough to be there, brains enough to compete, determination enough to excel in a junior-level class. Her midterm essay had been arresting for its unexpected insights and opinions.

"And what about Edith Wharton?" began Veronica for the third time, slowly, thinking Angela needed it repeated.

"What about Shirley Jackson?" interrupted Angela. "You never mentioned Shirley Jackson all quarter. I kept waiting for you to say something about her," she blurted in a quiet burst of deep feeling. *"The Haunting of Hill House* is the best."

She didn't talk in class often. When she did, it was always a short, passionate eruption.

"Well, Angela, you're right, Shirley Jackson is a very major name in the field," said Veronica, unable to conceal a smile of delight. "And her book is a milestone. She's just too modern to be included in this course. But her book uses all of the Victorian traditions. You've read so much, Angela."

From the look on Angela's face, she had struck some kind of nerve. Being the last day of class seemed to give her extra courage to speak. "I love books, Professor Glass," she said with ardor. "I love reading. More than anything. Books are the best things in the world. I read *The Haunting of Hill House* when I was eleven."

"You must have been terrified."

"It scared me so bad I couldn't sleep."

For a single moment they smiled at each other across the classroom, the two of them in complete understanding. Then the bell rang, students surged to their feet in a rumble, and their brief exchange ended.

4
Woman in the Library

Angela Harrow loitered in the open doorway, listening to Professor Glass answer the questions of the students crowding around her desk. She loved Professor Glass, loved her polish and confidence and smartness, the way she always knew exactly what to say.

At that moment her favorite teacher glanced up and noticed that she was lingering after class. Angela felt her cheeks flush. She was going to look ridiculous, like a child. Hefting her backpack up onto her shoulders, she darted out of the classroom .

Collar up around her neck, shoulders hunched forward, earphones strapped onto her head, Angela pattered recklessly down the stairs from the third floor. She was listening to Madonna on her headset. The other kids in the Early Entrance Program teased her about her musical taste. She didn't care. Madonna was the best. Besides, she wore the CD-player mostly as a disguise, to keep people from trying to talk to her.

Hurrying out the door, she left Thomson Hall behind her in a beeline through the rain toward the libraries. Her eyes were fixed straight ahead, her forehead creased in a forbidding scowl.

Darting under the bridge of the library arcade, she bumped through the turnstile and trotted up the big white staircase, making her way through Allen Library North. A long, yellow hallway connected up with the old part of Suzzallo Library that she liked best. On the far side of the lobby, she headed down an old, curving staircase of worn bronze tiles, following a yellow strip of tape on the floor through a maze of rooms filled with books to a last reading-room cut in half by wire-grid fencing and a "Staff Only" sign.

There was no going beyond the wire-grid.

It was her favorite place to study, down in the belly of the oldest part of the library, usually very quiet, seldom sought out by other students. The only sound that afternoon was a distant creaking which sounded like the wheel of a library cart but was probably just the ventilation.

She had the room to herself. Well, not quite.

She didn't notice the other woman until long after she'd turned off Madonna and pulled out her paperback collection of Edith Wharton stories. Busily jotting down notes, preparing for the final, she didn't hear her come down the stairs. She felt what seemed like a chilly breeze from outside, and glanced up just as someone quietly passed by her study carrel. A cautious moment later, Angela furtively glanced in that direction.

A tall woman in a weathered gray raincoat was standing at the end of the aisle, watching her. She was gaunt and bony, with washed-out features. Her hair was pulled back severely into a bun that had grayed to a nondescript hue. She betrayed no expression. She just stared.

Angela immediately looked back down into her book, hiding behind it, pretending to be deep in thought as she turned a page she hadn't read. When she dared to look again, the woman had slipped out of sight behind the last bookshelf. Since there was no other way out of the room, Angela knew she was still there, prevented from going any farther by the wire-grid fencing. She listened. No sound of books sliding back and forth on the shelf. The woman didn't make the slightest noise. She waited with increasing impatience for the woman to leave. Not a movement, not a rustle from the other side of the bookshelf.

Angela found herself becoming nervous. What was the woman doing? She became so curious she could no longer concentrate on her studies. Pushing back her chair, she rose to her feet and walked slowly down the aisle, past shelf after shelf, toward the last row before the wire-grid where the woman had stepped out of sight.

Pretending to be looking for a particular book, running her finger thoughtfully over the yellow number-tags on the book spines, Angela rounded the corner of the last bookshelf.

No one was there.

5
Elevator

For a moment it looked as though Angela Harrow was waiting after class to ask her something. The next time Veronica glanced in the girl's direction, however, she was gone.

Which was just as well. Veronica felt utterly depleted. The day was finally over! She wouldn't have to deliver another lecture until January sixth. She fled from the classroom, tugging loose from her last clinging students and their persistent questions, hurrying down the hall toward the staircase.

She edged and crabwalked down two long, crowded flights of stairs, bumped and jostled and nudged through a river of student backpacks, textbooks, dripping overcoats, jabbing umbrellas. Then, with a last shove, she was out the doors, for a quick run through the sprinkling rain, dodging two kamikaze students on bicycles coming up from behind. She skirted around the edge of Thomson Hall, cutting through the trees and across the parking lot toward the sanctuary of Padelford Hall.

The concrete ramp leading up to the door into A-Wing was slick with rainwater. The door thudded behind her. She pushed the elevator button. She could hear the cage inside groaning to a stop in response. A rumpled, unshaven graduate student nursing a styrofoam cup of cold coffee wandered out of the elevator as Veronica hurried in. He turned to stare at her with a squint of concentration, as though trying to memorize her face for his oral exams.

With a merciful whoosh, the elevator doors thudded shut, sealing her into the privacy of the humming, whining, rumbling black cube ascending toward her office.

That elevator! The memories were so thick, the years seemed to dissolve—

Twenty years ago, those same elevator doors had thudded shut on Veronica Cella, an attractive young graduate student, standing in the elevator next to Dr Samuel Glass, the lean, handsome head of the English Department. The moment the doors closed, the two of them had lunged for each other, clutching in a passionate embrace. It had been their private rite, their secret joke, the sudden, stolen elevator kiss.

Their affair during the last years of Sam's marriage had led them both to the altar after his divorce. Seven years ago, karma had caught up with her, and she had discovered her husband in bed with one of his graduate students.

She even knew the student. She sort of liked her.

Sam was long gone out of her life now, snatched up by the University of Chicago for some ridiculously high offer, stripped of his piousness and one of his two houses. Somehow Veronica emerged from that legal jungle with ownership of the old Glass family residence. She had moved there seven years ago, when she'd been hired onto the faculty of the UW English Department. She had lived there ever since.

The house was six blocks off-campus, a pleasant walk in fair weather to her office and classrooms. The three-story classic had been built in 1917 by her father-in-law, Dr Samuel Simpson Glass, long-time Comparative Literature faculty member. She had taken over the top two floors of the house, converting the lower floor into two rentals, a one-bedroom apartment in front, a one-room studio in the rear.

Over the years, Dr Veronica Glass had become a familiar university figure. Her intelligence and sense of humor had made her the most sought-after lecturer in the English Department. She knew the campus well enough to read a book while walking from lecture rooms to libraries. She had a remote, chilly smile. She remembered the names of her students, but never encouraged them to be familiar.

Life had disappointed her. She had turned to her academic career with a fiery gusto that led to the publication of a series of articles on her passionate new specialty, the Victorian supernatural tradition. Her first book of literary criticism, *The Ghost Stories of Henry James*, had received a rave review in *The New Yorker*. She had become a professional. She had given up all hope of romance. She always kept very busy.

As the elevator rose toward her floor, Veronica stuffed her cold hands into the depths of her overcoat pockets. One hand encountered a crackling obstruction.

She pulled out a crumpled sheet of paper. At first it looked like a grocery list. Much of it was covered with microscopic scribbling. Several portions of the sheet, however, were printed in large, childish block letters.

No need to frown
Busy lady slow down
Love is near
Dont live in fear

Sure theres pain
It keeps us sane
Dont miss the bus
When it comes for us

She stuffed the poem back into her pocket, oddly disturbed, wishing she had never looked at it. She stared at the crack between the elevator doors, willing them to open.

6
Long Way Home

The tall woman in the raincoat was no longer there.

Angela returned to her library study carrel and pretended that it hadn't happened. There had been no tall woman in a raincoat. For another ten minutes she squirmed in her chair, trying to concentrate on Edith Wharton. She finally gave up and closed the book.

The disturbing incident had left Angela with a knot in her stomach and a vague uneasiness. The look in the woman's eyes! Angela was too nervous to continue studying there. She'd had enough of the library for one day. Gathering up her books and zipping them into her backpack, she followed the yellow strip of tape back out of the reading room, up the stairs, and out into the last of the gray December afternoon.

Looking down at the ground as usual, headphones in place, frowning as she walked so that no one would talk to her, she left the spires of Suzzallo Library behind. She hurried across the bricks of Red Square, weaving through the other students without noticing them, as though the campus were swarming with phantoms. Crossing the last grassy banks and parking lots, she set off toward the main street through the University District.

There, on the Ave, she finally relaxed. The sidewalks were crowded with the usual colorful assortment of students, street people, drop-outs, druggies, homeless, elderly, and the pierced-and-tattooed, with the added commotion of Christmas shoppers. Included were plenty of other disoriented, distracted young teens like herself. One more short, skinny teenage girl was scarcely noticeable.

She walked up the sidewalk slowly, looking in all the shop windows, inhaling the delicious odors from the numerous ethnic restaurants, reading newspaper headlines at Bulldog News, admiring the movie posters outside the Varsity Theater.

At the far end of the Ave, she crossed Ravenna Boulevard into Cowen Park. Past the baseball field and the swings, down under the 15th Avenue NE Bridge, Angela walked through the ravine just as she always did to Ravenna Park at the other end. She knew every bend of the cinder-and-gravel trail, every curve and twist of the creek.

And why shouldn't she know the ravine by heart? Ravenna Park was practically in her back yard. That was the only thing wrong with it. It was far too close to her home.

She was hungry and cold. Shadows were lengthening, darkening. She had no choice. She had nowhere else to go.

Reluctantly leaving the park behind her, Angela set off past the tennis courts and empty wading pool and across the alley. She kept her eyes focused downward on the squares of the sidewalk. She bobbed her head, pretending to listen to music she didn't hear.

She could see the house now, halfway down the short neighborhood street. Park Road was a trim, tidy strip of well-maintained old homes, a short residential street along the border of Ravenna Park.

Every December the street changed. Already the annual transformation had begun. The fence around the house on the corner was lined with a whole battalion of giant marching Nutcracker Princes. Wreaths had sprouted on doors. Giant paper snowflakes clung to the windows. Soon, on the grassy mound around which the street wrapped in a circular drive, would rise an enormous revolving centerpiece. One year it had been a giant jack-in-the-box. Another year it was Santa's gift-filled sleigh pulled by eight flying reindeer.

The entire neighborhood was preparing, ready to erupt into its annual blaze of holiday cheer. Every house would become a sparkling, twinkling outline against the black winter sky.

Every house except one.

7
Neighbor Girl

Too much reading had ruined the girl.

Mrs Fredericks had seen it happen from two houses down, watched that poor, awkward Angela Harrow growing up miserable, nose always in a book, always by herself, wearing that terrible radio over her ears.

Like she was right now.

That December afternoon Mrs Fredericks had decided to string the lights around the two big juniper bushes in the front yard, so she saw the girl coming home. With a book in her hand, of course! Mrs Fredericks was cold and stiff and her arthritis was acting up, but she was stringing Christmas lights anyway, some yesterday, some today, some tomorrow. She always liked to do her part to make Candy Cane Lane a success.

Not like some people.

The home of Raymond and Grace Harrow was always the problem. It was a little nicer than the neighboring houses, a little better maintained, more recently painted, a little classier, pricier. Just like Ray. He was a little flashier and wealthier than any of his neighbors. He greeted them all with a quick hello. He was always in a hurry. But did he have the Christmas spirit? Was he part of the neighborhood? Not one bit.

He worked for some fancy law firm downtown. He was a partner. Business was apparently booming. He was always on the go. So was Grace. She had become active in her church's Women's Guild. She was currently fund-raising chairperson and organizer of the annual scholarship auction. Grace was frequently seen coming and going, usually running slightly late. She'd been wearing more makeup lately, probably trying to hide how much she'd been crying.

And then there was the girl. She was something else. Smart as a whip, too smart for normal school. She was already going to college! But did she act smart? No, like she didn't have a brain in her head. Daydreaming as usual, off in her own world, she would have walked right past her if Mrs Fredericks hadn't said something.

"Do you think your father will decorate this year?"

She startled the girl back to reality.

"Hi, Mrs Fredericks. No, I don't think so."

"Well, I didn't think so, either, but it's always good to be hopeful. It's a crying shame. Your house being right in the middle of things."

"You know what he's like, Mrs Fredericks."

"Well, what I *don't* know is how he ever got such a nice little girl. He must know how to do some things right." She yanked apart a tangle in a long black wire of Christmas lights. "Not that I don't see his point of view sometimes. It's a lot of work. But it's only once a year. We should find out this weekend what the centerpiece will be."

The girl seemed to have other things on her mind.

Mrs Fredericks scowled as she untangled the long string of lights. "Well, you'd better get home before you're late for dinner. And take my advice, go play with your friends more. A girl your age shouldn't be alone so much. Reading all the time! You've got to stop reading so much, you'll wear out your eyes—"

8
A Carol in Padelford Hall

"Joy to the world!"

The first sound to assault Veronica's ears as the elevator doors whooshed open on the third floor of Padelford Hall was that tired old Christmas carol being vocally tortured by several of her colleagues in an office down the hall.

Veronica hated Christmas carols. Those hideously hopeful tunes reminded her of the first twenty years of her life when she'd had a sister to share her world. Of singing Christmas carols together with Stephanie, harmonizing in the back seat of the car, carolling on the neighbors' front porches, practicing in the basement, performing on the high school stage at St George's. Of memorizing song after song together, clowning around together, laughing together. Christmas carols would always remind her of one heartbreaking, unchangeable fact. The most precious human being in her life had been snatched away from her twenty years ago. They would never sing together again about silent nights and winter wonderlands. But those horrible carols would never stop. They would come back year after year to torment Veronica and make her cry.

It was enough to put anyone in a bad mood.

She hurried away down the twisting, angling hallway. Not for the first time, she pondered why the corridors of Padelford Hall were so uncomfortably irregular. There was always the sensation of not being able to see what lay ahead, just around the next bend. Of being lost to sight between one curve and the next. As she felt right now.

Footsteps were approaching down the hallway. No one was in sight yet. Veronica happened to notice a French movie poster on a passing door and stopped. The footsteps stopped. She continued toward her office. The footsteps began again. She spotted a pen on the floor, and stopped to pick it up. The footsteps stopped, too.

Whoever it was remained out of sight. Veronica listened intently. Nothing. She felt ridiculous and uneasy at the same time. She heard a footstep, then another. The footsteps were coming toward her. Again the footsteps stopped.

Veronica began to hurry toward her office.

The footsteps started again. A figure stepped into her path just as she rounded the turn. The little woman with wispy white hair was as startled as she was.

"Muriel!"

"Oh, my goodness!" exclaimed the elderly woman, clapping her hand over her chest. She stared up at Veronica through wire-rimmed glasses, her bright, blue eyes greatly magnified.

"I'm so sorry, Muriel, I heard footsteps. They kept stopping and starting."

"So?" countered the feisty old woman. "A senior citizen like me has to take a rest, now and then. I didn't use the elevator. I came up the stairs to get some exercise."

"Three flights? Muriel Rose, you never cease to amaze me."

"I saw your car down in the parking lot, so I decided to bring you this article — the one about Edith Wharton and Spiritualism."

"You're the most incredible librarian on this campus!"

"And the oldest," said Muriel. "And the busiest. And the happiest. See you tomorrow for lunch."

9
Slap

An enormous candy cane was already posted in Angela's front yard as a harbinger of the twinkling, electric festivities to come. The Lane's trademark five-foot candy cane, constructed of metal piping, had sprung up in every front yard on the street like a localized infestation of pesty weed. It was the Harrows' one concession to the holiday spirit. There would be no other.

Angela reluctantly climbed the short flight of stairs to the front yard and proceeded down the neatly-clipped walkway to the door. Both cars were home. The house was silent, the draperies pulled shut. She knocked. No one answered. She tried the doorknob. The front door was locked. She reached in her pocket. She'd forgotten her key again. How could anyone with half a brain forget her key so often? How could she possibly be as smart as her teachers said and still act like such a child?

Shifting her backpack off the sore spot on her shoulder, she walked around the side of the house to the back door. In the corner of the back porch was a spare key hidden in a flower pot.

That was how she found out they were fighting again.

She could see them through the kitchen window. Her Mom's face was a tear-drenched mess. They were shouting at each other, only a few feet apart. They had been fighting more and more often lately. They were both so angry they didn't see her outside the back door, standing silently on the top stair.

She couldn't turn away. She couldn't make her body budge. She watched them, their faces red, shouting in the ugly bright light of the kitchen. She pretended she couldn't hear what they were saying. She'd heard it often enough. Her mother's face was swollen with crying, her mouth ugly with screaming. Angela got tears in her eyes just watching her mother through the window.

She couldn't make herself knock and interrupt them. She was afraid to let them know she was there watching.

Her mother slapped her father across the face.

Her father slapped her back.

Angela shook with each blow. She watched wide-eyed, chewing at her lower lip. They had argued before, yelled and cried, but she had never seen them come to blows. Her brittle family world was cracking apart. A chill rippled through her body. Her cheeks became cold and white. Drops of sweat dotted her forehead.

Inside the kitchen, the glass fruitbowl perched on top of the refrigerator suddenly tumbled to the floor and shattered.

10
The One Who Can Tell You

"If anyone in the U. District can give you an answer," said the rumpled, white-haired man sitting beside him, "that man right there is the one."

He nudged Matthew Braddon with the worn-out elbow of his dirty jacket, and pointed toward the volatile figure who was orchestrating the contents of four black skillets with half a dozen ladles and gleaming knives, a pinch of this, a sprinkle of that, over the leaping, unpredictable flames of the grill.

Matt absent-mindedly raised a forkful of grilled chicken and spinach, spilling thick globs of peanut sauce on the rice below.

A fleck of sauce already dotted one lens of the glasses perched halfway down his nose. His thatch of thick, unruly brown hair was tousled, ignored. The denim jacket stretched across his back outlining broad, bony shoulders, a lean, hunched frame. The upturned jacket collar concealed most of his weathered, fortyish face.

Matt turned away from his neighbor to discourage further conversation, hunching farther over the gray marble counter. Outside a chilly December breeze whipped mercilessly up and down the Ave, stinging the first wave of Christmas shoppers, periodically sweeping into the restaurant through the constantly-swinging glass door, where it icily crept up his spine.

Thai Tom was packed. Other diners bumped Matt elbow-to-elbow on either side. Would-be diners waited behind him for his seat. The narrow, crack-in-the-wall restaurant was wedged into the heart of the University District. Across one wall stretched a handwoven tapestry of an ancient King of Siam with his attendants on a journey down the Bangkok River. Matt sympathized with the King. He, too, had undertaken a momentous journey. He had left the East Coast behind.

Sandwiched into the Thai diner, he passed the last few moments of his meal admiring the culinary acrobatics of the talented chef as he cooked and prepared three simultaneous, constantly-shifting and revolving entrees, slicing, chopping, tossing, stirring, and serving his eager customers. Seattle grunge music wailed accompaniment on a nearby radio. He noticed Matt's lingering look.

"Is the Swimming Rama too hot for you?" He pointed at the fork which Matt had forgotten to remove from his mouth. Matt did so.

"The Swimming Rama is incredible," said Matt. "But I was wondering — I'm sort of desperate. Maybe you can help me. Do you know of any place to rent near here? Apartment? Even a room? I'm not choosy, as long as it's not too expensive."

"Here in the District?" The cook chuckled. "Nobody has a chance renting a room in the U. District two weeks before Christmas." He vigorously agitated the sizzling contents of a huge black wok, then added something to the frying pan which caused the contents to blaze into steam. "You need a place right away?"

"I'm about to find out," said Matt. "I'm on my way to a call-back interview at University Book Store. I've got an appointment in—" He checked his watch nervously. "—in exactly eleven minutes. Here's hoping it's my lucky day. Books! I love working with books. This could be perfect."

"I've got a good feeling. You're going to get the job."

"If I do, that's it. End of old life, start of new life. I'm moving to the U. District. I'll work here, live here, start over. But I've got to find the right place."

"The right place is waiting for you," said the cook with a grin. He gave a stir on one side, a measured dash here, a sizzling splash there. "Who knows, maybe I can help. Write down your name, somewhere I can reach you—"

Matt's anxious scrawl crossed the inside cover of a matchbook he dug out of the ashtray, his name followed by "Silver Cloud Inn" and the phone number. He slid the matchbook back across the counter toward the Thai chef. The busy man glanced at it, smiled, then snatched up his chopping knife and the matchbook at the same time.

"Thanks," said Matt. "Merry Christmas."

"Merry whatever," said the chef with a grin. "Merry today, merry tomorrow. Every day is Christmas. We just aren't smart enough to know it." He seemed to have six arms in a blur of culinary preparation. He disappeared in a sizzling explosion of steam.

11
Vacancy

"Deck the halls with boughs of holly! Fa la la la la—!"

Veronica closed her office door firmly behind her. She didn't immediately turn on the lights. Her English instructor's office in Padelford Hall, that cramped little cell of activity, was so swollen with her ever-increasing book collection that there was hardly room for her. Wedged between the shelves, where books of all sizes were packed two deep, was a semi-operable desk, semi-visible under a mound of ungraded term papers. She wasn't ready to see those papers yet. She liked the office better in the dark.

Unnoticed, the door of her office slowly, cautiously swung open behind her. A hesitant hand reached inside, groping its way blindly toward the light switch.

Click. The book-crowded office blazed into existence. Veronica spun around with a gasp.

"Sorry to startle you." Clarice Jackson was poking her head into the office. "I gave up on knocking. Didn't you hear me?"

Veronica blinked at her. "You were knocking?"

"And you, my dear, were in a different world. I tried phoning you from the English office, but you weren't answering the phone."

"The phone?" repeated Veronica incredulously. "That settles it. I'm heading over to the HUB for an espresso. Care to join me?

"Espresso this late in the day? I've got three kids and a husband. That's enough stress waiting for me at home without caffeine. So, what's the problem?"

"Nothing."

"Yeah, right. That's why you've gone temporarily deaf." She sat down beside Veronica's desk. "Let me guess. You're thinking about somebody. Someone who isn't here to share the holiday with you?"

Veronica looked at her in astonishment. "How did you know?"

Clarice burst out laughing. "It's no secret, honey. Holidays do that to you. That's what holidays are all about. Come on, let's hear it." She poked and probed the unhappy story out of her friend.

"I ought to be used to her being gone after twenty years."

"You never get over something like that, hon, not completely," said Clarice, squeezing her hand when she had finished. "And nothing you do can bring your sister back. But nothing can ever take her away, either, not really. You'll never get her out of your mind. So she'll always be with you. Let me give you a little advice. Stop troubling over it. There'll always be pain there, no getting away from that. But don't forget the wonderful times together. The good Christmas memories, you hang on to them."

Their confidential talk was interrupted by the appearance of Tyler Wates in her office doorway.

"Excuse me for interrupting," he said, with an awkward grin at Veronica and a nod toward Clarice. "I heard voices."

"I'd invite you in, Tyler," said Veronica, "but you already *are* in."

"Sorry." He shuffled his feet, but did not go away.

She sighed, and tried to be polite. "Clarice, this is Tyler. My downstairs tenant. And my student."

The good-looking young jock had been renting a room in Veronica's house since Spring Quarter the year before. He was an up-tight Business major, a clean-cut Methodist boy from a wealthy, rural Eastern Washington family. He was wearing, as usual, his perpetual baseball cap, brim facing backwards, as well as faded levis, a rock concert T-shirt, and an old athletic jacket.

This quarter he had surprised her by enrolling in one of her classes. He'd had no business doing so. He wasn't interested in Victorian literature. He didn't need the credit hours. He had only one motive. He clearly had a crush on her.

"Just thought I'd stop by and give you the bad news," said Tyler. "You had a visit this morning from Art Chang." This was the would-be renter for the vacant lower floor of her house. "He's found some-place else."

Veronica groaned. "But he was so positive! That means I'll have to start advertising and showing the lower unit all over again. Great!" She sighed in defeat, then rose. "Well, thanks for telling me," she said, hoping to nudge him out the door.

Tyler wasn't quite ready to be nudged. "I'm having a little trouble with the final exam question."

"Of course, you are," said Veronica. "You're probably having a *lot* of trouble. The course wasn't designed for Business students. It was suicidal of you to enroll."

Tyler grinned. "I like challenges."

"Too bad you don't like fiction."

"I like the professor."

"On your way, before I show you how Greek tyrants used to treat the bearers of bad news. Goodbye, Tyler." She closed the door behind him. "That boy is becoming bothersome."

"Come on, girl," said Clarice. "It's good for your ego to have an admirer or two."

"Admirer?" echoed Veronica. "I'm old enough to be his—"

"Now, you stop that," said Clarice sternly. "Woman, you need to get a little more self-esteem. Didn't you look in the mirror this morning? You're not Grandma Moses yet. And I know how sad your life has been — I know, I know — Christmas is tough, but you can be tough, too. Just grit your teeth, and get through it."

Veronica knew she was right. She would have to wade right through all the mucky emotional hassles and painful memories of that most dreaded holiday. No getting around Christmas. All she could do was endure it.

"Let me give you some good advice," said Clarice, taking her hand and rubbing it briskly between both of her own, as though trying to revive her. "I think, personally, that the very best thing for you to do, in this kind of awkward, painful situation, is just to stop, take a deep breath, and let go. Let go of it all, and make a simple agreement with yourself."

"Agreement?"

"An agreement to cancel any other plans, and accompany a dear, trusted, and wise friend out to dinner."

"But—"

"Don't worry about my family," said Clarice. "They'll jump at the chance to order pizza. Now, put on your coat. I know the perfect place. Get ready for some very tasty, inexpensive Thai food."

12
Hurting Each Other

The shattering fruitbowl seemed to wake her from a trance. Angela Harrow backed away from the kitchen window. She only got halfway down the stairs before her mother looked out and saw her.

A cry from inside. At once the shouting in the kitchen ceased. Before Angela could get one step farther away, the back door swung open and both her parents appeared in the doorway.

"Angela, honey, why didn't you knock?" said her mother. "We didn't know you were out there."

"Come inside here, Angela," said her father, "before you get cold."

Her heart sank. She trudged back up the stairs. She endured a hug from her mother, pretended not to notice her tear-reddened face, greeted her father politely, and bumped past them into the kitchen.

"Watch out where you step," cautioned her mother. "Your father just knocked against the refrigerator."

"I didn't touch the refrigerator!"

"Oh, you didn't?" said her mother. "I suppose the fruitbowl just fell all by itself."

"Well, it didn't get any help from me."

The jagged remains of the bowl glittered between them across the black linoleum tiles.

"Your mother and I were just having a disagreement."

"A difference of opinion. Since we don't agree on anything anymore."

Her father ignored her mother. Instead, he hugged Angela to his burly, barrel chest. "Did you get your chemistry midterm back yet?" He held her by the shoulders like a big specimen, squinting at her through glasses that had slid to the end of his nose and been forgotten there.

"I only missed two." Angela squirmed free.

"Next time don't miss *any.*"

Her mother brushed her cheek with a kiss, trying to pretend that her make-up hadn't smeared and streaked. "Dinner will be ready in an hour, dear."

"I'm not hungry," said Angela, escaping into the hallway and heading for the stairs that led to her bedroom.

"But you've got to eat something."

"I already ate." She took the stairs two at a time. She could still hear them below.

"I hope you're satisfied. Now that you've institutionalized fast food, that's all she lives on."

"And that's supposed to be my fault?"

She closed her bedroom door firmly behind her, desperate to be alone, knowing a closed door wouldn't be enough to keep them out. Her parents had forbidden her to have a lock. There was no place she could escape from them. Angela had tried. She had wallpapered the room with her own personal visual assault of posters, photos, and glossy magazine cutouts, covering every available space. She threw her coat across the bed, beneath her wall-sized poster of Madonna.

A light rapping on her door preceded her father stepping into the room.

"Am I bothering you?"

"No." What was she supposed to say? What other answer was acceptable?

"I hope you're not upset."

"No." She was upset every minute she spent in that house.

"I suppose you've noticed by now," faltered her father, sitting down on the end of her bed, "that your mother and I have been having a little trouble getting along."

She wouldn't look at him. Obviously, since she wasn't blind and deaf, she had noticed. He went on, as though she had answered.

"I just wanted to say that what's happening between your mother and I — well, it doesn't mean we don't love each other."

Love? If that was love, she wanted nothing to do with it. She tried to hide her trembling.

"Sometimes, Angela," he continued, struggling for the right words, "people just hurt each other without meaning to." He was using his reassuring, defense attorney voice, but it was breaking, cracking. "It's not always someone's fault. Even when you love someone, even when you love them very much, sometimes you just can't help hurting them."

The lightbulb in the bedside lamp exploded.

She screamed. Her father shouted. Both of them leaped away from it. A thin line of smoke trailed upward from the electrical outlet in the wall.

Angela's mother burst into the room. "What in God's name did you do?"

"I didn't do anything."

"You *must* have. You're breaking everything in sight."

"I haven't broken a single thing!"

"Did he hurt you, honey?"

"Hurt her? I didn't touch her."

A tear rolled down Angela's cheek.

"Daddy didn't hurt me," she whispered hoarsely.

The ceiling light fixture began to flicker.

"What's going on?" said her mother uncertainly, no longer so confident, taking a step backward toward the door.

"Nothing to worry about," said her father, regaining his composure, smoothing his thick, white hair back into place. "No need for anyone to get upset. Just some kind of power surge."

"I'm not upset," said her mother. "I just want to know who's going to clean all this up."

"I'm going downstairs to have a look at the circuit breakers."

"I guess that answers my question. I should have realized that men don't clean up messes."

Her mother and father continued down the hall, arguing. Angela was left alone in the bedroom, staring at the floor, at the sharp, gleaming pieces of broken lightbulb.

13
Bookstore Balcony

The harsh fluorescent lights overhead caused the walls and tables piled with bright, new books to gleam all around him in a rainbow blur.

"This is it," said the Personnel Director, "the heart of University Book Store. General Books. The reason we're all here."

Her voice betrayed genuine pride, a flicker of real emotion, the most she had shown since the beginning of Matthew Braddon's interview. The initial half hour had been spent in the personnel office, on the other side of the private glass wall. And now this. A casual, informative stroll through the bookstore departments, from pens and pencils and notebooks to calculators and computers. All of it culminating on the second floor with its two dramatic staircases sweeping down to converge in a colorful sea of glossy bookcovers.

The Personnel Director was a slim, attractive, well-maintained professional who had a particularly bad habit of standing too close to the edge of the staircase. Below stretched book-crowded walls, book-filled shelves, book-covered tables.

"I do have a last few questions." She licked her polished lips. "You've listed several titles here on your resume. You call them musicals. You performed in these musicals?"

University Book Store on the Ave

"I wrote them. I'm a playwright. Was a playwright. The first three were the big successes. *Hot Blood* was my musical version of Dracula. Then this one, *Fire from Heaven,* that was my Frankenstein musical. And then my biggest one, right here, *Wooden Boy,* the Pinocchio one. It ran for six months. You may have heard of that one."

He could tell by her polite smile that she hadn't.

"These next ones here, those were all flops. Then this was my big flop. My Arabic musical, *Magic Lamp,* ended up trying to open one week into the Gulf War. It was never heard of again."

He laughed. It was not a light-hearted sound.

"You get the picture. That's why I've come back to Seattle. I'm through with theatre."

"Book retail is hardly as exciting as theatre."

"But I want to go back to books. I had plenty of experience in book retail here in the Northwest before I ran off to Broadway and made a fool of myself. See here. Village Books in Bellingham. Powell's in Portland. I managed a Crown Books in Bellevue for two years."

"Yes, I noticed, Matt. That's why I called you back." She gave him a good view of her glistening, white teeth in an ear-stretching smile. "We have an unexpected opening. At our branch store on campus, a little bookstore in the student union building. We need an experienced buyer there immediately."

The Personnel Director took a step backward toward the edge of the staircase, smiling at him confidently. Matt tried not to watch her, tried not to notice the insecurity of her footing. "We have a place for you at University Book Store, if you're interested."

Matt grinned. The new life he wanted. A chance to leave theatre behind, to be happy with less, to change gears completely, to have realistic goals in the real world. All of it now within his reach.

Buying books for a college bookstore.

"I'm interested," he said.

14
Blue Moon

"And she said, 'You've got the job.'"

The stale air was clogged with cigarette smoke. The wooden tables were battered, carved, gouged, and wet with rings of stale beer. Rough, bearded men with long hair strutted heavily around the pool tables, chalking their cues fervently and remembering happier times.

"To my new life in the bookstore!" said Matt, raising his dripping stein of beer.

Outside the window, an attractive, half-clothed young woman lounged on the lower horn of a blue crescent moon on a painted wooden sign hanging above the tavern. That same beckoning young lady had been contentedly swinging on the moon for twenty years, since the long-ago nights Matt had spent drinking in the Blue Moon in his college days. Then, as now, the eternal night traffic rumbled outside the windows on 45th, streaming out of the University District, trying to connect with the real world again.

"To your new life." The other stein rose and clinked into his obligingly, but without enthusiasm. "Now, tell me again, what exactly made you want to meet here?" said Tino Rodriguez, regarding the surroundings with distaste.

Tino was immaculately dressed, as always. His snug, stylish lime green turtleneck sweater and Calvin Klein jeans showed off a well-maintained body that looked ten years younger than thirty-seven. Short, black hair clung to his skull like a form-fitting cap. His black eyes sparkled with silent laughter.

"The Blue Moon is a college tradition." Since the fifties, the tavern had been a notorious hangout for existential bikers and collegiate badboys, famous poets and philosopher wannabes.

"But I thought you said it was a classy place."

"Classic, not classy," said Matt. "It just seemed like the Moon would be the appropriate spot for an old seventies man like me to drink a toast to the start of his new life."

"I suppose." Tino winced. "That doesn't make it a pretty sight. Everything is so macho. The men are all so butch and old and grumpy." He turned back to his friend, punching Matt affectionately in the arm. "You, on the other hand, are holding up nicely. It's great to see you again."

Tino had played a fatally handsome Count Dracula in Matt's first big success, the Seattle production of *Hot Blood*. He'd been plagued for weeks after the show by lovesick teenage girls camping outside his home. They had camped in vain. Tino's tastes ran elsewhere. His performance as The Creature in the Los Angeles production of Matt's Frankenstein musical, *Fire from Heaven*, got rave reviews, stole the show, and cemented a lifelong friendship between actor and playwright.

"You're a sight for sore eyes, pal," said Tino. "But this place! I haven't been to a straight bar in so long. I forgot how depressing they are."

29

"All bars are depressing."

"I can think of exceptions. Come on, let's go dancing. You've always been popular with the gay crowd."

"If only I were half as successful with women!"

"You can't always get what you want."

"I don't want anyone anymore. Women, men, anything."

"A nice, healthy relationship would do you good."

"In my dictionary, relationship and disaster mean the same thing. Every woman who falls in love with me suffers for it. I'm a walking mine field. It's like I want things to go wrong."

"You just need to get out and meet more people."

"I need to keep to myself. Romance isn't my department. Whereas it's your specialty. So, is there a current flame?"

"Oh, there are always a few admirers. They aren't important right now. You are. How long are you in Seattle?"

"I've returned to Eden for good," said Matt, refilling his friend's stein as well as his own.

"Sure, sure," said Tino. "At least, until the first theater in New York gives you a call."

"No chance of that. I'm back in Seattle to stay."

"You're really going to settle down here?" said Tino. "Good news for us locals. This calls for a real celebration."

Matt regarded him skeptically. "Oh, is that what it calls for? Not a funeral march?"

"Hey, I thought this was a celebration."

"Talking about theatre always depresses me."

"Snap out of it, old man!" Tino gave him a slap on the back to bring him to his senses. "No wonder you're depressed, hanging out in places like this. Too much brooding about life. Come on, you ever been to a little place down in University Village called Delfino's?" He didn't give Matt time to answer. "Wait till you taste their stuffed spinach pizza! Then you're going back to your motel. You need a good night's sleep. And me? I'm going out dancing, where people know how to have a good time."

15
On Impulse

By the time Tino finally dropped him off in front of the Silver Cloud Inn, Matt had eaten far too much pizza and it was much later than he'd intended.

A message waited for him in his room at the Silver Cloud Inn from someone named Veronica Glass. Without taking off his jacket, he dialed the number. The receiver was lifted on the fourth ring. A voice mumbled something.

"Is this Veronica Glass?"

The voice mumbled, "Speaking."

"Matthew Braddon. Sorry to be calling so late."

"Matthew who? Oh, yes! What time is it, anyway?"

"Almost eleven, I'm afraid. I just landed a job today. I was out celebrating."

"Congratulations," said Veronica. "Well, yes, it is late. I got your phone number at Thai Tom. The cook must have heard me talking. He said, 'Your new tenant has been here looking for you,' and handed me a matchbook with your name on it. So you're looking for a place in the U. District?"

"Yes, I am. I very much am."

"Well, I've got a place to rent. I'll warn you, the walls of the house are thin. I'm looking for someone who wants to live a quiet life."

"That's me."

"Someone who has very few parties, listens to music at low volume, and doesn't have the television blaring every night."

"I'm your man."

"Someone who doesn't take singing lessons or play a musical instrument."

"I'm passing the test with flying colors," said Matt. "Mind if I ask exactly what kind of housing we're talking about?"

"The lower floor of an old house."

"How old is old?"

"Fifty years or so. Old enough to have high ceilings and big, walk-in closets. Some furniture, nothing fancy. Covered porch. Separate entrance. Separate bathroom. Separate kitchen. We share a washer and dryer. Five hundred a month."

"Am I dreaming? Tell me more. Where are you located?"

"Six blocks from campus," said Veronica. "Ravenna Boulevard. The house is surrounded by trees. Quiet, secluded, but in the heart of the District. Other than the student renting the back room, you'd be sharing the house with me."

"Well, you sound fairly sane and reasonable," he said. "At least I like your voice." They both laughed. "I'll take it."

It happened that suddenly. The words were out of his mouth before he realized he was going to say them.

"But you haven't even seen it yet!"

"You'll have my personal check in your hand tomorrow. I don't suppose you happen to be available shortly after three?"

The phone line was silent for a moment.

"See you shortly after three," said the unreadable voice of Veronica Glass. "Do you have a pen? Here's the address."

CHAPTER TWO

Thursday, December 12

1
Time-Clock Rules

"This is the time-clock, and you're expected to be on time," said his boss unpleasantly.

Matt had come dangerously close to being late on his first day at the bookstore. Though campus was still familiar from his college days, it had been transformed by startling new structures upthrust like mushrooms. Not until the last minute did he see the familiar old building up ahead.

The Husky Union Building was the fifty-year-old student activity center. The solid brick stronghold squatted defiantly in the center of campus, its wings reaching out indecisively in different directions, a sprawling conglomeration of renovations and additions. The north wing of the HUB was occupied by University Book Store. Through the windows, in an overly-bright interior, he glimpsed headless mannequins modeling University of Washington sportswear.

He quickstepped through the drizzle to the HUB doorway and down the hall. There he took an abrupt turn to the left, past a large sign for Doctor's Choice cosmetics half-concealing the door of the bookstore.

At first glance, the HUB branch of University Book Store looked more like a large convenience store. Its colorful stock of school supplies, souvenirs, and greeting cards were displayed beneath blazing fluorescent lights on every available inch of wall, table, and aisle. Only a skylight at the back of the store revealed in a gray shaft of natural light the location of the books.

Lunging into the office, Matt collided headlong with a frowning, sixtyish woman whom he recognized at once as the bookstore manager. "Oh, excuse me! I didn't see you."

"So I noticed." Her silver, grandmotherly hair picked up no accompanying twinkle in her eye. She was no one's grandmother.

"Martha Ironwood." She thrust out her hand, more as a warning than a signal of goodwill, daring him to put his hand into hers.

He submitted, winced. "I'm Matt Braddon, the new book-buyer." It sounded like an apology, a confession.

"I see." Her worst suspicions were confirmed. Her nostrils flared in righteous annoyance. "Take off your coat, and hang it over there. We've wasted enough time. I despise wasting time."

Every second he wasted hanging up his jacket seemed to cause her personal grief.

"I'll be blunt," she said. "I've been the manager here for five stressful years. I've increased sales every year. I spend every Thursday afternoon in therapy to prove it. I've got all the trouble I can handle right now. I don't want any trouble from you. You were almost late this morning. Don't let it happen again." She leaned uncomfortably closer and lowered her voice to a hiss. "I despise tardiness."

After introducing him to the time-clock, she marched him straight to the front cash register. "You'll be a cashier four days a week. One day a week, you'll manage the book department."

"One day a week?"

"Books never need more than one day a week," interrupted a loud, chipper voice behind her. "Pens and notebooks take much longer. And photo orders. And you make a lot more money on greeting cards and candy bars and Doctor's Choice cosmetics and—"

"When I need additional information, Dolly," said Martha patiently, "I'll ask for it." When the woman failed to leave, Martha sighed. "This is Dolly Wrangles, my assistant manager." Her tone of voice made it clear that Dolly was her particular thorn in life.

"My pleasure," said Dolly, a pear-shaped woman in her fifties. Her toothsome Midwestern grin was topped by two tiny, bullet-hole eyes. "Welcome aboard."

"Now, step behind this cash register," said Martha. "Let's see how much you know."

She didn't sound hopeful.

Martha spent the next hour initiating him into the rituals of his new job. When she left for her afternoon appointment with her therapist, Dolly Wrangles eagerly took over. She showed him in painstaking detail how to fill out the tax exemption form, the credit form, the return form, the photo order form, the gift certificate form, the reserve form, and the special order form.

"Just don't make any mistakes," she said. "If you have any questions, ask me. It's easy, really. Just remember one simple fact. There are rules for everything."

34

2
EEPer

Angela had almost made it up the front stairs into Suzzallo Library when she felt someone grab her arm. Her earphones were in place, she was frowning, hunched forward, consciously looking at no one, moving briskly. No one should have been able to stop her.

Which was exactly what Angela wanted. After yesterday's distresses, she wanted nothing to do with anyone. She'd left the house early before her parents were awake. She wouldn't be anywhere near them when the verbal knives started slashing.

Everything in her life was suddenly in unpredictable turmoil. Her body was changing before her very eyes. Her skin felt like it was on pins and needles all the time. None of her clothes seemed to fit right anymore. Her parents were changing. All the rules were changing. She was stranded in the middle of a college campus, and — and that wasn't all.

Something else was changing, too. Something she couldn't put into words, something she didn't want to admit, that she kept trying to forget. Things she didn't understand about herself. Things that started getting worse yesterday.

She spun around on the library stairs.

Short, plump Ellen Wu was blinking at her through the huge lenses of her black-rimmed glasses, which made her look like a ruffled owl. Standing one step lower than Angela only accentuated her shortness. She was looking up at her now from under ink-black bangs, her square, sensible face trying to smile but losing confidence halfway. "Hi, Angela."

"Hi, Ellen." Angela had been able to rebuff and avoid all the other Early Entrance kids, but not Ellen Wu. When the others gathered at Guthrie Annex 2 in the afternoon, in the lounge of the Center for the Study of Capable Youth, Angela went home. Her father had made that condition very clear. The other kids, aged twelve to fourteen, had learned to trust each other. Angela trusted no one.

She wasn't exactly weird. She just didn't know how to connect with people. Angela Harrow was always lost in her own world.

Ellen Wu had not given up on her. She had decided immediately on the very first day that she wanted Angela for her friend. Nothing Angela had done had quite succeeded in discouraging her.

Turning her back on her, Angela bolted up the library stairs two at a time. Ellen hurried after her.

"Are you going to study?"

"Yes."

"Can I study with you?"

"No."

"But EEPers should stick together." Ellen was repeating a maxim that the director of the Early Entrance Program had tried to instill in them. Support each other. Be there for each other. Help each other.

"I need to be alone today," said Angela, without slowing down. She had nothing more encouraging to say than that.

"Don't you like me?" Ellen blurted out candidly.

"I just study better alone," said Angela, forcing her words to be hard, to hide the quaver in her voice. She was afraid to like Ellen. Angela was afraid of liking people.

She kept going up the library stairs and didn't look back. The library door whooshed shut behind her.

3
"Did You Just Hear Something?"

Angela started toward her usual studying place, and then paused. Her experience downstairs yesterday with the mysterious woman in the raincoat was still fresh in her memory. The thought of returning there made her feel ill at ease. Instead, she crossed the lobby and climbed up the elegant curving stone staircase to the third floor. Swinging open the heavy door into the Graduate Reading Room, she slipped quietly inside.

Dozens of long tables lined the aisle like pews in a cathedral, with light spilling down upon them through towering stained-glass windows. Angela sat at one end of a table, snapped on the light, and immediately set to work, opening her notebook, getting out her pen, organizing her notecards. She didn't look on either side of her until she heard a very faint snoring.

Just to her left, slumped over in one of the deep armchairs, was a slender, elderly woman sound asleep. Her white hair was drawn back in an untidy bun, from which numerous strands had escaped.

After studying for a while, Angela noticed that the soft snoring wasn't the only sound in the Graduate Reading Room. She could hear some kind of metallic tapping, like slow clanking footsteps inside the walls. Angela looked around. She could see no obvious source. The man on her right didn't seem to be aware of anything. She noticed that the temperature seemed to be dropping. The air was becoming cold and clammy.

The old woman suddenly sat up straight in the armchair with an alarmed snort. She listened. She seemed to hear something, too. She peered in all directions, as though looking for the hand that had awakened her.

Angela quickly lowered her eyes, but not before the old woman spotted her. She scrambled up onto her feet, patted her dress into place, and came over to Angela, bending down beside her so that her lips were scarcely an inch from Angela's ear.

"Did you just hear something?" she whispered.

Something about the old woman terrified her, as though she were reading Angela's mind.

"No," lied Angela.

"Like something hitting against metal?"

"No."

"Does it seem cold in here to you?"

"No." Angela's voice cracked slightly as she said it.

The old woman gave her a long, assessing look. Then she raised her glance beyond Angela, seemed to be listening intently, and hurried out of the Graduate Reading Room.

4
Stair #13

The light drizzle of rain wasn't worth an umbrella. Veronica was hurrying across campus toward her lunchtime appointment with Muriel Rose, not watching where she was going, when she unexpectedly looked up and found herself facing the homeless man.

He appeared to be as startled as she was by their abrupt face-to-face meeting. Unshaven, windblown, straggly-haired, he wore the same torn green parka as before, with a pack of belongings slung over his back.

"There you are!" he cried. "I've been looking for you."

She felt like bolting, but stood her ground. "You have no business looking for me."

"No business at all," he echoed. "I agree. I completely agree. But I do have something for you. This."

His arm suddenly thrust toward her, too fast to dodge. She was already in motion, moving past him, hurrying away in the wrong direction.

She didn't look up until she reached the stairs leading up to the gargoyle-infested Quad. He was nowhere in sight. Scolding herself for her fearfulness, she circled back toward the libraries over slippery, red-brick walkways, beneath baleful gargoyle stares.

She noticed ink was running along her fingers. The homeless man had shoved another poem into her hand. Rain was causing the ink to dribble and smear. She read what she could on the wet paper.

Lose it all
World to gain
Love will find you
In the rain

Pain today
Here to stay
All our sorrow
Gone tomorrow

What dreadful stuff! Raindrops smeared and blurred what few words were still legible, creating a crumpled, dripping wad of ink-wet paper. What had once been a poem was now a soggy mess. She deposited the remains in a trash receptacle, and hurried up the entrance stairs of Suzzallo Library. The Reference Desk was straight ahead. The white-haired librarian wasn't where she said she'd be.

A well-dressed Asian woman behind the counter approached. "Muriel said to watch for you. She's got a mystery on her hands."

"Mystery?"

"Noises of some kind. Don't ask me. I didn't hear them, she did. In the Graduate Reading Room." Her voice was just barely audible as she guided Veronica aside, out of hearing. "We've had a couple of reports lately about that room. Bangs. Tappings. We thought maybe echoes. But then this morning Muriel took a nap there, and when she woke up, she heard the noises, too."

"I don't understand. What can she do about noises?"

"She thinks they're coming from up above, from somewhere over the ceiling. The ceiling is suspended, you know. There are catwalks up there."

"You've got to be kidding me," said Veronica. "At her age, she's going out on catwalks?"

"Maybe you can stop her before she gets that far. Do you know where Stair #13 is?"

"Never heard of it."

"You get there from the staff work area behind Government Publications. There's a door that leads up to the tower. That's where she was heading. Can you find it?"

"I should think so."

"She said she'd be back by now, but you know Muriel. Once she sets her mind on something, there's no stopping her."

*

Veronica was familiar with Government Publications, in the oldest, original portion of Suzzallo Library. She found her way there easily. But she had never been beyond the service counter at the back of the room.

"Looking for Muriel Rose?" said a short, dapper man peering into the green data of his computer screen while fiddling intently with his mustache.

"Yes, I am."

His eyes never left the screen. "Hmm," he said reflectively, and tapped several keys which caused an influx of fresh green data. "She was talking about Stair #13. It's on the other side of those desks, in the corner. It looks like a closet. The light switch is on the left."

Veronica found the door easily enough. It was boldly labeled, and open a few inches. The light was already on, though essentially ineffectual. Stair #13 was a small enclosure entirely filled by an ancient metal spiral staircase.

"Muriel?" she called softly up the tight, dizzying spiral.

No answer.

Impatiently, Veronica took hold of the railing and began to climb. The cramped stairwell was dusty with disuse. Her footfalls on the metal grill stairs clattered and echoed. They were the only sounds of life.

"Muriel?" she whispered, as she reached the dark landing. "Oh, my God!"

The spiral staircase had come to an end. The next stairs continuing upward were the rungs of a metal ladder attached to the wall. She squinted up at the ascending rungs. It was too dark to see the top of the ladder.

"Muriel, are you up there somewhere?"

She abruptly answered her own question.

To one side of the ladder, where a door led out onto the roof, was a section of flooring that looked unfinished. There was Muriel Rose,

39

in a crumpled tangle of untucked blouse, disarranged white hair and buckled limbs. The old librarian was struggling her way up onto her feet, propping herself up against the wall in the shadows. With a cry of alarm, Veronica hurried to her side.

"Muriel! Are you all right?"

Her friend blinked, took a deep breath. "Fine, fine." Veronica helped her into a more comfortable position. Muriel brushed back a wild wisp of hair, tucked in her blouse. "Nothing to worry about. Just lost my balance."

"Take your time. So, what's all this about noises?"

"That's just it, I'm not sure." The old librarian tried to laugh. "Strangest thing. For a moment there, this morning, when I woke up from my nap in the Graduate Reading Room, I actually thought — Well, it's your fault. You've got me reading all these Victorian ghost stories."

Veronica smiled. Her interest perked up. "You saw a ghost?"

"No, no, no!" the old woman quickly denied. "It's just that, well, your imagination starts to wander. What is causing those noises? I was starting to get cold. I thought I heard something—"

"What did you hear?"

"Clanking. Tapping. I couldn't tell what it was. So, that's why I'm here. I've been out on the catwalks before — well, it didn't seem like very many years ago. I thought something might have come loose. Because otherwise, what could that sound be? I came up here to find out. You know me."

"I certainly do." The two women smiled. They liked each other. They'd been going to movies and plays together for years. Both of them were very private single women, and knew exactly how to respect each other's boundaries. Veronica helped her back onto her feet.

"Think you can get down these stairs okay?"

"Easy as pie." Gripping the dusty rail, the old librarian began a cautious descent. Veronica went down the stairs in front of her, ready to catch her if necessary. "Now, don't go telling everyone how Muriel Rose is having paranormal experiences in the Graduate Reading Room. They'd have me retired in six months."

"Your secret is safe with me."

"I knew I could trust you, dear. Old people only blab about things like ghosts to extremely trustworthy friends."

"Can we possibly eat lunch now?"

"How about Delfino's?" Muriel worked her way spryly down the staircase. "You know what sounds good? A stuffed spinach pizza!"

40

5
A Shock

That afternoon, after his discouraging first day at the bookstore, Matt brushed his mop of hair into some semblance of order, turned up the collar of his denim jacket, hunched his shoulders against the cold, and set off across campus to take his first look at his yet-unseen apartment.

Beyond the towering antpiles of the dormitories he found his way to NE 45th. Cutting through the fraternity and sorority houses of Greek Row, he followed the winding, tree-lined boulevard across the Ave, the address clutched in one hand.

The house wasn't there.

Matt came to a standstill. There was the neighborhood grocery store, right where she said it would be, but the house numbers were all wrong. Somehow he had gotten himself mixed up. Twisting the owner's words around, he'd confused one grocery store with another, and come out blocks away from where he wanted to be.

He set off in the opposite direction. He was so upset from his miserable first day at the bookstore that it was no surprise he couldn't find a simple address. Craning his neck to look up the side of the hill, descending along the bends and turns of Ravenna Boulevard, he found himself suddenly facing the right numbers, carved into the fourth stair of a zigzagging stairway up the hillside. He stopped abruptly, gaping at the dozens of stairs winding up to the three-story house above him, his features rigid with shock.

He knew that house.

He recognized it at once. It couldn't possibly be the same house, and yet it was!

He felt like walking straight past it. Instead, he couldn't make himself turn away. He stepped up the first stair. Then another. How could he possibly recognize it, after all those years? He should turn around right now. But there were no other available rentals. It couldn't be the same house. And yet if it was, then maybe if he just didn't think about it. If he didn't look down at the stairs. If he didn't remember—

He continued up the second flight of stairs, and then the third, higher and higher up through the ivy and ferns to the house towering over him. He managed to take three strides across the small front porch and knock on the door of the empty apartment. He knocked once more before he had to brace himself against the doorframe, just as the door swung open.

*

She had nearly finished writing the final chapter of her new book, *The Ghost Stories of Edith Wharton*. Unfortunately, it had taken her two weeks longer than either she or her publisher had expected. Veronica had gotten another impatient call from Chicago. A polite but firm encouragement to deliver the manuscript immediately.

Consequently she was so deeply in thought, so intently puzzling how to phrase her insights in exactly the right words, that at first she wasn't sure she heard knocking downstairs. She finished jotting down a last note and looked up from her desk.

She hadn't noticed the library around her becoming dark. Winter afternoons were so short, they were over before they got started. She rose slowly to her feet, waiting for a repeat of the sound, for a clue, for an explanation. She pulled on her sweater and stepped out of her library onto the third floor landing.

Knocking.

That time she was certain she heard it. She glanced at her wristwatch. Of course! The new tenant was so late she'd forgotten about him. That must be him now.

Veronica called, "Coming!"

She hurried into her kitchen and opened the door next to the cupboard. Wooden stairs lit by a naked electric bulb led down into the laundry room, deep in the heart of the house. At the bottom of the stairs, she stepped around the old boiler to the other side of the washing machine.

Opening the door into the vacant apartment, she passed quickly through the cold, odorless kitchen into the deadly hush of the living room, through the few scattered pieces of furniture toward the front door. She fumbled with the doorknob.

The door groaned open.

The man slumping toward her was propped against the doorframe as though he were drunk, and that was her first conclusion. "Can I help you?" she said hostilely, ready to slam the door in his face.

He turned toward her, eyeglasses tilted slightly crooked, forehead glistening with perspiration, looking straight into her eyes. "I'm sorry, I'm all right."

"You don't seem all right."

"I just lost my balance for a minute, that's all. You must be Veronica Glass."

"Matthew Braddon, I assume?" She guardedly kept the door half-closed between them.

"Yes, of course," he mumbled. "Matthew Braddon, your new tenant—"

Before he could say another word, however, his forehead struck the edge of the doorframe as his knees buckled.

*

She helped him stretch out on the sofa in the cold, half-dark apartment.

"I hope you're feeling better," she said, returning promptly from her kitchen upstairs, regarding him warily.

"You've got to excuse me. I'm fine, really."

She handed him a steaming mug. "Here, take a sip of this. I gambled that you might like a little cream in it."

"A good gamble," he said. The coffee was delicious and quickly revived him. "Sorry to cause you all this trouble." He sat up with an effort. "You're going to worry about what kind of tenant you've landed."

"Not at all," she lied. That was exactly what she was worrying.

"I'm not prone to toppling through people's doorways," he said. "Honest." He straightened his glasses on his nose. "You see, I didn't realize until I got here that I'd been in this house before. Must be twenty years ago, when I was in college."

"Really?" Perhaps he was only imagining it, but her attitude toward him seemed to harden slightly into a frosty reserve. "What a coincidence!"

"I was only here once," said Matt, in a voice scarcely above a mutter. "But once was enough. There was a party here."

"Yes," she said.

"You probably know all about it. Back in the seventies, it must have been. The wild days."

She seemed uncomfortable with the topic. "Usually I try to spare tenants that unsettling bit of news."

"I was there," said Matt. He nodded his head, remembering more than he wanted to. "I only wish I hadn't been."

She avoided looking him in the eye. "So you know the worst. Seeing the house again must have been a shock."

"Yes, a shock." He remembered the tiny kitchen sandwiched full of young people, the bags of pot and mushrooms in the freezer, the sheets of acid in the silverware drawer. It had climaxed in over two

43

hundred terrified students trying to evacuate the house at the same time, surrounded by sirens and lights and police cars. "It took me years to forget about it. But I managed to forget. Until I got to the foot of the stairs just now, and took one look up at this house."

The mere sight of the house had caused it all to rush back to him, that tragic party, three floors full of crazy students, every floor with its own stereo blasting, every room packed with laughing, drinking, smoking, horny college kids celebrating the end of finals, the start of the holidays, being alive. And then eleven of them were in jail at the Wallingford Police Station. And one of them wasn't alive.

"The night before Christmas Eve, nineteen seventy-something. Was it seventy-six? That horrible night—"

"You're shaking."

The coffee mug was beginning to tremble in his grip. A dribble of coffee sloshed over the edge. She reached out to steady the mug, and her hand closed over his. For one brief, awkward moment, neither of them dared to pull away, for fear of spilling the coffee between them.

"Sorry if I'm interrupting anything," said a voice that didn't sound sorry.

Both of them pulled away their hands at once. The coffee mug crashed to the floor between them, snapping off its handle, splattering both of them.

"Oh, I'm sorry—"

"It was my fault."

Tyler Wates, the student renter, stood in the open doorway of the laundry room. "The door was open, so I thought I'd better investigate. Gotta watch out for intruders, you know."

"No intruders, just us," said Veronica, picking up the broken pieces of mug. "Thanks, Tyler. Everything's under control. This is the new tenant." Tyler took a step into the unrented apartment, hand extended for introductions. Veronica blocked him. "He's not feeling too well. I'll introduce you to him later, when he's up on his feet."

"Later," said Tyler, not entirely pleased.

She closed the door on his scowling, handsome face and began using some stray sheets of newspaper to mop up the spilled coffee on the floor.

"You introduced me as the new tenant. I haven't really earned that title yet." He pulled a folded check out of his pocket, smoothed it out, and handed it to her. "First and last month's rent, with damage deposit. Sorry the check isn't local, but I just flew into town. It's my New York account. It's good."

"But you haven't even seen the place."

"I'm looking, I'm looking." He strode around quickly in all directions, hands folded behind his back, examining, inspecting. A big living room with a high ceiling. The front picture window looked down on Ravenna Boulevard. The woodwork floor tipped slightly. A crack in the ceiling. Tiny kitchen on the left. Tiny bathroom on the right. Big, old-fashioned white porcelain bathtub with claw feet. Boxy, spacious bedroom. The entire lower unit patched together with remodelings, renovations, crooked joinings. "I'll take it. I'm ready to sign any papers you want me to sign."

"Wonderful," she said. "Well, the rental lease is up on the third floor, but I haven't photocopied it yet. It can wait for your signature till tomorrow." She reached out and helped Matt slowly rise up off the sofa onto unsteady legs. "Let me give you a lift back to where you're staying."

"I need the fresh air," said Matt. "By my calculation, the Silver Cloud Inn should be just down the hill. A walk will do me good. Thanks again." He buttoned up his jacket, and stepped out the front door onto the porch. She followed him out. He took a deep breath. "They don't have air like this in New York City. It's like breathing straight caffeine. I feel better already. I plan to get my things out of storage and move in after work tomorrow."

"Better go to bed early tonight," said Veronica, shaking his hand to finalize their arrangement. "There are fifty-two stairs. You'll get to know each one of them personally. No one ever forgets moving into this house."

CHAPTER THREE
Friday, December 13

1
A Bad Habit

Matt Braddon carefully backed the rental truck up to the curb at the bottom of the stairs. He had changed out of his bookstore clothes after work into an old pair of sweats. He had checked out of the Silver Cloud Inn. Jumping down to the street, he looked up at his new home, at the three flights of backtracking stairs meandering up the ivy-cloaked hillside. Too bad Tino was in rehearsal that afternoon. Well, he would manage on his own.

Something rubbed against his leg. It meowed before he could accidentally step on it.

"Well, hi there," said Matt, squatting down to its level. The lean black cat rubbed up against his knee. "Are you the official welcoming committee?" He gave it a scratch under the chin, which increased the volume of its purring. "Watch out now, fella. If you're not going to help, stay out of the way."

Time to stop playing with cats and get to work.

Sliding open the truck's back door, Matt gathered up two dining room chairs on one arm, scooped two more onto the other arm, and with a glance to make sure the cat was safely out of sight, began making his way slowly up the first flight of stairs like a giant wooden crab with four mahogany legs.

He forced his mind to focus on the here and now. He refused to let his thoughts drift back to what he had seen on those stairs. He would no longer dwell on the past. The whole horrible business was over and done with long ago—

Because of his struggle, he didn't notice the bicycle on the third flight, propped against the short brick wall lining the stairs. His foot stepped between the wheels. He gave a cry of surprise and another of shock as he lost his balance. Like an enormous porcupine bristling with wooden spikes, he toppled forward onto the stairs. The chair

47

underneath him gave a sharp crack. A front leg snapped off and he was collapsing on top of the broken chair when a muscular arm wrapped around him from behind.

"Whoa, gotcha!"

Tyler Wates had appeared out of nowhere in T-shirt, sweatpants and sneakers.

"I'm really sorry!" He helped Matt regain his balance, bracing him up against the brick bulkhead. Then he hauled the bicycle out of the way, up onto the ivy bank under the camellia tree. "It's a bad habit of mine. Don't tell Professor Glass, please. She told me not to leave my bike there. I was just going to be here for five minutes, and didn't want to haul it all the way up."

"I'm afraid I've ruined your bike."

"My own fault for leaving it there." Tyler scooped up the pieces of the broken chair, hooked his arms through the other chairs, and carried them all up to the front porch. "Is that your truck down there?" Before Matt could answer, Tyler was bounding down the stairs. "You're moving in. Let me give you a hand unloading."

"But you were going somewhere."

"Nowhere that can't wait."

Tyler continued to give him a hand for almost an hour, hauling heavy boxes up the stairs with a rambunctious, athletic enthusiasm that was exhausting to behold.

2
Knife

The truck was finally empty. After an hour of trekking up the stairs with Matt's possessions on their backs, both of them were bone-weary. While Tyler took a shower in his studio at the back of the house, Matt rinsed off in his old-fashioned bathtub.

He was soon busy in the kitchen, searching among the cardboard boxes and wads of crumpled newspaper for enough matching food items to throw together a meal for two.

Tyler's place connected with the rest of the house through the laundry room. A staccato rat-a-tat announced his arrival before the laundry room door swung open.

"Now, don't make a lot of food," said Tyler. "Nothing much for me." He stood in the kitchen doorway, still damp from his shower, wearing gym trunks, not wearing a shirt. "Gotta watch it, I'm getting fat," he said, slapping a belly that was obviously without a spare ounce. "Don't want to get out of shape before I marry, and I don't plan to get married for a long time. I may look like a fraternity boy, but I'm not. I study all the time. You won't have to worry about me. I keep to myself. Don't party. Don't bring home girls."

"I don't date much, either," said Matt.

"Of course, I'm horny all the time," qualified Tyler promptly, with a grin. "But I'm saving it for marriage. Ever since I took Jesus as my personal savior."

"I see." Matt concentrated on peeling potatoes.

"So what are you cooking?" asked Tyler. "I'll help." He took three strides forward into the heart of the tiny kitchen, and was immediately in the way. A round table clogged the far half of the kitchen, making the high shelves inaccessible. Sink, refrigerator, drainboard, oven and range were all crowded into the other half.

"Please, sit down, Tyler. There's not enough room—"

"I'm a good cook, really." He seemed to be looking for something to do wrong. "Here, let me chop up the onion. Really, trust me, an onion I can chop." He pulled out the chopping board, blocking any escape from the kitchen. "What's wrong with this knife?"

"Nothing's wrong with it." Tyler had selected the biggest knife in Matt's collection.

"It's so dull it hardly cuts. Look, it's like sawing. I'll sharpen it."

Matt tried to dissuade him. "No, no, that's not necessary."

"I can do it. Look, here's the sharpener."

"But there's no need." He reached for the knife.

"This knife is too dull to cut any—"

Matt gasped.

An unexpected slice. The blade painlessly opened a tiny red line across the inside of Matt's palm. Bright drops of blood splattered the linoleum floor.

"God, I'm sorry," said Tyler, his face white.

"So, have you finished moving all your—?" began Veronica, standing in the open laundry room doorway, surveying the piles of pans and dishes everywhere. Then she saw what had happened. "Get your hand over the sink and apply pressure to it. I'll be right back." She bolted upstairs for disinfectant and bandages.

He thrust his hand under a stream of water from the faucet, sending pink swirls eddying down the drain.

3
Superstition

"Hasn't exactly been my day."

"Friday the thirteenth," said Veronica, with a wise nod and a solemn raised eyebrow. "Speaking of bad luck, sounds like you've had your share. Tyler just let it slip, as he was running off to the library, that this is actually his second attempt on your life today."

"I feel confident he's not a hit-man," said Matt. He tried to laugh as she bandaged his hand.

"Looks suspicious to me," said Veronica. "First you nearly fall down the stairs over his bicycle. Then he nearly bleeds you to death with the chopping knife."

They were no longer in the kitchen. The close quarters made them both uncomfortable. They were sitting now in a confusion of chairs and tables that would ultimately be Matt's living room.

Veronica finished her bandaging, and regarded her First Aid handiwork with approval. "That blasted Tyler! Whether he knows it or not, he's trying to kill you. Subconscious aggression. Male wolves battling it out to be the Alpha of the pack."

"Male wolves don't help each other move in. He was just being careless. Besides, he's obviously jealous. If I was his age, I'd have a crush on you, too."

"Crush?" His comment caught her off-guard. "Crush?"

"Hard to miss noticing the way he looks at you," said Matt. "Didn't you ever get a crush on one of your teachers? That fascinating, aloof, attractive older person?"

For a terrible moment, she remembered how she'd first felt about Sam Glass twenty years ago. The lean, sexy radical English prof! It took her a moment to regain her sense of irony. "I see. And you're old enough so that you *don't* have a crush on me?"

He became embarrassed. He tried to make a joke out of it. "I was hoping it didn't show."

"Well, there's no law against crushes," she said philosophically, trying to brush the awkward topic aside.

"All guys his age are in a state of crush," said Matt. "Testosterone isn't easy to deal with. He doesn't seem any crazier than most." He yawned, quickly covering his mouth. "Sorry. It's been a long day. I'm not used to running so many stairs. My legs are in shock."

"If it's any comfort, my calf muscles finally stopped hurting after the first year. Now they're just perpetually numb. I think that means I've adapted to life here."

She gathered up her medical supplies and turned toward the door. "Sweet dreams."

"Thanks for being such a great resident medic."

She went out through Matt's kitchen and up the laundry room staircase leading to her floor.

*

He made his way down the short hall to the bedroom, where he tugged off his shirt and pants and dropped them on the floor. Taking off his glasses and setting them on the bedstand, he snapped off the bedside lamp.

He lay in the dark, feeling the throb of his bandaged hand, staring up at the ceiling. His first night in his new home in the U. District. A new life. In a house with such unpleasant memories. He was so tired that getting to sleep wouldn't be a problem. The problem would be forgetting—

Brad. Crazy Brad.

There he was again, his wacky dormitory roommate, in the thick of the party, always where the action was the wildest and the noisiest, shouting and laughing in his own hazy, blurry world, living life as though it had no consequences.

Long stringy black hair, lean horsey face, scrawny body that could bend in any direction, always listening to music wherever he went, always listening to it loud. Changing his major every two weeks, changing his girlfriend just as often. This time he'd had too much to smoke, too much to drink, which was not unusual, but he was yelling into the telephone receiver, "Officer, I want to complain about a party," trying to be heard over the blaring stereo beside him.

Not until then did Matt realize his roommate had actually done what he'd been comically threatening to do, that he had really phoned the police. "Officer, there's a stereo up on the second floor that's too loud."

Matt tried to get there in time. Too many people were squeezed into the house. He couldn't reach Brad, he couldn't stop him, he couldn't knock the phone out of his hand because everyone was shouting and running and jumping, pushing and elbowing and kicking as he tried to stop that idiot Brad.

"That's what I said, officer. I can't hear my own stereo. I demand that something be done —"

With a gasp of horrified protest, Matt sat up in bed. That awful Christmas party!

He lay back down again, drawing the covers around him, forcing himself to calm down, to breathe slowly and deeply. A few nightmares were to be expected. Living in that house was bound to stir up old memories.

He wrestled his pillow into a comfortable lump and tried to slip back into sleep. No luck. After an hour of tossing and turning, he groaned and gave up. He sat on the side of the bed, swinging his bare feet down onto the cold floor. He put on his glasses, but he didn't feel like reading. He didn't turn on the lights. He wasn't hungry. He didn't know what he wanted. He was restless. He walked around nervously in his undershorts, feeling his way in the dark, shuffling his way toward the closet to get dressed.

Being careful not to bump his bandaged hand, he managed to pull on a shirt and was bending down to locate his pants and shoes when he accidentally banged his head on the edge of the open closet door. "Ouch!" As the door swung closed, he glimpsed something in the mirror attached to it, something reflected in the windowpane. At first he thought it was someone outside trying to break in through the window.

Another look. It was a reflection, but not his own. The reflected figure was a woman standing in the bedroom doorway.

He spun around. "Hey, who's there?"

The doorway was empty. He'd only glimpsed her briefly in the swinging mirror, but it could have been only one person.

"Veronica?"

No answer. He rushed to the bedroom door, out into the dark apartment. Not a breath of movement. Piles of unloaded boxes loomed unpredictably. His hand patted along the wall, batting toward a light switch. A blaze of light — the disordered, cluttered living room clogged with packings and crates.

He stood frozen, watching.

He was about to turn away, then listened. A soft, almost inaudible murmur. He scowled with concentration. It was laughter — a ripple of laughter, a soft rill of chuckling, another even softer, the enticing, provocative laughter of a woman.

A sound. A creaking board under a shift of weight. It seemed to come from the kitchen. He considered the possibility of someone else actually concealed in the house with him, hiding in the kitchen, waiting for him. He approached the kitchen doorway, half-blocked by the corner of the refrigerator. As he rounded the glossy white coldness, he heard it again. It clearly came from the end of the kitchen. From the laundry room door.

He swung the door open. The hollow darkness on the other side was chilly and still. He reached in and pulled the light cord. Bright lights revealed cement walls crowding around the clothes washer and laundry basin. Wooden stairs wrapped around the ancient boiler leading up to the second floor. The weight of his foot was creaking down on the first stair when he heard the sound again.

This time it wasn't laughter. The sound he heard now, faintly, from some other room, some other floor, was heartbreakingly sad, a sniffling, sobbing wretchedness, pure human pain.

Matt's heart was hammering wildly. He was so scared he could hardly move. Who could possibly be so sad? Tyler's door beyond the boiler was dark. The sound seemed to come from above.

A creak on the stairs.

"Who's there?"

No answer.

Before he had time to think about what he was doing, Matt bounded up the first flight of wooden stairs, lunging toward the switch-around above the boiler to see who was on the other side. He froze on the landing. No one there. He heard what might have been a very soft sob. He listened, not daring to move in the hushed laundry room. Not a rustle, not a breath.

The door at the top of the laundry room stairs was open a crack. Through the crack, he saw something move.

Was it her? Suddenly aware of how suspicious he looked, creeping about in the darkened laundry room in his undershorts, he stepped rapidly backward to retreat down the stairs. Too rapidly. He felt something grab his shirt from behind. Something metal and sharp snagged at his shirtsleeve, slid icily along his side. A ripping, tearing sound as he lost his balance. He slammed backward against the plasterboard retaining wall behind him. It stopped him with a bone-rattling grunt, knocking the breath out of him.

Then he felt the side of his shirt where it hung open, slashed wide in a long tear, sliced away to the skin. Poking out from the window ledge in front of him, from between two cans of dried house paint, were the long, gleaming blades of the garden shears. He had come uncomfortably close to stabbing himself in the ribs.

Matt retreated down the stairs paying careful attention to his footing. He tried not to think about the sharp blades of the shears. He tried to forget how close he had come to impaling himself. He tried to stay calm. Calm was what he needed. If he wasn't careful, his new home was going to kill him.

CHAPTER FOUR
Saturday, December 14

1
Ice Cold

Matt woke up Saturday morning with one issue completely resolved. He was moving out. He couldn't remain there. Living in that house was out of the question.

He lay in bed for an hour, an emotional wreck, thinking about what had happened the night before. He was crazy to have rented the place considering what he knew about its past. He should have turned around the minute he *saw* the house.

But he didn't, and there he was. Could he be tough enough to make do? It was, after all, a place to rent in the U. District. There weren't many others. Obviously there would be a few bad memories stirred up. The weird coincidence of discovering himself trapped in the middle of his long-buried past was extremely unsettling.

That didn't explain the woman. Who had he seen last night? That wasn't a dream. That wasn't his imagination. He had seen the reflection of someone who could only have been the owner of his building. Veronica Glass was a fascinating woman. Attractive enough, in a cold, distant way. But why would she come down uninvited in the middle of the night?

After a short morning jog through Ravenna Park, Matt took a quick bath, removing the bandage from his healing hand. Then he started his first load of laundry. Leaving the washer filling, he found a forgotten, unwashed pair of jockey shorts half-hidden under the bathtub. He snatched them up and headed back to the washer to throw the shorts in with the rest of his clothes.

He opened the laundry room door.

Dripping wet, wrapped in her bathrobe, Veronica was halfway down the laundry room stairs, reaching toward the washing machine.

"Oh, excuse me—"

Matt's sudden appearance startled her. Her wet foot slipped out from under her on the wooden staircase. She fell down the remaining two stairs. With a cry, he stepped forward and caught her before she hit the washer. His arms closed around her.

She pulled away, clutching her robe in an angry attempt at decency.

"My God, are you all right?"

"How embarrassing!"

"I hope you're not hurt."

"Only my pride. I'm smart enough to know how slippery these wooden stairs can be."

"You look upset."

"I am upset. You would be, too, if you were taking a shower, and the water turned ice cold." She glared meaningfully at the washing machine.

"You don't mean that I—?"

"When you turned on the washing machine, you cut off my water pressure. Suddenly all I had was cold water. I was just coming down to pause the washer long enough to finish my shower."

"I'm so sorry."

"Well, I'm completely mortified."

"It will never happen again. I'm still just figuring out how the house works." He hesitated. "By the way," he said, "there was something I wanted to ask you. I was just wondering — I don't suppose, for any reason, you might have — well, last night, I couldn't sleep, and — well, I saw you downstairs."

She seemed to take a moment to fully realize what he had just said. "You saw me? Inside your apartment?"

"In my bedroom, actually."

"Your bedroom!" she echoed in exasperated amazement. "Really, Matt! I don't make a habit of visiting my tenants during the night in their bedrooms." She looked at him quizzically. "Is this some kind of weird joke?"

"Actually, I'm serious. I figured it must be something I didn't understand. With an old house like this, it could have been a problem with the electricity."

"Or a serious problem with your landlady, maybe."

"Listen, I wasn't suggesting—"

She tried to ease the tension with humor. "Sounds to me like you're dreaming about me, and don't want to admit it."

"That must be it." Her humor relieved him. He regretted bringing it up. "Listen, clearly I was mistaken. I'm sorry to cause so much unpleasantness on my first morning here. Let's put all this behind us and start off on a better note. Let me take you to breakfast."

"That's very kind of you," said Veronica, caught off-guard by the invitation. "I would accept, but we don't need to go anywhere. I was just getting ready to make breakfast. You can come up and join me."

"But that would mean I'd just invited myself to eat with you."

"Wrong. *I* invited you." Veronica started carefully back up the wet laundry room staircase. "See you in half an hour. And watch out for these stairs. They're slippery."

2
Cemetery View

He had to knock three times. He could see her in the kitchen, glimpses of her moving back and forth, oblivious to his knocking. When she finally did hear him, she hurried toward the door at once, wiping her hands on a dish towel.

"Did I keep you waiting?" she apologized, swinging the door open. "I was expecting you to come up through the laundry room. You didn't have to go outside. Those of us who live here use the inner stairs — especially in cold weather like this!"

"This is why I don't write plays anymore," he said. "I can't even get my own entrances right."

"You wrote plays?"

"In another lifetime."

Wiping his shoes on the doormat, he stepped inside. A thick carpet insulated the floor of the living room. One big armchair by the fireplace, surrounded by a cluster of little endtables, was clearly a favorite place to read, judging by the piles of books. He had dreaded his first sight of the upper part of the house, fearing that it would trigger more memories of that tragic party, but he remembered only rooms crowded with loud, laughing, dancing students. None of the house looked familiar. He sighed with relief.

Scrambled eggs and bacon were already waiting on the dining room table, which was set for two. Each plate had a glass of orange juice waiting beside it.

"Wow," he said. "A real breakfast."

"How was your first night?"

"A little bumpy. A nightmare, actually. Guess a few memories are to be expected. Nothing I can't handle. Takes a while to get used to a new bed, that's all."

"A new bed." She nodded in agreement.

The word *bed* caused the conversation to falter. They both quickly switched to safer, saner topics — their favorite authors (hers was Iris Murdoch, his was Jim Thompson), their favorite movie directors (hers was Fellini, his was Spielberg). All too soon breakfast was finished.

"Thanks. That was a real feast," he said. "You mentioned earlier that you'd had a book published. I'd love to see a copy. I don't suppose you have one around."

She grinned. "Have you ever known an author to *not* have a copy around?" She rose to her feet. "There's always one up in the library. Come on. You haven't seen the third floor yet, anyway."

His features immediately changed. He rose to his feet, the smile abruptly gone from his face, one hand raised in objection. "Say, look, it can wait," he said. "Don't bother."

"No bother at all," said Veronica, mildly surprised at the sudden change in his attitude. "Come on," she said, heading toward the staircase. "It's up here."

"No, please," said Matt. "I don't mean to intrude. First I practically invite myself to breakfast, and then—"

"You're not intruding."

"It doesn't have to be right now."

She didn't seem to hear him. She preceded him up the broad, dramatic staircase to the third floor.

He hesitated, took one step, then another, then followed her. His heartbeat hammered in his ears with every step. He reached the landing, turned, and started up the second flight. To his left, the open door to the bathroom. To his right, the door to her bedroom. Directly ahead of them, the room at the top of the stairs. The largest room, with two French windows looking out over the front of the house. The walls were solid books.

"This is my favorite place in the house," she said. "My personal writing space and primary book collection."

"But this is so much larger—" he began, looking confused. "In my memory, which is clearly wrong, there were two rooms."

"Your memory is right." Veronica smiled. "There were two rooms. I had the wall removed when I moved in seven years ago." She stepped to one side. "Welcome to my library." She noticed the pale look on his face. "Is something wrong?"

He was staring at a small door tucked away in the corner. "If I remember correctly," he said, "there's an enormous closet — that door right over there."

58

"You're right, it's huge," said Veronica. "Your memory is in very good working order. That's where I store all my junk, the guilty, sentimental stuff I can't throw out."

"A walk-in closet big enough for a bed. A closet with a window inside it—"

Veronica stared at him. Then she crossed the library, opened the closet, pushed aside hangers of forgotten clothes, and pointed. "There's the window. Right where you remembered it." She stepped back out of the closet, and re-crossed the library toward the two French windows. "I suppose you remember the view out here?"

Before he could stop her, she had unfastened the latch at the bottom of one window, swung it open, and stepped out onto the narrow third-floor balcony.

"Wait—" began Matt, but she had already walked to the end of the narrow deck. The far too narrow deck, hardly a balcony at all, protected by a rail not quite waist high. He missed part of what she was saying. Clenching his jaws, focusing straight ahead, he crossed the library in a few quick strides, trying not to remember anything at all from his past, trying to see only what was really there now, trying to concentrate on the two French windows ahead of him. He stopped at the open one.

"What are you looking at?"

"Oh, nothing."

"Don't worry, it's safe. It's not going to give way. And I'm not going to push you off." He grinned back at her uncomfortably. She stood at the far end of the railed walk, right where the roof tucked under the heavy boughs of the maple tree. "Every spring you can watch raccoon cubs playing in the branches."

"No kidding?" He climbed through the window and took a step toward her. He did not look down. He did not glance over the balcony's edge.

"That's Calvary Cemetery," said Veronica, pointing toward the green hillside covered with tombstones several miles beyond. "My family's graves are all over there."

She took hold of the balcony railing. She did not look down. She leaned out over the sheer drop to the stairs. Matt broke into a sweat along his forehead.

"My grandmother has already paid for my grave. Can you believe it? I'm looking over from this side now, but in thirty or forty more years, I'll be over on that side." She leaned on the balcony railing. She did not look down at the stairs yawning below. "Have you ever lost someone close to you?"

Matt tried to stammer some kind of answer, but no words would come out. He backed away from her, managing to stay on his feet, reaching out behind him for the frame of the open window. Before he could lose his balance, he grabbed the open shutter and swung back through the French window into the solid safety of the library.

She didn't seem to notice. "People tell you it gets easier with time. People tell you you'll forget. But you never do." She stared across the valley at the cemetery, at the evergreens and graves against the gray December sky, as though she were attempting to read the inscription on one particular gravestone. She blinked, seemed to come out of a trance. "Silly me. The book. I forgot all about it."

Matt was halfway across the library, backing toward the door. He stared at her. "The what?"

"*The Ghost Stories of Henry James.* You asked to see it."

"Oh, yes. Of course, your book."

3
Under the Tree

Angela studied for as long as she could Saturday morning, until the words on the page began to blur and she could no longer remember what she'd been reading.

She sat at a carrel next to the wall-high windows at the modern Ground Level end of Suzzallo Library. It was a well-lighted place with plenty of rustling jackets and scraping chair legs and foot traffic. The plastic-looking Ground Level of the library was too modern and well-lit and boring for spooky noises or disappearing women. She'd been studying there all day.

Zipping up her books into her backpack, she left the library and set out into the cold, crisp day to walk around campus and the District until the fresh air revived her. She kept walking for almost two hours, thoroughly reconnoitering the Ave, combing Ravenna Park from one end to the other.

She was in a grassy grove on the far side of the ravine when she realized she was getting tired. She only intended to rest for a moment, settling down at the base of a large leafless maple, curling up between two giant, ground-breaking roots. She didn't realize how exhausted she was, didn't realize she was falling asleep, until her head nodded forward with an awakening jerk.

Her eyes snapped open. The sky was moody, overcast. The wind-rattled leaves were hissing and rustling all around her. She heard a crackling and snapping of dry grass. She peered into the branches on every side. Ahead of her the evergreen boughs parted. A figure crouched in the bushes in front of her, eyes wide, watching her.

"Stay away from me!" she hissed.

"I won't hurt you," said the creature. He seemed to be composed primarily of a navy-blue stocking cap pulled down to his eyebrows, with worn-out, muddy denim knees protruding on either side. Hunched over in a crouch, the creature waddled toward her with a popping and breaking of weeds.

"Don't come any closer."

"I won't. I won't."

But the snapping fronds and crunching twigs told her he was getting nearer. A bare, bony knee bulged out through frayed denim threads. Bloodless, unshaved cheeks were shadowy brown with fuzz. Tendrils of unwashed hair, dusted with bits of leaf and burrs, wormed free of his cap and squiggled down over his pale forehead.

She caught a whiff of something human, dangerous.

"You stink. Don't touch me!"

"Do I really stink? I just wanted to show you this."

"Stay away from me."

"I *am* staying away. But just look at this. I think you'll like it. Maybe you will. Look and see. It's a poem."

CHAPTER FIVE

Sunday, December 15

1
Black Cat

"I've fallen in love with my neighbor," said Matt, grinning up at Veronica from where he was sitting on his porch that afternoon.

She was coming down from the second floor, descending the side stairs. "In love with your neighbor?" she echoed. She was wearing her black overcoat, clutching her purse, and clearly didn't know what he was talking about.

Matt was comfortably ensconsed, legs outstretched and crossed, on the wooden bench that bordered one side of his porch. A cold cup of coffee was forgotten beside him. He'd spent most of the day, as well as all of yesterday, emptying boxes, arranging drawers and shelves, stocking cupboards, creating a home. He'd just read the first twenty pages of an Iris Murdoch novel that Veronica had loaned him.

It had been a stark black-and-white Sunday. Frozen, half-dead fern fronds rattled crisply all around the house. Though the afternoon breeze had a chilly sting, he was bundled in his fur-lined denim jacket. The air was a heady rush, a Northwest delicacy worth sitting in the cold to savor.

"Which neighbor is that?" said Veronica. She spoke guardedly, not exactly sure what her new tenant was trying to tell her. Then she saw the black cat beside him, nuzzling its head under Matt's dangling hand, licking at his fingers.

"It's so friendly," said Matt. "Where does it live?"

"As far as I know, this little rascal is without a home," said Veronica. She approached slowly and quietly to avoid alarming the cat. "I get the impression he's wild. I've seen him visiting other houses around here, turning on the charm, asking for donations."

"Wild cats aren't usually so trusting." As though inspired by Matt's comment, the black cat jumped up into his lap and settled into a comfortable ball, purring loudly.

"There, you see," said Veronica. "Shameless."

"Well, hello there," said Matt, scratching under its chin which the cat extended toward him for easy access. "Aren't you the friendliest guy on the block!"

Veronica smiled and waved goodbye as she continued down the hillside. "I'd say that cat is seriously considering you for a roommate."

2
Not Listening

Angela hated Sundays.

She hated being walled up alive in the house with her parents, pretending she didn't notice the fighting behind closed doors. If she totally concentrated on the book in front of her, if she walled out everything else except studying for her finals, Angela could pretend that she didn't hear her parents downstairs. She hunched forward over her bedroom desk, her back firmly to the door.

Weak December sunlight filtered through the window onto the pages of her open textbook. The voices of her parents got louder. Angela began chewing on a fingernail. When the finger began to bleed, she jumped up, knocking her chair over backwards. Grabbing her earphones, she pulled them down over her ears and turned the music up loud.

But the frustration and rage filtering through the walls of the house were louder and meaner than any rock music she could play. Not even Madonna, pouring out her heart into Angela's earphones, could drown out the bitter words, the hateful accusations.

Angela began pacing, trying not to hear the ugly things her parents were saying, trying not to care. Let them destroy their marriage, if they wanted to! She would get along just fine without them.

The sound of her mother crying always upset her. If her father was such a smart man, why couldn't he figure out how to save his own family? She was nearly ready to scream. She clenched her fists. When would they stop? When?

A sharp, splintering crack.

The sound startled her, seemed to snap her out of it. She turned off her CD-player, took off her earphones, looked around in bewilderment. Nothing had moved or fallen. Then she saw the framed photograph of her mother and father on her bureau drawers.

The glass had cracked down the middle.

Angela stared at the broken picture, her lower lip trembling. Why had the glass cracked?

Footsteps approached. A knock at the door.

"Angela are you all right?" said her father, standing outside her room.

"I'm fine."

"What was that sound?"

"I dropped a picture," said Angela. "The glass cracked. It's okay."

"You be more careful."

"I will."

She waited until the footsteps retreated. Then she pulled a folded piece of paper out of the plastic inner pocket of her three-ring binder. The paper was covered with graphically printed words, some bold and clear, others less so. The largest words were in the center of the poem.

Whatever your doing
Is what you get
No need to be crying
No time to fret

At least your not dying
Its not over yet
So try to keep smiling
Im glad we met

The rest of the poem was crowded down at the bottom of the page. The words were too crunched and tiny to be legible.

3
Secret Place

After an hour of searching, Angela found him down in the ravine, sitting on a huge boulder out in the middle of the creek, surrounded by a zigzagging wooden walkway. She stood at the end of the walkway, watching him. He glanced in her direction, then looked away. She approached and sat cautiously near him, on a low wooden stair.

A dozen scowling, sweaty men in their thirties thundered down the ravine trail in a blur of gaudy, expensive running gear. Somewhere nearby an old woman was patiently calling her wayward dog.

"I like your poem," she said.

His face brightened, and he turned to look in her direction. "You do? My name's John. What's your name?"

"Angela."

He scrambled up onto his feet on the boulder, his dirty green parka flapping open at his sides like tattered plastic wings. "You really like it?"

"Really. And the way you print it out. It's like calligraphy."

"That's what it is!" he cried excitedly, jumping down onto the wooden boardwalk beside her. "The word you just said — that's exactly what it is!"

"I like it." She lowered her defenses. He seemed harmless. "Sometimes I don't understand poems. Sometimes it seems like they go around and around in circles trying not to say things. But I like your poem."

He grinned broadly. "My poems don't go around and around. You understand my poems. Poems are the only reason for living. Come on, I'll show you my secret place."

Angela was immediately wary. "I don't think so." She had been warned about situations like this.

"Don't be afraid. You can trust me."

"It's not that I don't trust you—"

"Come on, you'll like it."

She couldn't help being curious to see how he survived without a home. "Where exactly is it?"

"This way," he said, taking her hand. "Not far."

She pulled her hand away from him. "Are there going to be other homeless people there?" She had seen them sleeping under the bridges in the ravine, anonymous lumps in dirty, torn sleeping bags, their heads tucked under like snails. She'd seen them sitting on the shadowy bridge bulkheads under the spans, talking loud and drinking from mysterious bottles in paper bags. They scared her.

"No way," said John.

When he took her hand again, she gave up resisting. He led her up a winding trail out of the ravine, toward the upper grassy banks of Ravenna Park.

"I stay away from other homeless people," said John. "They're like animals. They don't write poems. Do you know what the law of the pack is?"

"No," said Angela cautiously, trying to remain very aware of where he was leading her, ready to turn and bolt at the least sign of danger.

"Well, that's how they live. The law of the pack. It's not pretty." He seemed to think that summed it up. "I'm not like that. I don't live in a pack."

The ravine was bleak and winter bare. Banks that a few months ago had been lush green with vegetation were now trampled flat and hard with dead leaves and dirt.

"Do you go to shelters?"

"No way. Never go to shelters. Never beg. You're always safest around universities. I can pass for a graduate student." He giggled. "Sometimes I find a way to hide in empty classrooms before the night doors get locked. Those are good nights. A nice warm place to sleep. Otherwise — well, here it is."

They had reached the top of the ravine bank, where the grassy fields of the park began. Just beyond a weathered bench was a low tunnel through a thicket of branches. He ducked down and led her after him. Crunching and stumbling around stumps of laurel, prickly holly and a few sparse ferns, he led her over broken, rotten branches, through ivy and moss, on a vague, half-defined footpath. Overhead, against the gray sky, the intertangled bare twigs closed around them like a web. Below, at one end of the soccer field, she could see white goal-posts like prehistoric skeletal remains.

His secret place was a couple dozen steps into the trees down the ravine bank. He had carefully, methodically, marked out his place on the ground in an orderly frame of twigs. It was about six feet long and three feet wide, like a grave, covered with cut fern leaves laid flat.

"This is my bed," he said. "And these are my closets." He showed her his hiding-places in the bushes where he stashed his belongings in plastic bags. He proudly raised a broken umbrella, with one metal spine sticking out. "And this is for keeping dry on rainy nights."

In spite of herself, Angela was impressed. She could feel herself relaxing. "I like it here."

"Me, too." He sat down on a stump with a casual familiarity that showed he had sat there often. "So, what's on your mind?"

She regarded him warily. She was about to reply that nothing was on her mind, and instead said, "I've been thinking of running away."

He nodded, as though he understood perfectly. "Don't blame you." Suddenly he stiffened, lurched to his feet, and began pawing at his bundles. In a moment, he had pulled out a pen and a sheet of paper, and at once began scribbling down words as fast as he could until he had finished.

"Inspiration," he explained. "When it comes, you have to go with it." He handed her the poem.

Doesnt matter
Where you run
No way out
Until your done

Your salvation
Wont be fun
Dont give up
Until youve won

"You're spooky," she said, backing away from him.

He smiled. "Just gotta be me."

She started to run.

He waved goodbye. "Don't worry," he called after her, as she hurried toward home, "I'll teach you the ropes."

CHAPTER SIX

Monday, December 16

1
Final Exams

Nothing could have prepared Matt.

Not for the shocking difference between his first two days on the job — the half-deserted bookstore, the occasional customer — and what happened to the bookstore on Monday.

Monday morning was the beginning of finals week.

At least he'd gone to bed early the night before. No more strange women had visited him during the night. Though a sound had awakened him in the wee hours of the morning, and a shadow had crossed his window, a leap out of bed and a curious look had revealed only his new feline friend, tail stiff and straight up, rubbing its shoulder against the glass.

So he'd had plenty of rest. Fortunately!

The doors of the bookstore slammed open at eight o'clock to an invasion of frantic, sleepless, nervous, red-eyed young people assembling in impatient lines at the cash registers to buy their multiple choice answer sheets and examination blue books, before rushing out again toward their individual destinies.

Suddenly, in the midst of it all, Veronica appeared in front of his counter, her cheeks flushed from the morning air. Bundled in her black overcoat and a midnight blue wrap-around scarf, she was as surprised as he was.

"I had no idea you worked at *this* University Book Store. I assumed you worked on the Ave. My office is just across the parking lot. In Padelford Hall."

"Hello, neighbor," he said. "Something in the universe seems determined that our paths should cross."

"Does this customer need special help?" interrupted Martha Ironwood, thrusting her professional smile between them. "We're always happy to help faculty members."

"I've been helped, thank you," said Veronica. Clutching a Christmas card for her parents, the only card she would send that holiday season, she hurried out of the bookstore.

As the next wave of students started gathering in anxious lines, Matt ran to the back of the bookstore to check the price of a bestseller. In the process, he noticed a figure loitering in the Fantasy and Science Fiction corner, spellbound over a new sword-and-sorcery epic. She was younger-looking than most students, a slender girl with long, lustrous brown hair, scowling, wearing headphones.

When he noticed her again an hour later, back in the same corner, she was in the same position, clutching the same paperback, in the grips of the last few pages.

The day was long and furious.

In the frenzy of running the cash register, he almost failed to recognize his fellow renter, Tyler Wates. Baseball cap on backwards, silver cross swinging against his T-shirt, red-eyed, unshaved, Tyler was buying a box of No-Doz and clearly needed a tablet immediately. Nearly dozing on his feet, he counted out his money laboriously, spreading it slowly and carefully on the counter, much too tired to distinguish the difference between dimes and pennies.

"Good luck on your test," said Matt.

"Luck has nothing to do with it," said Tyler grimly. "It's just learning to accept the Lord's will."

The onslaught of exam-crazed students was repeated throughout the day. Matt's idealism about a budding career as a bookseller crashed and burned. He faced the bitter truth. He was a cashier.

*

Angela sailed through her chemistry final without a hitch. She was one of the first to gather up her belongings, turn in her exam, and walk out of Bagley Hall into the bright, chilly morning.

The windblown spray from the high, aquatic spires of Drumheller Fountain misted over her as she walked along the edge of the pond. She had paused for a moment to watch the ducks when she heard footsteps hurrying after her. Ellen Wu chugged up beside her, snugly bundled in a red overcoat, still pulling her red woolen gloves onto pudgy fingers.

"How did you do?"

"It was easy."

Ellen's eyes grew huge behind her glasses. "You thought that test was easy?"

"Chemistry is pretty simple."

Ellen Wu was having trouble walking fast enough to keep up with her. "Maybe, if you like chemistry. I like physics better."

"Physics is okay," said Angela in a neutral voice, adding impulsively, "I like relativity."

"I *love* relativity," cried Ellen. "Time dilation is so cool!" Suddenly she thrust a folded piece of paper into Angela's hand. "Call me over the break. Maybe we can do something together." The act caught Angela by surprise, stopped her in her tracks. Ellen looked up at her candidly. "I think we should be friends."

Angela stared at her. "You do?"

"Call me," said Ellen and hurried away. Her red coat disappeared into the hundreds of exhausted, disoriented students pouring out of the chemistry final.

*

Not for the first time, Veronica struggled to remember what it was like to be a student. Exhausted from lack of sleep, jittery from too much caffeine, nervous from cramming, students in various states and conditions of suspended animation came bumping and jostling into the classroom. None of them looked capable of writing a coherent sentence, much less doing any serious thinking.

She waited at the podium in front of the classroom for backpacks to thud to the floor, for coats to flop over the backs of chairs, for the last flurries of chatter. Tyler had been up all night, and looked it. Bethany looked appropriately somber.

The Early Entrance student had been, as usual, the first one to arrive in class. Lately Angela had been looking increasingly troubled. But, after all, it was the end of the quarter, it was finals. The draining last week often wore down students. Veronica had other things to occupy her thoughts. In spite of herself, she couldn't get her new tenant out of her mind.

Even the cat liked him!

While the class wrote their finals, she worked on the troublesome last chapter of her Edith Wharton book. Her thoughts kept wandering. By the time the bell rang at the end of the exam, she'd composed three messy, crossed-out paragraphs which couldn't be tortured into expressing what she wanted them to say.

She collected the bluebooks. Angela's chair in the back row was empty. Her neatly-written bluebook was all that remained.

71

2
Night Lights

"We've got to stop meeting like this."

They both laughed. They had just met again in the laundry room. He was wearing a black sweatshirt with *Hot Blood* splashed across the chest in dribbly red letters. She was still dressed from a long day in her campus office, black slacks, turquoise Italian silk shirt. She moved an armful of clean, wet clothes into the dryer, while he dumped in his dirty clothes to take their place.

"I'm still shaking from finals assault on the bookstore. I've got to get back my sense of humor." He shook a stream of blue detergent into the washing machine. "I'm heading out for a short walk in a minute. Feel like joining me?"

She came close to saying an automatic, "No, thank you," but the idea was appealing. "Let me grab a coat."

They headed toward the park, but the evening was coming on quickly, and the ravine was nowhere to be walking after dark. Hesitating uncertainly at the bottom of the boulevard, they were lured by a twinkling, brilliantly-lit home, its front shrubbery and trees transformed into a glittering rainbow of lights. Another house drew them a little farther along, and then Veronica noticed the house with the Nutcracker Princes marching around its fence.

"Of course," she said. "Come on, up this way. We can take a walk down Candy Cane Lane."

"Candy Cane Lane?"

*

Angela crouched in the bushes at one end of Park Road, watching unseen. John was behind her across the alley, in the thickets of Ravenna Park.

"Come here and look," she whispered.

"I don't want to," whined John, hidden in the tall, dead stalks of grass. "I thought you hated Candy Cane Lane."

"Sometimes I do."

"Well, I don't like it here. Too many people. Let's go."

"Oh, my God, there's Professor Glass," she hissed, ducking her head behind the thicket of branches.

"I told you we shouldn't have come," hissed John.

"Yes, we should have," said Angela, taking another peek through the branches at her teacher. "I'm glad we came." Professor Glass was walking with a man, walking slowly, the way people walk when they like each other. She watched them until they were out of sight.

"Too many people," said John unhappily.

Angela didn't say anything. She knew what Candy Cane Lane could be like, and this was nothing yet. Soon the sidewalks would never be empty. Soon the line of cars would never end. But the lights! So twinkling, so cheerful—

Rising from her crouch, she hurried back across the alley to the edge of the park where John was waiting impatiently.

"You have to admit it's pretty!" she said.

"Let's go," said John. "I need to write a poem."

"No, I want to go closer. I want to get a better look at the man walking with Professor Glass."

She grabbed for John to pull him along. He shoved her away. "Leave me alone."

"Well, stay here if you want," she said. "I'm going closer."

"Go closer if you want. I'm staying here."

She left him in the bushes without a backward glance. There was no sign of Professor Glass and her man friend. She looked toward her own house. Completely dark, no lights inside or out. No one home. She turned toward the centerpiece.

Around the base was a ring of moving toys — a giant rocking-horse, a giant dolls' house, a giant jack-in-the-box bursting out of his box. Rising above them loomed the enormous head of a Nutcracker Prince, jaws stretching from ear to ear, opening and closing, big enough to snap up and swallow one of the circling cars.

Soon she forgot all about the lights and Christmas decorations and even the jaws of the Nutcracker Prince. Far more fascinating were the passing cars. Cars full of families, of adults and children sharing an evening together, loving each other, trusting each other. She tried to think what it would be like. Family after family. The sight made her sad. Candy Cane Lane made her sad.

She turned away. When she got back to the bushes on the edge of the park, John was gone.

*

Each of the slender, ornamental trees that lined the winding sidewalk wore a large red ribbon. Elves and Raggedy Ann dolls peered out of frosted windows. Angels and shooting stars swept by overhead. Lights, swarms of lights, glittering galaxies of lights made the street blaze and twinkle with color.

They walked up one side of Candy Cane Lane and down the other. They came back out where they had gone in, and slowly made their way toward home.

Veronica abruptly stopped.

"What's wrong?" said Matt. "See somebody you know?"

It was him again. Across the alley, in the bushes and wild grass on the edge of Ravenna Park, half-hidden in the shadow of the trees, stood the homeless man. He saw her at the same time. He turned and walked quickly away.

"That man over there," she said. "Last week I found him sleeping in the parking garage. He was probably as scared as I was. He gave me a poem."

"No kidding. A homeless poet. Was it any good?"

"Pretty crazy. I've still got it. I'll show it to you when we get back."

He gasped and stopped abruptly, as though he'd been stabbed from behind.

"What is it?" she asked, looking at his face for the answer.

"The mountain," he said, pointing. "Look at that! Isn't it incredible? It's so beautiful."

The dark silhouette of Mount Rainier rose up in the southeast, sharp and clear in the icy air, blue-white against a sky flushed pink.

Veronica felt closer to him at that moment than she had felt to anyone in so long. Before she had time to think about it, to analyze her motives, to consider the repercussions, to inhibit herself, her knuckles bumped against his and she took hold of his hand. His fingers clasped back. He turned to her and smiled. Her heart leaped.

They didn't let go all the way home.

CHAPTER SEVEN

Tuesday, December 17

1
"What Happened to You?"

Clarice Jackson glanced up from her computer screen, and then couldn't stop staring. From the moment Veronica walked into the English Office to pick up her mail, Clarice could tell that her friend seemed different.

"Well, what happened to *you?*"

"What are you talking about?" said Veronica, looking up over the edge of an opened letter. "Absolutely nothing has happened to me."

"Is that so?"

"Yes, of course that's so." She gave Clarice an amused look of exasperation. "What are you getting at?"

"Nothing, nothing," said Clarice. "Just wondering. How was your night last night?"

"Fine. Went for a walk down Candy Cane Lane."

"Oh, isn't that fun! We drive through every year. Who'd you go with?"

"The new tenant. He moved in Friday."

"Ah, ha!" said Clarice triumphantly, like a detective spotting a fingerprint. "So that's it! I knew you had something up your sleeve. He's pretty nice, huh?"

"Oh, come on, Clarice, don't make something out of nothing," said Veronica. "You're being silly."

"Who's being silly? You come in here smiling from ear to ear, beaming like a lighthouse, I'm supposed to think you had another boring Monday night?"

"Beaming?" echoed Veronica in confusion. "Am I smiling? I don't mean to be."

"So, when did I stop being your friend? When did you stop telling me everything?"

"Clarice, you know I always do—"

"Well, then, this tenant who's walked into your life—"

"He hasn't walked anywhere."

"Of course not. And he's a hunk?"

"Clarice, not all attractive men have to be hunks."

"Ah, ha! You admit he's attractive. And?"

"And?" Veronica sighed in defeat, abandoning all hope of concealment. Suddenly the two friends were laughing together. "Okay, I admit he seems very nice. He's kind and intelligent. And sensitive. And literate. I confess, I think I'm going to like having him in the house."

2
Metamorphosis

Angela left campus in the afternoon, earphones clamped on securely. She headed straight past the fraternities and sororities out the tree-lined length of Greek Row. When she got to Ravenna Boulevard, she turned toward the park.

Last night at home had been one of the worst. She was still in shock. Her parents had shouted such mean things at each other. Life, as she knew it, was coming to an end. She hated going back to that house. Hated it!

She crossed the alley into Ravenna Park and set off past the tennis courts and the few scattered picnic tables into the trees. Instead of going down the gravel trail into the ravine, she glanced behind her to make sure no one was watching, then darted around the park bench into the bushes. Making as few crackling footfalls as possible, she worked her way down through a tunnel of brittle, half-frozen branches on a vague trail descending into the thickets on the ravine bank.

The sky flickered nervously. A brief, shuddering brightness overhead. A rumbling thundercrack.

John was sitting on a stump near his fern bed. He made no acknowledgement of her presence. His brow was furrowed, his pen working busily. He glanced up at the moody, darkening sky, squinted, frowned, and popped open his umbrella, which he hooked into the branches over his head. He had scarcely done so when he gave a startled cry, and jotted down a quick phrase. Then a few more words. Then several more lines. Then one last word. He made a sound halfway between a laugh and a shout, and looked up at her in relief.

"Done!" He grinned. "You'll like it. I mean, I really think you'll like it. I mean, I know you will, but I mean, really. Well, here. Take a look. Go ahead. I wrote it for you."

She took it from him, and stared in amazement at the complexity of the columns and columns of microscopic print. She could read the larger words.

Heart on fire
What you desire
Dark is whole
Out of control

Cant get away
All must pay
Life is strange
Time to change

"What's it supposed to mean?"

"Don't ask me," said John. "Never, *never* ask the poet. The poet is the last one to find out. The poet is doing his best, just getting it all down on paper."

She didn't want to talk about poets. She took a deep breath. "I've decided to run away."

"I thought you might."

"But I've got a few questions."

"I like questions," said John. "You can't really be friends if you don't ask questions. Smart people ask lots of questions. My teacher told me that. Questions show you're smart. Questions are what we need in this world."

"I'm trying to ask you one."

"Fire away."

"How do you manage to eat?"

He tucked in his shirttail, then stretched and pulled it out again. He scratched the back of the stocking cap over his head. "You manage. You worry about it a lot. You do what you have to do. I'll show you where to find food. I'll show you how to stay dry and warm. There are tricks. You learn them. Slowly. I'll show you what places to avoid. I'll show you where to go when the cops drive through the park. I'll teach you right. I'm an expert."

"Why?"

"Why what?"

"Why do you want to help me?" said Angela. She stared at him unflinchingly, looking for the slightest sign of deceit.

He stared back. "Because I'm not afraid of you."

"Why should you be?"

"I'm afraid of most people," he stated matter-of-factly, "but I'm not afraid of a girl like you. You're probably only twelve years old."

"Thirteen!"

"Well, I'm not afraid of a thirteen-year-old girl. That's your problem. Nobody in his right mind is afraid of a thirteen-year-old girl."

"Obviously, that's a problem," said Angela contemptuously. "This world is not designed for thirteen-year-old girls. Not much I can do about that."

"Oh, yes there is."

"But I can't help what I am," said Angela.

"You can help what people think you are," said John.

Suddenly he seemed to forget about her completely. He began intently rummaging through his belongings. He went from one plastic bag to another, from bush to bush, dragging out all kinds of rags and rubbish, little bottles and jars, odds and ends, forgotten parts and broken things, muttering to himself, whining and groaning with frustration. Then he cried out. He raised something sharp and metal and gleaming.

Angela took two stumbling steps backward in a panicky retreat before she realized what it was.

Scissors.

"The solution is simple," he said. "Haircut."

She stared at him, not knowing whether to run or laugh.

"Cut my hair? You? You don't know how," she managed to protest.

"What's to know? Clip-clip. Don't have to be an expert. It's easy. I mean, people have cut their hair for thousands of years. It's legal. And your hassles will be gone, like that!" He snapped his fingers. "Believe me, you'll look just like a boy."

"A boy?"

"People are afraid of thirteen-year-old boys. Thirteen-year-old boys can be scary. They're unpredictable. They can be dangerous. Therefore, they're respected."

She started to say, "But I don't want to look like a boy." She almost said, "But I don't want to cut my hair." Her mouth opened in protest, full of objections, but none of them came out. The structure of her world was collapsing. Suddenly she felt like being an active agent in the mess. There was one thirteen-year-old girl in the world who preferred breaking the rules on purpose before all the rules were changed. Even if the price was her long, pretty hair!

When he took her by the hand, she didn't pull away. He led her to a fallen tree-trunk. "Really, it's the perfect solution!" he said. His confidence in the plan reassured her so much that she didn't protest. "Just sit down here. Don't worry, it doesn't hurt. I'll take care of the whole thing for you. Honest, it's easy. Just a couple minutes, and presto! No one will know it's you."

Lightning flashed across the sky, brighter, throwing bigger shadows. The following rumble was louder and closer, with an angry edge.

"Come on, before it starts raining," he said. "It's hard to cut somebody's hair in the rain."

She allowed herself to be seated. She tried not to think about what her parents were going to say when they saw her. She stared straight ahead, as though waiting for a gunshot. She almost jumped up and ran as the first clump of hair plopped at her feet in the slick, wet mulch of dead leaves.

Another. Another. Curling, scattering little pieces of herself that weren't her anymore. Clip-clip. Another. Clip-clip.

"Now, don't move, or I'll make a mistake. You don't want to lose one of your ears, do you?"

Angela took him seriously and froze, trying to believe she was doing the right thing. Clumps of hair dropped around her on every side like little dead mice.

"So, when are you going to run away?"

"Don't want to talk about it."

"Are you finished with school?"

"Don't bug me with questions. You're just like my Dad. Questions, questions, questions."

But the mention of her father caused a delayed reaction. It suddenly struck her what she was doing. She surged to her feet with an anxious cry.

"Hey, watch out!" he protested. "Do you want a bald spot?"

"My Mom and Dad are going to see stars!" she said, with a gasp of horror. "They're going to go into orbit. How can I show up with my hair chopped off?"

"Is that all you're worried about?" said John. "No problem."

Setting down the scissors, he darted to one of his plastic bags, thrust in an arm, rummaged about, and pulled out something that could have been a place-mat or a purse. It was neither. He shook it out, and thrust it onto her head. It was a big floppy purple hat. "It never looked very good on me, anyhow."

Angela was only slightly relieved. "I can't go around wearing a weird hat like this."

"There's nothing weird about my hat," said John with authority, pulling her back to the tree trunk and sitting her down again. "Now, stop worrying and running around half-done. Sit still, so I can do this right."

Clip-clip, clip-clip.

"Goodbye, thirteen-year-old girl," he said, with a snip here and a snip there. "Hello, somebody else. Hello, mystery person. Who are you going to be now? Time to chop off that name of yours. Clip-clip. Now that you've got a new haircut, you need a new name. Clip-clip. You can't be Angela any more. Well, what'll it be? Clip-clip." He concentrated on his haircutting for a moment, then gave a sharp, excited cry, like the squawk of a startled bird. "I've got it! All we have to do is chop off the end of your name, just like we chopped off your hair. Chop off the last letter, and we've got a new name."

"Angel isn't a name."

"Angel is a name," said the homeless man with confidence. "Angel is a very good name. And it's yours."

"Angel?"

With a park-rattling thundercrack, the sky dissolved into sheets of rain.

CHAPTER EIGHT

Wednesday, December 18

1
Confused

After consciously avoiding him all of yesterday, to her surprise she discovered Matt seated over against the wall in Espresso Roma that afternoon, as though they'd had plans to meet and he was waiting for her. His wet denim jacket was draped over the chair beside him. He looked up from the paperback he was reading, and smiled.

She closed her dripping umbrella as she walked toward him through the wooden tables. Intense, graphic concert posters loomed on one side, giant primitive oil nudes on the other. Several struggling table lamps along the way lit the leaves of a few long-suffering houseplants. Jazz thrummed and purred from state-of-the-art speakers in every corner.

"Fancy meeting you here."

"This thing is incredible," he said, marking his place in the Iris Murdoch novel.

"She's the best," said Veronica.

They were both awkward, very aware that they hadn't seen each other yesterday, that they hadn't spoken since their stroll through Candy Cane Lane the night before.

"I'm having another cappuccino. What can I get you?"

"A short double mocha would be perfect."

She watched him from across the coffee house, amid the scattering of graduate students, street kids, aging hippies. He managed to carry both steaming glass mugs back to the bench without spilling a drop.

"How's the bookstore?"

"Well, let's say I'm past the idealistic stage. I've seen how ugly it can get. Thank God finals are over."

He sipped his cappuccino. She sipped her mocha. They glanced at each other and smiled awkwardly.

"I think we got a little carried away on our stroll through Candy Cane Lane," she said softly. "Hope you don't think we're getting serious. Or that I want to be in a relationship."

"Not at all," he said. "Thanks for being honest. I feel the same. It's not a good time for me. I've got enough complications in my life."

"I enjoy your company so much, it's easy to start letting things slide. Including common sense! It's ridiculous to be acting that way with someone I've just met."

"You're a very easy person to be around, and I guess I started getting confused."

"Believe me, I was the confused one," said Veronica.

"Actually, I'm still very confused," said Matt.

He reached impulsively across the table and took her hand. His fingers wrapped around hers, held on, didn't let go. She tried very hard to deal with it intellectually. She could rationalize it. She could explain it. But she couldn't pull her hand away. Her emotions washed right over every attempt at control. Suddenly her hand was clasping him back.

"It's too soon," she said.

"It's not very smart."

"It just leads to a lot of pain."

"Someone is going to get hurt."

"I don't know what's happening," she said awkwardly, "but it's pretty clear that *something* is happening."

He nodded. "Something is definitely happening."

2
Sudden Vacation

She was someone different the moment she woke up.

She rolled over in bed, raised a hand to brush her hair back out of her eyes, and there was nothing there to brush away. She lurched out of dream-fog into immediate consciousness with a jolt of alarm. Angela Harrow, the helpless, unhappy daughter of divorcing parents, was gone forever. Someone new and unpredictable was in her bed, taking her place, someone who was no longer quite so helpless because she had decided to take her destiny into her own hands.

Someone named Angel.

She looked at herself in the full-length mirror on her closet door. A skinny stranger with chopped-off hair looked back at her, a stranger with secretive eyes who seemed to be keeping secrets even from herself.

She'd gotten in last night wearing the floppy purple hat without her parents seeing her haircut. To her amazement, they had yet to notice it. Her act of rebellion was going undetected. But it was only a matter of time, a bomb waiting to go off, a house-rocking explosion temporarily delayed.

She climbed into long, loose jeans, an old favorite pair. She pulled on a dark, baggy sweatshirt with sleeves that were too long. Wearing her black Keds, laced tight, bundled up in the fleecey depths of her navy blue jacket, her face engulfed by the tipping, wobbly sides of the purple hat, she grabbed her backpack and a copy of *Wuthering Heights,* and managed to escape from the house before her parents got up.

She spent the day in Suzzallo Library, even though her finals were over. She didn't have anything else to do. She'd brought along one of her favorite books, but was too restless to read more than a couple of chapters. Instead she browsed the shelves and poked and wandered, the floppy purple hat crushed down on top of her head.

By three o'clock her stomach was rumbling. She'd gone all day without food. She headed reluctantly toward home. She'd put off thinking about her haircut all day. Now she found herself dreading the inevitable showdown with her parents.

But she could postpone it a little longer. At that time of the afternoon, she would have a clear shot at the refrigerator. Her father would be at the office with clients, her mother still at the charity drive. With luck she could scamper out of the house again and delay the unpleasant encounter until that evening.

Luck seemed to be with her at first.

With her purple hat pulled down low over her head, she opened the door with her key and called, "Hello?"

No one answered. The house seemed to be deserted. She went up the stairs, called "Hello?" again, and looked into her parents' bedroom. The sight brought her to an unexpected halt. She backed up a couple steps and looked again, blinking.

The room was just like always, the television on its rolling table, bedlamps standing guard on either side of the king-size bed. But with one confusing difference. Spread out across the middle of the white bedspread were two open suitcases, half-packed. A chill shivered over her that had nothing to do with the icy December weather outside. Her father's neatly-folded underwear. Her mother's summer blouses and short pants.

She was still staring down into the suitcases when she heard the car pull into the driveway. She bolted out of her parents' bedroom like a guilty thief, and into her own room, closing the door behind her. She tried to forget what she had seen. Whatever the explanation, she was afraid to hear it. She didn't want to know.

She was considering climbing out the bedroom window, to escape before they discovered she was home, when she realized she had dropped off her backpack downstairs on the kitchen table. Which was right where her parents found it when they came in through the garage door.

"Angela, are you home?" called her mother, knowing the answer in advance from the evidence before her eyes.

There was no escape. She could already hear her father's heavy, anxious footfalls coming up the stairs, followed by her mother's lighter, quicker steps.

"Let me handle this," she heard her father mutter in a voice she was not intended to hear. A quick rapping at the door before it swung inward and they were both standing in the open doorway, blocking the one escape route.

"I suppose you've noticed that we're packing," said her father awkwardly, gesturing in the direction of the suitcases in the other room. "Sorry not to have told you before, but we just found out ourselves this afternoon."

"Angela, honey," said her mother, "I know you realize that your Dad and I haven't been getting along very well lately."

Her father closed in, cutting off her mother. "You're old enough and smart enough, Angela, to know that all relationships have their difficult times. When the rocky spots come, the two people in the relationship have to work them out together." He glanced significantly at his wife, as though imparting this bit of wisdom for her sake, too. "Well, you'll be glad to know that your mother and I are going to work it out."

"We've got to, honey," said her mother urgently. "We've got to make one last try to patch up our differences."

She tried not to look at them. She looked across the room, at the glass pig filled with hundreds of pennies on the shelf above her dresser. The pig began to tremble.

"And we've been very lucky," said her father. "By sheer luck, there's been a cancellation and your mother and I have managed to get two tickets to Hawaii. I just confirmed our hotel reservations. It's going to be our second honeymoon." He put his arm around his wife and drew her toward him.

She could hear something. She listened. The pennies in the glass pig were softly clinking together.

Her mother took hold of her father's hand. "The two of us haven't had any time alone together in so long, Angela."

"For thirteen years, to be precise," said her father.

Angel's eyes filled with tears. Suddenly she understood. The fault was hers. They were flying to Hawaii to get away from her.

The glass pig shuddered on the edge of the shelf.

"Angela, honey," said her mother, "I hope you can see that it's all for the best."

"Obviously we won't be leaving you here alone," said her father. "Aunt Debbie said you can spend Christmas with her in Tacoma." Her heart sank. Aunt Debbie's idea of a good time was watching soap operas all day. "How does that sound?"

"Okay," she managed to get out.

"Our flight leaves tomorrow morning."

So soon! Angel was trembling. "Okay."

"We'll take you to Aunt Debbie's before we go to the airport."

The pennies in the glass pig jingled louder.

"I know it's sudden," said her mother. "But you'll have a great Christmas with Aunt Debbie." Angel couldn't look up. Her mother noticed. "Honey, I can't see you under that awful hat. Where did you get that thing, anyway?"

"Angela," said her father sternly, "take off that silly, ugly hat so we can see your face."

He didn't wait for her to obey him. He reached out and in one quick, impatient swipe snatched the hat off her head. Her mother screamed at the sight of her chopped-off hair.

"Oh, Angela, how could you!"

"Why, you crazy little—!"

The glass pig tumbled off the shelf. It shattered, in an explosion of pennies across the floor.

Her mother screamed.

Angel lunged out the doorway. The bedroom door slammed behind her with such force that the house shook.

Her father grabbed the doorknob and yanked. The door wouldn't open. "Angela!" He twisted and jerked the knob. By the time it came loose and swung inward, she was already out of sight. He thundered down the stairs, lunged down the hallway, flung open the front door.

"Angela!" he shouted from the dark front porch. "Angela, you get back here! You are *not* going to ruin our vacation. *Angela—!*"

3

"Something Bad in Me"

Without knowing exactly where she was heading, she ended up deep in Ravenna Park, on the far bank of the ravine on a back trail no one used anymore. There she lunged to a stop, gasping for breath, her whole body trembling. She had just snapped her life in two, and left everything else behind. Her bedroom, her clothes, her place at the table, had all abruptly become things of the past.

Dark winter clouds thickened and shifted across the sky.

Angel was too shaken to remain still. Not knowing where to go or what to do, she paced up and down in a small, tree-strangled glade, getting her wind back, trying to think straight, trying to stop crying. Too many emotions were colliding inside her. Her skinny chest heaved to accommodate each gulp of air.

She was so upset she hardly knew where she was. And where would she go from here? Not home! Not back to her parents! She ran one of her hands back through her chopped-off hair. She stopped pacing, and stood completely still.

A chilly blast rattled the branches of the trees on the edge of the grove. It seemed to come out of nowhere. The shifting sky overhead darkened, thickening with moody clouds, the air sharp and electric, crackling with tension. Angel made a soft wailing sound. She doubled over, hugging her stomach. The wind whined around her like something alive. The seething current of disturbed air picked up twigs, broken branches, fragments of bark, dead leaves, hurtling them around the grove like an angry swarm of hornets.

"No," she moaned. "No, no, no—"

She realized she was no longer alone. The unnatural wind abruptly died. The airborne rubble dropped to the ground. The leaves ceased their whispering rustle.

The homeless poet stepped out from behind the drooping fronds of a giant fern. Bits of burr and leaf clung to the stocking cap covering most of his forehead. His eyes were huge, staring in disbelief. He opened his mouth to tell Angel what he had just seen. No words came out.

"What are you doing here?" She made no attempt to hide the irritation in her voice.

"That's a very good question," he said nervously, scratching his head. "The kind of question that makes you think. What am I doing here? I ask myself that question every day. I ask myself that question every hour."

"Oh, shut up. You've ruined everything!"

"I — what?"

"You made me look ugly." With tears suddenly running down her cheeks, she lunged at him, grabbed him by the front of his parka, shook him. "My parents hate my haircut!"

Her strength surprised them both. John was stammering. "Hate it? But it's — it's a fine haircut."

"They hate me!"

"How could anyone hate anything about you?"

A stinging wind sliced through the glade. The sky rippled with rapidly shifting shadows. Something was disturbing the grove. She pounded on his chest with her fists.

"They hate me because — something's wrong with me."

"Nothing's wrong with you," said John. "You're absolutely fine. You're perfect. You're nice."

"I'm not nice!" she snapped. "I'm weird. I'm scary. Sometimes I get so mad, so depressed. Sometimes I make things break. There's something bad in me. Something bad. And it's getting worse."

"Angel, Angel, you're not bad," said John. "There's nothing bad in you." He gently reached out and touched her hand.

Something slammed John square in the chest. He was flung to the ground in the weeds like a broken rag doll.

She ran toward the bridge.

4
Kid in the Ravine

They parted in front of the coffee house, each going their separate ways. Veronica returned to finish some last Edith Wharton research in the library. Matt, with scarcely an hour of daylight left, walked back to the house and began changing into his running clothes.

Already, after only a few days, he was developing a few rituals and routines. The bathroom had some pattern to it. The kitchen had a sense of where things ought to be. He was determined to make that house with a troubled past into a comfortable and trusted home.

The great surprise of his new life was happening inside him. Without the slightest intention of finding someone, in a house haunted by the unhappiest memory of his college years, he had discovered Veronica who was rapidly filling both his mind and his heart. Should he warn her about his disastrous batting record in love? Should he urge her to stay as far away as possible before he hurt her, before he added her unkindly treated heart to his collection of shattered relationships?

Locking the door behind him, Matt trotted down the front stairs to the sidewalk, with a glance up at the darkening sky. He trotted down the blocks of wet parked cars. There was still time left, before it got too dark, to run through Ravenna Park. He'd been trying to make a habit of regularly jogging out the tree-lined trail through the ravine, out to Cowen Park at the other end and back again. A perfect way to unwind after a stressful day at the bookstore.

Another jogger ran by in the other direction. He passed two women walking their dogs. Two teenagers whizzed by on bikes. Mostly he was alone. The trail was crackling hard underfoot, the ravine in the chill grip of winter. He heard something crashing toward him through the leaves.

Suddenly a kid bolted out of the snapping underbrush directly in his path. He wore a baggy, black sweatshirt and muddy-kneed levis, with a navy blue coat flapping open. His smooth, flushed cheeks were smeared with dirt and tears, his eyes swollen red from crying. Caught off-balance by Matt's unexpected presence, the teenager skidded off his feet, hitting the trail in a tangle of limbs. Matt helped him up onto his feet.

"Hey, are you all right? Do you need help?"

The kid was hardly grateful. He smelled of sweat and fear. Without a word, he pulled free of Matt's hold with a defiant jerk.

"What are you afraid of—?"

The kid scrambled away from him, skidding across the trail and over the side, down into the thickets and ferns of the ravine bottom.

"Hey, you okay?" shouted Matt.

But the kid was already out of sight.

Matt backtracked. That kid was in trouble. He loitered, waiting for some sign of him. The boy was nowhere to be seen.

Shaking his head in disbelief, Matt continued jogging out the main ravine trail. He crossed the low wooden bridge hovering less than a foot above Ravenna Creek. He was heading toward the open amphitheatre of trees ahead, where the high, graceful spans of the 20th Avenue NE Bridge crossed the ravine overhead at the height of the treetops. That was when he noticed the boy again.

This time the kid was leaning over the bridge railing a hundred feet directly above him.

Immediately cautious, suspecting a prank, Matt slowed his pace, keeping his eyes fixed upward, convinced that the little punk was in-

The 20th Avenue NE Bridge

tending to drop something on him. Then he realized that the kid had nothing of the sort on his mind. He was climbing over the railing.

Matt almost shouted at him, then decided that would be the worst thing to do. The very thought of what the kid was doing made Matt's stomach knot. He bolted off the trail, scrambled frantically up the side of the ravine, clutching roots and branches, using ferns for footholds. Clawing his way upward, he stumbled onto a bumpy, uneven footpath leading up. With luck, the kid would be too busy staring down into the deadly drop underneath to see Matt advancing. Once he made his way onto the bridge, Matt would have to keep his sight turned away from the edge. A wail of terror began to build in his chest at the very thought. He did not want to go close to the railing. Not for any reason.

Matt had nearly reached the top of the trail. Only a few more feet. The bridge seemed to slide and tip uneasily before him. The bitter taste of fear burned the back of his throat. His arms were already extended, trying to reach out for the kid who was very much on the wrong side of the railing.

When the kid heard him coming, he would let go. The kid would see him first. Matt couldn't get there in time. If Matt could only get one arm extended out over the railing far enough to hook around the crazy kid. But the boy was sure to kick and struggle.

Matt had almost reached the top of the ravine and was still frantically trying to plan his one slim chance at a rescue when his foot struck an unsteady rock on the edge of the path. The rock pulled free. Matt's foot skidded out from under him in a spray of wet leaves. Tumbling off the trail, he crashed over the edge of the embankment, over a fallen tree trunk, and down through the fronds of a giant fern. And another fern. And another.

His head thudded against the rock that stopped his fall.

*

Her sweaty hands refused to let go.

Angel stared down from the bridge at the dizzying tops of the tallest trees, at birds flying underneath her, at the trail winding below her through the bottom of the ravine. She tried to make herself succumb to the invitation of the effortless plunge, the sudden, soothing fall into nothingness.

Her hands, slick with perspiration, suspended her above the drop. Readying herself for the final act of her life, she was interrupted by the sight of a jogger on the trail below her — the same man she had nearly collided with moments ago — suddenly veering up the nearest footpath that climbed the ravine bank toward the bridge. He was looking up in her direction.

She would tolerate no interference.

She loosened the fingers of one hand, trying to make them disconnect from the railing. Her fingers refused, becoming claws with minds of their own. Before she could pry them free, before she could relinquish control of her life and let go, to her amazement, the jogger fell instead. Suddenly he went tumbling down the bank of the ravine. His body came to an abrupt stop in a crumpled pile of limbs.

Angel stared down, waiting for him to move, to change position, to scramble to his feet. The body didn't budge. The silence of the ravine roared in her ears.

The stillness of the jogger's body seemed to bring her to her senses. She carefully clambered back over the railing onto the bridge. How good the bridge's solid cement sidewalk felt under the rubber roles of her Keds! She hurried the length of it, hesitating at the end of the bridge. She looked down the bank.

The jogger hadn't moved.

She scrambled under the bridge, onto the highest of the several embankments. From that distance she couldn't tell if the jogger was breathing. Half-clambering, half-sliding down through tree-roots and ferns, she got as close to him as she dared.

She looked up and down the trail. No other joggers or bikers or people walking their dogs. He would die of the cold if she left him. She crouched down, trying to see his eyes. He was covered with mud. A line of blood ran across his forehead. He moaned faintly. The sound startled her to her feet with a pounding heart, ready to run. His head slowly turned to face her.

She recognized him. The man she had seen in Candy Cane Lane, walking with Professor Glass.

5
Unexpected Arrival

"You can call Edith Wharton a great writer," said Tyler grudgingly, "but from my point of view, she's just gloomy." He was standing in the laundry room door of her kitchen, defensively discussing his final exam. "Everybody suffers. Everybody is doomed. There's no hope for anyone. Is that supposed to be heavy literature? She's just a big sourpuss. Talk about a negative attitude."

"That's called a tragic vision," said Veronica patiently, washing the dishes while she listened to him, trying to be reasonably polite. "A tragic vision is one way of being honest about life, Tyler. Not being afraid to say the truth, even if it's unpleasant."

"Well, sometimes the truth can be pleasant," said Tyler, blinding her with his most charming grin, "if you just let it happen."

They were interrupted by a knock at the front door.

She promptly grabbed a dishtowel to dry her hands, taking advantage of the opportunity to extricate herself from the conversation. "I'll talk to you later, Tyler," she said, backing him out of the kitchen toward the laundry room. "Sounds like I've got company." He was still trying to get in a last word as she politely closed the door in his face. Then she quickly left the kitchen, crossed through the dining room, and opened the front door.

She went quietly into shock. A shabby teenage boy stood on her porch, supporting a filthy, groaning man who was splattered with mud, his vaguely familiar features contorted with pain. It took her a moment to recognize her new tenant.

"Matt!" she cried in alarm. "Matt, what happened?"

He struggled up onto his own feet, managed to maintain an unsteady balance, and tried to smile. "I'm okay." He winced. His glasses were tipped crookedly on his nose, and one of the lenses was cracked. "Ouch! oh! oh! oh!" he groaned, as various cuts and bruises and bumps over his body announced themselves. "I just wasn't watching where I put my feet."

"You could be seriously hurt. Let me take you to the hospital."

"No, no, no. It's not that bad."

"Well, come in off the porch, at least."

"Not yet. Let me clean up a little, okay? I can make it down to my place on my own. Besides, I think I'm going to throw up."

Before anyone could stop him, Matt staggered away across the porch, and down the side stairs in a stumbling, loose-footed hurry to his own front door below, which slammed.

She turned to the kid. "My God, what happened to him? Who are you? Come in here." Veronica opened the door wider, hustling him inside. The boy looked away from her, never straight in the eye.

"He fell."

"Fell? Where?"

"On the side of the ravine."

But Veronica was intently watching the boy's face. Something was bothering her. He looked familiar. She brought her face closer to his, peering into his eyes. "Who are you?"

92

The boy hesitated. "Angel."

"That's quite a name. Angel. I like it—"

That was when she realized who the kid was. This wasn't a boy at all. It was Angela Harrow, her bashful Early Entrance prodigy. Her hair chopped off, looking like a runaway, pretending to be someone else. She could sense the poor thing's distress.

"Are you in trouble, Angel?"

"No."

"Do you need a ride somewhere?"

"No."

"Do you live near here?"

"No."

"Angel, do you have somewhere to spend the night?"

That question took longer to answer. "No."

What came next out of Veronica's mouth was as much a surprise to her as it was to the girl. "Would you like to spend the night here?"

Angel looked at her with huge eyes. She shivered, wrapped her arms around herself, and nodded.

6

Head in Pieces

When no one answered her knock, Veronica poked her head into the lower apartment. "Hello? Are you okay down here?"

A lamp was lit in Matt's living room. The rest of the apartment was in shadows. She stepped over a discarded pile of rank and filthy clothes, dropped in a muddy heap by the laundry room door.

"Matt—?"

An answering groan came from the hallway. She crossed through the living room and down the short hall. The glow of the bedlamp spilled out through the open door . She entered quietly and stood by the bedside. Her scratched and battered new tenant emerged with a grunt of pain from under the blankets.

"How's the head?"

"In pieces. Does it show?"

She inspected the damage, wincing at what she saw. "You look like Humpty Dumpty." She tried to hide her concern in humor. "You've got to stop using your head so much. Does it hurt?"

"Not since you got here. I'll be fine. I'm just lucky to be back home. Where's that kid?"

"You mean your young rescuer? Upstairs."

"Better keep an eye on him. He was getting ready to jump off one of those bridges over the ravine."

Veronica drew in her breath sharply. She shuddered, then decided to change the subject, to lighten the tone and talk about Angel later. "So *you* decided to jump instead?"

He grinned weakly. "Something like that. I was trying to keep him from jumping, but I've got a bad problem with heights and — well, I never got there. So at least he's still here. Good. We've got a real troubled teen on our hands."

"Now, no one is on our hands," corrected Veronica. "Let's get a few things straight. First of all, your rescuer is not a boy. She's a girl."

"You've got to be kidding!" said Matt.

Veronica raised an eyebrow. "You find the idea of being rescued by a woman so amazing? Hmmm. Next topic. It turns out she's one of my students."

"You already know her?"

"And I'd be glad to help her, but there are a lot of weird laws. I don't want to be sued for interfering with some troubled kid. It's a matter of contacting the university, finding out who her parents are, and returning her to where she belongs."

"You're making her leave?"

"She can stay here tonight," said Veronica, speaking in a steady, sensible voice, "but tomorrow she goes home. Letting her stay is asking for a law suit. Legally I'm harboring an underage runaway."

Matt looked at her oddly. "Strange to hear a woman worry about the law instead of the welfare of a child."

His words brought her up short. Why was she speaking so coldly about the girl? Something in Veronica was pulling away from Angela, not wanting to grow fond of her, not wanting the unhappy kid in her life.

"You're right," she said, giving his hand a brief squeeze. "I can hardly believe it, but you're absolutely right." She smiled at him. "I hate to think I've hardened my heart so much that even a man can give me advice."

"Even a man?" said Matt.

She found herself closer than she thought. The sheer proximity of his body under the blankets made her dizzy. "Still, we can't harbor a runaway."

"I'm a runaway, and you're harboring me."

"You're not underage."

"Lucky for me."

Neither of them intended to kiss.

94

7
Questions

"Tell me, Angel, where did you plan to spend the night?"

Veronica drew the living room curtains against the December blackness outside. She had left the girl sitting in front of a crackling fire. When she'd come back upstairs the girl had scarcely budged, even though the fire had collapsed into glowing ruins.

Angel had picked up the open book abandoned on the armchair, and was now immersed in a Victorian ghost novel. The girl's scruffy head poked up from behind the thick volume. Her face was a fortress, betraying no emotion, no weakness, no crack of vulnerability. "I don't want to talk about it."

Veronica tried another approach. "Won't your parents worry about you?"

The girl made a point of not looking up from the book. "My parents have other things on their minds."

"What about your finals?"

"Finished."

"What about your friends?"

"Don't have any."

Veronica looked at her sadly, a frail, remote creature hunched over the old book. She could feel the kid's desperation. "Hungry?"

Angel shrugged. "Starving."

"How about some soup and a sandwich?"

"Awesome."

Angel followed her into the kitchen, watched her intently as she opened a can of soup and emptied it into a plastic container, mixing it with milk.

"What is that stuff, anyway?"

"Cream of broccoli."

"Ugh," she exclaimed. "Sorry. No way. Out of the question. I should have asked first, but I could never, ever, possibly—"

"How about just a sandwich," said Veronica.

"Super." She grinned, then the grin abruptly faded. "Do I have to leave tomorrow morning?"

Veronica took the girl's hand. "Angel, I don't want to make you leave. I want to help you. But if I let you stay, I'd be breaking the law. Do you realize that? I have an obligation to contact your parents. You won't go to jail for staying here. But *I* could go to jail."

"You won't go to jail," said Angel, with wide, sad eyes. "I would never let you go to jail."

They carried their sandwiches and mugs of hot chocolate up to the library, where they sat together, just the two of them.

"You've got so many books!" In open-mouthed amazement, she rose to her feet and turned slowly around, trying to read all the titles on the book spines, from one wall to the next wall to the next.

"I've always loved books," said Veronica, sipping her hot chocolate. "I can honestly say that reading has been the greatest joy of my life."

"Me, too!" said Angel passionately. "I love books, too."

Veronica smiled at her. She rustled her fingers through Angel's short-cropped hair. "Last quarter I had a student who loved books just as much as you do."

Angel blushed, and looked away from her.

"Tell me, has something bad happened at home, Angela?"

"Don't call me Angela," the girl snapped. "My name is Angel now, and I don't want to talk about it."

"All right, all right," said Veronica. "You don't have to talk about anything. It can all wait till morning."

"Thanks."

"And you're welcome to spend the night. I'm happy to have you here. But sooner or later, your parents have to be told."

Angel gasped. "Yes, of course." An idea had come to her like a slap. "My parents have to be told." She suddenly knew exactly what she wanted. "Please, Professor Glass," she faltered, "I was wondering — I was thinking — let me stay here with you. Please! Just until they get back from Hawaii. They're going for Christmas—"

"Who is?" interrupted Veronica.

"My parents. They're going to make me stay with my Aunt Debbie in Tacoma. But I could stay here with you. I'm quiet. I read. I could help. I don't want to be left in Tacoma alone—"

"But you'd be alone here, too. Except for me."

"With you, I would never be alone. Call them and tell them I can stay with you."

Veronica wanted to shout that the very idea was out of the question. Under no circumstances could anyone expect her to give up her privacy to harbor this precocious little brain-child. Especially with her new book's deadline breathing down her neck.

She looked into the girl's eyes.

"What's your telephone number?"

8
When Someone You Love Dies

With a little compacting and rearranging, Veronica was able to convert her library on the third floor into a reasonably comfortable guest bedroom.

"I don't believe he actually said it was all right."

"It took him a long time to say it," said Veronica, sliding a pillowslip around a fat pillow. "It's a good thing we had that phone conversation back when you signed up for my course. At least he recognized my voice. Although the whole thing would have been easier if you hadn't upset them so much by giving yourself that haircut." Angel made no comment. "Well, it's only right they should be concerned. He sounded like a nice man. He was very anxious about your safety. They really wanted to see you before leaving."

She responded sharply, without looking Veronica in the eye. "Well, I didn't want to see them."

"You made that very clear. They didn't want to force you. Besides, I think your poor father was willing to compromise. He didn't want to give up those tickets to Hawaii. And, really, what better risk — your daughter's college teacher. So he's happy, and we'll be happy. Everybody's happy."

"Too good to be true," said Angel. "Something's got to go wrong."

"So cynical!" said Veronica. "You're too young for such a gloomy outlook."

"Maybe I just haven't hit the happy times yet."

"Well, this old couch may not be beautiful," said Veronica, covering it with a sheet and tucking in the edges, "but it's extremely comfortable, as I can testify after falling asleep on it far too many times."

"It'll be fine," said Angel.

"And this comforter is nice and warm," she said. "It was my grandmother's. It's got goosefeathers inside — the perfect thing for a winter night like this."

Veronica's back was to the girl, and she was flapping out the comforter over the improvised bed, so she didn't see Angel walking over to the framed photograph on the wall.

"Who's this?"

Veronica turned and looked. Angel's nose was about three inches away from the photo. She was examining the picture intently. "That's my sister."

"She's so beautiful," sighed Angel.

"She was my favorite person in the world," said Veronica, in a voice she had trained not to break.

"Why do you say *was?*"

"My sister died," said Veronica. She said it bluntly and quickly.

"When was that?"

"A long time ago. Twenty years ago. She was just finishing her first quarter here at the U."

Angel paused awkwardly. "Did she die on campus?"

Veronica hesitated. "No, actually she died here in this house."

"She did?"

Veronica gazed at the picture of her sister without seeing it, seeing the real sister instead, the living, breathing memory that had been frozen in the frame. "Maybe that's why I moved here. To be near her and not to forget."

"If my sister died somewhere, I would never want to live there. It would make me depressed."

"I suppose it should, but it never has. I've always loved this house. It's been seven years now. At first I thought, since it used to belong to my ex-husband's family, there would be bad memories. But not at all. Sam and I didn't live here. Our house was in Laurelhurst. I never think of him here. Just her."

"She must have been incredible."

Veronica nodded. Yes, Stephanie had been incredible. "One of the things I've realized in life is — well, when someone you love dies, how much they stay with you, in your thoughts, in your heart. I'm closer to my sister who's gone than I am to my living parents in Arizona. My folks and I haven't gotten along since Steph died. I think they always blamed me. Maybe I blamed myself, too."

She looked at the picture sadly, then turned away. "Sometimes I feel like Steph is still here with me, keeping me company."

"How did she die?"

Veronica stared out the French windows, as though maybe she hadn't heard Angel's question, as though trying to see through the darkness all the way to Calvary Cemetery. "Let's not talk about it anymore. It's getting late." She turned back to the couch. Her facial muscles tightened with restrained emotion.

"You don't understand," said Angel.

Perplexed, Veronica turned away from the impromptu sleeping quarters she was creating, and stared at her. "What did you say?" One look told her something was wrong.

Angel's cheeks had gone pale. All the blood appeared to have drained from her face.

"Oh, Angel, I'm sorry," said Veronica. "Am I scaring you, talking about my sister's death?"

The girl's eyes rolled back, as though she were attempting to see something behind her on the ceiling.

"What's wrong?" said Veronica, trying to conceal her alarm. She put her arm cautiously around Angel. The kid was very cold. "What's happening, Angel? Is there something I don't know about? Do you have some kind of medical problem? Are there pills you need? A glass of orange juice?"

Angel had no answer. All she could do was repeat the same words, tonelessly. "You don't understand."

"Why are you saying that? Angel, look at me."

"You don't understand."

"What don't I understand?" Her voice was slightly shrill.

Angel appeared to be in a trance. She added one more word. "You don't understand, Ronny. Ronny, you don't understand."

Veronica cried out. It was a reflex of painful memory and pure shock. She could no longer pretend it was just a coincidence. "Stop it," pleaded Veronica. "Please, Angel, stop."

Angel couldn't stop. "Ronny, you don't understand."

Veronica whimpered. "Angel, you're frightening me."

"You don't understand, Ronny!"

All she could say over and over were those words — exactly the same words that Veronica's sister had said, the last words Stephanie ever said to her, on the night before she died.

9
Haunted Library

Long after leaving her young guest, Veronica remained wide awake and pacing in her bedroom.

How could Angel possibly have known the words Stephanie shouted that night? With police sirens wailing, with blue lights flashing through the windows, being bumped and jostled, elbowed and pushed by frantic, frightened, drunken students, as she dragged her sister out of the house, Stephanie had cried those same words over and over. "Ronny, you don't understand!"

Veronica finally managed to stop pacing, to undress, to lie down in her bed, to sleep. But it was only to dream.

She found herself back in the days when she had believed in happiness, far too high above the ground at the top of the towering water slide at Lake Wilderness, with dozens of people standing in line on the ladder watching her freeze, waiting while she gripped the sides of the slide in terror, refusing to let go.

"No! No, I can't. I don't want to. No—"

Her sister's mocking voice came from directly behind her, in her ear. "Scaredy cat!"

Then the shove that broke the grip of her hands, the sisterly push that sent her shooting down the water slide, plummeting faster and faster—

She woke up abruptly.

At first all she could do was lie there and consciously try to slow down her heart, calm her breathing. Of course she had dreamed of her sister! First Matt had reminded her of the party, and then her troubled young guest had stumbled on the very words Stephanie had said at the end. But how could the girl have known? Why, twenty years later, was the death of her sister suddenly as painful as though it had happened yesterday?

She tried to go back to sleep. She was uncomfortable, restless. Something was bothering her, a nagging worry at the back of her mind. Why did she feel like something was wrong with the house tonight? She tried not to think about Angel. She tried not to remember the way she had looked at the picture of Stephanie—

Veronica folded back the covers, and sat up on the side of the bed. She couldn't get away from that nagging suspicion that everything wasn't all right. There was only one way to put her mind at rest. To prove that the house was perfectly safe. To prove that she was not a scaredy cat.

She hurried across the cold bedroom floor, and bundled up in her bathrobe and slippers. Grabbing the flashlight she always kept in her bedside drawer, she took a deep breath to anchor herself, resolutely crossed the bedroom, opened the door, and stepped out onto the third floor landing.

The house was still, but it was not a peaceful quiet. It was an anxious hush, a breathless silence. She turned the beam of light toward the library door.

Inside the library, a floorboard creaked.

*

Angel sat on the side of her impromptu bed, staring around her at the dark, book-crowded walls. The distant glow of the streetlamp across the street filtered through the French windows, edging the spines of the volumes, glinting off the frame of the photograph on the wall.

Something had happened to her that night. She had been feeling stranger and stranger. She had frightened Professor Glass so badly that she had started crying.

A shadow shifted out on the balcony. She caught a glimpse of movement through the French window. She listened. A footstep. Something crossed in front of the glass. Something the height of a human being.

A face was looking in through the French window.

She stared in panic, her heart hammering. Not a face. Only a reflection of the moon in the sky. But she had to be sure. Angel rose and walked cautiously through the room to the window. Her fingertips touched the cold glass.

No one was outside.

She reached down for the latch of the French window, turned it, and stepped out onto the balcony.

The cold night wind gusted at her, chilled her.

A terrible emptiness took hold of her as she gripped the balcony railing. It reminded her of the bridge, of what she had nearly done that afternoon. For one awful moment, she had not wanted to be alive. Angel felt dizzy. She tried to step back, away from the edge of the balcony, but her feet wouldn't budge.

Something lurched out of the shadows behind her.

Angel threw up one arm in front of her face to protect herself, but lost her balance. Her foot skidded out from under her. Her arm whacked against the wooden railing as she tumbled back against it. For a moment she lay stretched on the narrow third-floor deck, afraid to breathe, afraid to budge. What had come at her? Whatever it was, it was up there with her now.

It brushed against her foot.

Before she could scream, she saw its tail flick into the air, and then its fur brushed against her arm. She stroked the cat's head. "Thanks a lot, for scaring the life out of me."

It purred.

"You've got nine lives, so it's no big deal for you. You can afford to lose one. Where did you come from, anyway?"

She was examining the sloping rooftop along the balcony where an overhanging tree branch provided access when the cat suddenly bolted in terror, and vanished.

A beam of light came through the library door. Behind the light she glimpsed the dark figure of a woman.

10
Shadow of a Woman

Matt woke up groggily.

The bedroom was dark. The luminous hands of the clock were more blurry than usual, but indicated some ungodly hour in the middle of the night. The lower floor of the house was hushed and still. Yet he had the distinct impression he was no longer alone.

"Veronica?"

No answer. But one of the shadows at the far end of the bedroom seemed to detach itself from the wall and slowly approached the bed. He blinked, but his eyes refused to focus. He tried to force his vision to make sense, but his eyelids kept sliding shut. Why was he so tired?

The movement, the footsteps, were those of a woman. Someone was in his room! She reached the side of the bed and bent over him. The touch of cold fingertips.

"Veronica—"

She kissed him. He felt her hands moving over him. He kept trying to hold on to her, to clasp her in his arms—

He sat up with a gasp. He was drenched with sweat. He thrust out his hand into the darkness, and switched on the bedlamp.

He was alone. He let out a shout of sheer terrified disbelief.

In a moment footsteps thundered down through the heart of the house toward his apartment below, followed by a banging on the laundry room door. "Matt? Matt, are you all right?"

The door was flung open. Veronica hurried through the darkened apartment, her flashlight beam leaping ahead of her. She was wrapped in her bathrobe and followed by a pale, wild-eyed Angel.

"Were you just here in this room?" cried Matt. "Veronica, tell me. Were you here with me just a minute ago?"

"How could I have been?" said Veronica, staring at him in confusion. "I just got here. Matt, why do you keep asking me that? What makes you think I would prowl your room in the night?"

"Angel," he said, without bothering to answer Veronica, "were you in my room just now?"

"No," said Angel.

"Please, Angel, tell me the truth," he begged. "I won't be angry. I promise."

"No!" cried the girl.

He sank back onto his pillow, his forehead gleaming with sweat, his cheeks pale yellow in the light of the bedlamp.

"God, help me," said Matt.

CHAPTER NINE

Thursday, December 19

1
Left Behind

"Time to wake up, sleepyhead," said Veronica.

She drew the curtains. Morning light streamed into the library from the east, pouring through the French windows, spilling across the lump under the comforter. The cold sunlight gleamed along the edge of Stephanie's framed photograph.

Angel poked out her tousled head from under the covers, squinting into the brightness. "I don't want to wake up. I want to keep dreaming."

"You do, huh?" Veronica didn't have time to be playful. She had office hours in Padelford Hall that morning. "I'm on my way to campus. You feel like coming along?"

"No."

Veronica tried another approach. "Angel, I want to be sure you're okay before I leave you here."

"I'm okay."

"Are you feeling better?" Veronica regarded her intently. "Tell me, what happened to you last night? You kept saying, 'You don't understand.'"

The lump under the covers didn't move. "I did?"

"Don't you remember saying that?"

"No" she said.

"You seemed like you were starting to get sick."

"Really?"

"Yes, really. You got all white in the face."

Angel avoided looking her in the eye. "Must have been something I ate."

"You don't remember any of it?"

The kid's patience snapped. "No, I told you," she barked. "Stop asking so many questions."

"How else am I supposed to understand you, if I don't ask you questions?" Veronica sighed. "Okay. One last question. You feel like having some breakfast?"

Angel nodded. "I'm starving."

*

Suddenly she was alone.

Professor Glass had walked out the door, heading for campus. The door had thudded shut behind her. Ten minutes later Matt had slammed and locked his door downstairs, leaving for the bookstore.

Angel found herself in a silent, unknown house.

The empty rooms seemed to call out to her to explore them. She snooped everywhere. The medicine cabinet. (Very few pills, compared to her mother.) The vanity. (Where did she keep the rest of her makeup?) The bedstand. (No eyeshades or earplugs, like her father.) The drawers of the desk. (Notebooks, folders, boring stuff.) The huge, walk-in closets. (Lots of old-fashioned dresses.) And that was just the third floor. She explored the second floor just as thoroughly — every corner of the living room. (No magazines anywhere!) Every cupboard and shelf in the kitchen. (So many different kinds of tea!)

Then she went down into the laundry room, where the rust-red boiler whooshed and boomed. Half-used, half-hardened buckets of paint. Rusty saws and hammers. Rake, broom, mop.

And two doors, one door on either side.

She silently turned the doorknob into Matt's apartment, swinging open the door just enough to slip inside. She found herself in his kitchen. She switched on the overhead light. (Unwashed dishes in the sink.) Then she wandered into the living room and back down the hall through the bedroom and bathroom. (Socks and underwear on the floor. Towel hanging over the side of the bathtub.) She turned out the lights as she walked out, and closed the door as quietly as she'd opened it.

There remained only one other door, just beyond the boiler and the hot water tank. She was about to try the doorknob when the door swung open in front of her.

"What are you doing here?"

A young guy in a T-shirt and baseball cap, student backpack slung over one shoulder, parka tucked under his arm, stood blocking her way. She recognized him at once from her Victorian Lit class. She avoided looking him in the eye.

"Professor Glass said that I could—"

"Oh, I remember you," said Tyler. "What did you do to your hair?"

"I was ready for a change."

"I can't remember your name."

"Angel."

"Angel?" He blinked, taken aback. "My name's Tyler. You always sat at the back of the class, didn't you? Wait, I remember now. Your name's Angela."

"My name is what I say it is," she said, with an edge of aggression that caught him off-guard.

"Sure, whatever." He shrugged. "So what did you get on your paper?"

She'd gotten one of the highest grades in the class. She told him. He scowled. A vein stood out on his forehead.

"It had lots of punctuation errors, though," she added, hoping to make him feel better.

It made him feel worse. "How'd you do on the final?"

"Okay, I guess. I like Edith Wharton."

"Figures."

Tyler Wates wasn't smiling. The grade on his paper had been miserable, and he feared no better on his final. He wasn't happy with the way things were changing at the house, either. He was starting to feel like an outsider in his own home. Veronica was spending all her time with the new tenant. Tyler was being ignored.

He turned his back on Angel long enough to lock the door of his room. "You believe in luck?"

"Sometimes," she said.

He opened the door out of the laundry room, letting in a gust of cold air. "Wish me some," he said, as he stepped out into the chilly, bright light of noon. "I'm about to take a chance on looking like a fool."

2
Seeing Ghosts

"Two students were looking for you this morning," said Clarice, sipping at her mug of coffee. "They wanted to know if you'd changed your office hours."

Veronica was red-cheeked and breathless as she moved quickly through the English office, absentmindedly sorting a handful of mail. "Sorry. I was late."

"Again?" Clarice looked up with a casual, glancing morning smile. "Must be that new love life of yours." The smile faded as she continued staring at Veronica's face. "Hey, what happened?"

"What do you mean?"

"You look a little green in the face." Clarice walked around her desk and took hold of Veronica by both shoulders, looking her square in the eyes. "What aren't you telling me?"

"Nothing," lied Veronica, unable to meet her direct gaze.

"Nothing, nonsense — something has happened to you," said Clarice. "Something's scared you, I can tell."

"No, no, it's nothing," insisted Veronica. "I haven't been taking my vitamins lately. I guess I'm wearing down."

"Vitamins? Honey, how stupid do you think I am?"

The need to tell, to receive comfort and encouragement, was too great to resist. "Clarice, you know how much I love ghost stories. I mean, Victorian supernatural thrillers are my specialty. But literature is one thing, and life is something else. Ghosts aren't real. I don't believe in ghosts. Do you?"

The English Department secretary regarded her with raised eyebrow. "Well now, honey, you may be asking the wrong person. Ghosts are part of my heritage. African ghosts are nothing to fool around with. My granny told me all about haunts and jack-o'-lanterns and plat-eyes. When somebody dies, I still cover all the mirrors in the house, just like granny did. But I don't go around telling folks I believe in ghosts. You don't say that if you want to be considered sane in the twentieth century."

"How about seances?"

"What *about* seances?" said Clarice. "Seances are playing around with trouble."

"I mean, do you believe that a medium can receive—?"

"Now, what's with all these questions? It's time you stopped asking so many, and started answering a few. Like what happened?"

Veronica hesitated, uncertain how to explain. "Well, yesterday my new tenant had an accident. He fell in Ravenna Park. Hit his head."

"How awful," said Clarice.

"And this runaway kid brought him home. At first it looked like a boy, but it was actually a girl."

"Hard to tell these days," said Clarice. "I can hardly tell with my own kids."

"And she didn't have any place to stay, so I let her spend the night, and—"

106

"You what?" said Clarice. "You let some teenager you don't know sleep in your house?"

"No, you see, I recognized her. She was one of my Early Entrance kids. So I called her folks and told them she could stay with me."

"You what?" Clarice knew Veronica well enough for her mouth to genuinely fall open.

"She was desperate. But then she's hardly been in the house for an hour, and all of a sudden she turns white in the face, goes into a trance, and starts saying over and over the last words my sister said before she died."

"You've got to be kidding me!"

"Over and over. *Ronny, you don't understand, you don't understand.* Now how could she possibly know that?" Veronica smiled lamely, trying to swallow her anxiety. She would have liked to forget she ever heard those few terrifying words come out of Angel's mouth.

"Whew!" Clarice blew out a long breath, and just stared at her. "Don't look at me. All I know is, you just made the hairs on my arm stand on end."

"And that wasn't all," said Veronica. "My new tenant screamed in the middle of the night. He said someone was in his room. A woman. Can you believe it?" She tried to laugh. "What am I supposed to think?"

"Sounds like a good ghost story." Clarice chuckled.

"That's just what people will say," said Veronica. "People will think I'm cracking up. They'll say, 'That girl has read one too many.' But Clarice, I'm telling you, I don't believe in ghosts. They're fiction. They're not real life. Big difference. Ghosts only happen in books and movies."

"Except that it's happening to you," said Clarice. "Now, if this were a book or a movie, there'd be a simple answer. Your house is being haunted by your sister."

"But that's just it!" cried Veronica. "I can't believe it's her. I mean, I've been there seven years, and nothing's happened. Why now? No, that house isn't haunted by anyone, least of all my sister."

"If you say so," said Clarice. "Well, that leaves only one other woman who could have woken up your tenant." She gave Veronica a meaningful look.

"Clarice!"

"I rest my case," said Clarice. "Just one thing I want you to keep in mind. That girl may not be in contact with a ghost at all — but with you. The human brain is a strange and wonderful thing. Emphasis on strange. That kid may be reading your mind and not knowing it. What comes across as a ghost could just as easily be telepathy. Who knows all the tricks your mind can play? All the ways it can fool you?"

"So you think ghosts are just mental tricks?"

"Now, I didn't say that." With a deep-throated, reassuring chuckle, she gave Veronica a little hug. "Let me give you a little advice. Assume that there are such things as ghosts. If ghosts are real, then the very worst thing you can do is give them power. You do that every time you're afraid. They feed on fear. That's how they get to you. That's how they drive you crazy. It's all done with fear. So, my advice to you, honey, is to stop wearing yourself out worrying. You can't let it get to you. Live your life with a smile. And whatever you do, don't show you're afraid."

3
Closet Door

She kept on the move. She found herself getting slightly ill at ease if she stayed in any one room too long, as though someone were secretly watching her from somewhere behind her back, from empty doorways, through the windows, through the keyholes. But if she kept moving, if she kept drifting from the kitchen to the living room, from the bathroom to the library, if she just kept turning on lights and opening doors, being active and busy, the house was fine.

Angel poked around in the front closet, found one of Veronica's jackets that she liked, and borrowed it to sit outside on the wooden swing, reading in the bright winter sunlight.

A blood-curdling cry caused her to drop the book and leap to her feet. Tyler came bounding up the hillside stairs toward the house whooping with excitement, punching at an invisible punching bag. As he took the stairs two at a time, he whipped off his baseball cap and hurled it victoriously into the air, catching it at a leap.

"Hey, hey, hey!" he cried to her. "You're looking at the luckiest dude on this campus!"

He charged up the wooden side stairs to the front porch. Before Angel could pick up the book she'd dropped, he grabbed her by the arms and spun her around. "I did it! I did it!"

"Did what?" she asked helplessly, the words jiggled out of her. He grabbed her up in his arms, heaved her off the ground, and almost threw her into the air. Angel burst into a wild, delighted burst of laughter.

"You know that babe in our class, that blonde sorority chick who is so totally beautiful — well, you are looking at a guy who just got up the guts to take a walk down Greek Row and knock on the door of the most nose-in-the-air sorority this side of the Mississippi, and ask out that foxy honey on a date."

Angel's smile slowly faded.

Tyler didn't notice. "Do you realize who her Daddy is? These people have money. And she's a Christian! She's got everything a guy could want. And she said yes. Yes! I've got a date tonight with Bethany White."

Laughing and crowing, whooping and singing, his noisy celebration followed after him as he trotted down the side stairs and around the house to the rear door leading to his room.

Angel picked up the book that she'd dropped on the porch, brushing it off as she went inside. Tyler and Bethany deserved each other — let them do whatever they liked! It couldn't matter less to her. She ran upstairs to the third floor to put as much distance between herself and Tyler as she could.

The day was darkening outside, threatening rain. The third floor hall was in shadows. She thought she had left on some lights. She clearly hadn't. She turned on the hall light, the bathroom light, and the main overhead light in the library. She didn't remember leaving the French window open. It might rain, and she certainly didn't want rain blowing in on the books. She pulled the window shut, and fastened the latch.

She read in the library for a while, then became restless and began starting one book after another, unable to find one that held her attention.

She decided to take a shower. She poked through Veronica's clothes, found a bathrobe she liked, and took it with her into the bathroom. She undressed, climbed into the tub, pulled the plastic shower curtain all the way across, and turned on the hot water. The small bathroom quickly steamed. The water power was weak, and what should have been a brisk spray came out in a dribble. She was trying to adjust the shower head and sprayed herself in the face. She was wiping the water out of her eyes when a tall shadow moved across the shower curtain.

She gave a scream of panic. She yanked aside the shower curtain. The bathroom was empty.

Angel stared in disbelief. The rattling hiss of water spraying over the bathroom floor brought her to her senses. She quickly turned off the shower, dried herself off, and used the towel to mop up the wet linoleum. All the time she kept an eye on the bathroom door, listening. Tying the bulky bathrobe securely around her, she cautiously approached the doorway.

The third floor landing was silent. Nothing moved in the house. She was so certain she had seen someone that it was very difficult for her to admit that it had all been her imagination. She left the bathroom and was crossing the hall to the library when she froze, staring in terror.

The library lights were off. She had left them on — she was certain of it! At first she couldn't move. She managed to take a cautious step toward the doorway, and another.

A creaking sound came from inside the library.

"Tyler." The word came out as a hoarse croak. "Tyler, you're not funny." No response from the hushed library. "It's not nice to scare people. It's mean. Please, stop it."

No response.

She rushed forward, reached inside along the wall for the light switch, slapping at it in panic. The library burst into light. No one was in the room, just walls of books.

A French window swung open. It creaked on its rod, swinging wider. She knew she had locked it. Angel slowly approached the window, peering through the glass panels as she pulled the shutter closed, trying to see if anyone was outside on the balcony as she latched it shut.

The balcony was empty.

She heard something behind her. Something was moving in the room with her. Angel scarcely dared to breathe, waiting for the sound to repeat. When it did — a faint, metallic tinkling and scraping — she turned slowly to stare at the library closet door. She listened intently.

The latch was jiggling up and down. As though someone was on the other side of the closet door, trying to get out. She stared at the latch. It jiggled. She reached out and took hold of it.

The latch stopped jiggling.

The closet door swung open. It was a huge, old-fashioned closet, big enough to hold a bed, packed wall-to-wall with more books. She pulled a dangling cord attached to an overhead light bulb. It glimmered uncertainly.

Something dark and low moved at the end of the closet, like a cat. Angel smiled, and waited for it to move again. At last, the culprit — how had that cat found a way into the house? Animals she could handle. "Here, kitty, kitty, kitty!"

Silence. She took several cautious steps closer, and started to crouch down. She felt the whoosh of the closet door closing behind her before she heard the slam.

The light bulb shattered. She was in total darkness. Something else was in the closet with her. She tried to scream, but no sound came out. She felt an icy chill invade the small room. She clawed at the closet door, trying to find the latch.

Whatever touched her was very cold.

4

Greek Philosophy

After getting off work at the bookstore, Matt stopped by the optometrist to get his glasses repaired, then continued up the Ave to the Continental Cafe. He was sitting in front by the long flower-box as the afternoon darkened, looking out the window at the endless stream of humanity hurrying from one end of the Ave to the other, students and street teens and homeless intermingled with shoppers, bags and packages rustling and bumping toward Christmas.

"I was afraid I was going to be late. I got tied up in a conference with a troubled dissertation student."

"At least we got a table."

They placed their orders and then sat together awkwardly. Except for their plan to meet at the old family-owned Greek restaurant, they hadn't spoken since last night.

"Before I forget, I've been meaning to ask you," he began. "I know it's none of my business, but I can't help wondering. The tenant before me — what happened? Why was this place for rent?"

She smiled. "I don't blame you for asking, after last night. I wish I had a more satisfying answer. I didn't know him very well. He only lived here for a year. Family emergency. I think someone took a serious fall. He moved back to Pittsburgh."

"Doesn't shed much light."

"No light at all," said Veronica. "I hardly know what to say or where to begin. When I remember what happened last night, I think I must have been dreaming."

"Dreaming is the only sane explanation," said Matt, "except for the fact that it happened to all three of us separately."

"But what *did* happen?" urged Veronica. "That's just it. What exactly occurred? And why last night? And why us? Why not Tyler, too? Why did Tyler sleep right through it?"

"The lucky dog," said Matt.

"How are you feeling?"

"Splitting headache." He massaged his temples delicately. "I really cracked the old noggin in the park."

"That must have been quite a spill."

"I felt like this after getting mugged in New York."

"Any more feelings of not being alone?"

"Nope." He appeared to be staring straight through the restaurant table into the floor. "Definitely alone."

"What was it, do you think, Matt?" She leaned closer to him across the table. "What did we experience last night? Are we talking psychic manifestation? Or are we talking indigestion?"

He grinned. It trailed off into an uneasy shrug. "I wish I knew. It wasn't a dream. Someone was in my room, right beside the bed. Believe me, she touched me. I could feel her hands."

"You're sure it was a woman?"

"She was kissing me. Yes, I'm sure."

"Kissing! But how could anyone possibly—?"

"I know, I know. Don't ask. I've been trying to explain it to myself all day, and coming up with nothing. Kisses in the night from a woman who wasn't there."

"You don't think it was Angel, do you?"

"She was upstairs with you. And my front door was locked."

"Well, then, what could it possibly—?"

"I think we've ruled out just about everything."

"Well, not exactly everything."

"Everything sane," he said. "Everything believable."

"Well, then, maybe we'll have to look for explanations that aren't quite so sane and believable."

He looked up from the silverware he'd been nervously idling with, directly into her eyes. "I hope you're not talking about ghosts." The word, once spoken, made both of them uneasy. "Because I don't believe in ghosts."

"Neither do I," she agreed. "Which leaves us right back where we started. Unfortunately, we may be forced to change our beliefs."

Their conversation was interrupted by shouts, a screeching of tires. A grubby, baby-faced teenager leaped through the tight passage between two stalled cars. He got as far as the sidewalk before shouts on either side froze him in place. He started swearing up a storm, then unexpectedly burst into tears. Policemen converged on him from all directions. In a moment, both his hands were pressed up against the window as he was methodically searched.

"When are we going to stop hating our children?" said a sad, gruff old voice.

Not until he spoke did Matt and Veronica realize that an elderly Greek man was standing nearby puffing unhappily on his cigar, his bushy white eyebrows scowling. "The children today, they need so much love, and what do they get?" He gestured toward the police action on the sidewalk. "They get frisked." The old Greek shook his head sadly, folding his arms across his stomach in dismay. In silence he watched unhappily through the window as the teenager was interrogated.

A red-headed waitress served Matt and Veronica.

"Speaking of children, I wonder how Angel's doing." She sipped cautiously at a hot yellow spoonful of avgolemono soup.

Matt crunched into his Greek fries. "I'm sure she'll be fine on her own. We'll go home as soon as we're done, and make sure everything's okay."

The old Greek scratched thoughtfully at his thick, white moustache. "Why is it so hard to love your own children? That's what I want to know. I love my son, even though he's a hopeless lunkhead." He cocked his arm with a little twist, some ancient Greek gesture of hopeless resignation, toward the younger man with a similar, black mustache standing behind the cash register. "You have to love your children. It's a law of nature."

5
"No One Was There"

They had almost reached the house when they heard the scream. They didn't have to say anything. They both started running.

Veronica hurried ahead of him up the hillside to the house. He followed her up the side stairs onto her porch. She fumbled the key into the front door. They lunged into the living room, froze there in the silence of the house, listening. When the next cry rang out, there was no doubt where it was coming from.

Matt's face turned pale with dread. Veronica didn't take the time to ask why. Together they dashed upstairs. For one terrible moment, they both stopped in their tracks in the library doorway, staring at the closet. The sounds were coming from inside it. Matt clutched the library doorframe for support, unable to approach any closer. Veronica lunged across the library and flung open the closet door. Angel tumbled out.

The sight seemed to relieve Matt from his temporary paralysis. He rushed to the girl's side. Together they helped Angel up onto her feet and away from the closet. She was shaking. Her face was wet with tears. "Angel, what happened?"

She took a moment to compose herself, to swipe at her nose and eyes with the back of her sleeve. "I — I think someone else was here."

"Someone else?" repeated Veronica, not understanding. "You mean, someone else was in the house?"

She nodded solemnly. "Playing a joke on me. Scaring me. Locking me in the closet."

"But nobody else was home," objected Veronica. "Nobody except possibly Tyler downstairs in his room. And he would never dare come up here on his own. Not if he knows what's good for him."

"Someone turned off the light."

"You mean, the lights went out while we were gone?" said Matt. "Could have been a power shortage."

"Not all the lights," said Angel. "Just the library light. I'm sure I turned it on."

"You probably turned it off, as well," said Matt. "It's so easy to forget. We do it automatically, without thinking."

"But I couldn't have turned it off," explained Angel. "I was in the bathroom. And someone came in there with me, because I saw them through the shower curtain."

"Someone came in the bathroom?" repeated Matt. "Did you catch a glimpse of them?"

"No," said Angel. "I — I just saw their shadow. But why would anyone try to scare me like that?"

"Oh, Angel, you probably just scared yourself."

"But someone opened the French window."

"The French window was open?" Now Veronica was getting alarmed. "Do you think someone tried to break in?"

"No one was there." Angel had run out of answers. She started crying again, hardly making a sound. "No one was there."

"Well, we're here now," said Veronica with decided warmth, "and we'll be staying with you."

"I don't know what happened to me," said Angel. "I just got scared, that's all. I'm not usually this way. It'll never happen again. Please don't tell my parents."

"Nobody's going to tell anyone."

"You don't have to worry about me. You can leave me alone. I'll be fine. It was an accident. The door slammed. And the lightbulb — it broke. I don't know how it happened. I didn't do it, I promise."

"Don't worry," said Matt reassuringly. "Anyone can get scared. Accidents can happen to anyone." He was trying to build her confidence, but something about his tone, about the way he said the words, betrayed him, made him sound as scared as she was.

"Are you upset with me?"

"Not at all," said Veronica, putting her arm around the girl's shoulders. "You're just being human, like the rest of us."

6
Wrong Doors

Two hours later the hush of the house was interrupted by a knock at the front door. Veronica and Angel were peacefully reading before a crackling fire in the library.

Their evening together had been free of turmoil. Once Veronica had gone downstairs and made certain Tyler hadn't been prowling around the house, she and Angel had walked up to the girl's house on Park Road to pick up some of her belongings. Much of the time they had walked in silence, peacefully, without words.

Angel had led her to the only house on Candy Cane Lane without decorations. She had wandered through the deserted living room and kitchen like an unauthorized intruder while Angel packed up clothes, a bathrobe and slippers, assorted necessities. After the hearty walk with Angel that evening, she was glad to be reading in the library now with her legs up on the hassock, basking in the warmth of the fire. At least until the knock jolted them out of the spell.

"Now, who in the world can that be?"

Veronica set aside her book. Cinching her houserobe around her waist, she went down the house's big central staircase to switch on the porch light and open the front door. Standing in the doorway was Bethany White, open-mouthed in shock. With her long, blonde hair and the bright, plastic colors of her ski pants and parka, she looked like someone in a poster for a Scandinavian airline.

"Professor Glass!" she gasped. Instead of the door being opened by sexy, attractive Tyler Wates, her date for the night, the door had been opened by her most dreaded teacher. "But I thought Tyler—"

"I'm sure Tyler is expecting you, Bethany." Veronica smiled. "His door is around the back of the house. All you have to do is—"

But Bethany wasn't listening. She was staring past Veronica at someone behind her standing halfway down the staircase.

"Oh, my God," whispered Bethany, "I didn't recognize you."

"Good." Angel glared at her, bristling like a cat. "I'm glad you didn't recognize me." Her cheeks flushed with defiance, Angel ran back up the stairs into the library.

Bethany turned to Veronica. "I didn't mean to upset her."

"She was already upset."

"Does she live here, too?"

"Just for the holidays. Good night, Bethany."

"I'm so sorry to bother you—"

"Everyone gets the wrong door at first," said Veronica, edging the door closed. "Tyler's place is easy to find. Just go back down the stairs and take the cement path around—"

"Thanks," called Bethany, hurrying away, not listening to the rest. "Sorry to bother you."

*

Matt had changed into his sweatpants and an old yellow *Wooden Boy* sweatshirt from the original off-off-Broadway production. He was stretched out on the sofa trying to read *Publishers Weekly* without falling asleep when he heard knocking at the front door.

He opened it to find a beautiful young blonde regarding him with a horrified grin. "Oh, no! Not again. Isn't this Tyler's room?"

"Tyler is just around the side of the house."

But she didn't hear him. She was staring at his chest. "I saw that show in New York. It was fabulous. Did you see it, too?"

Matt grinned. "Yeah, I saw it a few times."

"Really, you loved it, too? I used one of the songs for my audition piece, the one the Blue Lady sings, 'Boy.'"

"Oh, you gotta believe, you are what you dream," he sang, imitating the stiff movements of the show's wooden star.

She was impressed. "You even know the words."

"I wrote the words."

"You what?"

"*Wooden Boy* is my show. I'm the playwright, Matthew Braddon."

"You've got to be kidding me." Her eyes grew huge. "I'm so excited to meet you. My name is Bethany White." She shook his hand. "Are you visiting Seattle?"

"I'm living in Seattle," he said, "I've moved back home. Just got myself a job at University Book Store."

"No way!" she cried. "You work on campus? Incredible! Listen, I'm a reporter for the UW *Daily*. You've got to let me interview you. Please. This would make a fantastic story."

"You can find a lot more exciting topics," he said. "I doubt if any-one on campus even remembers who I am."

"After my story, they will," she said confidently. "Please." She took hold of his hand, clutching it persuasively in both her own. "Please."

"Hi, Bethany." They both turned to see Tyler standing at the corner of the house. "I've got a separate entrance back here."

Bethany turned back to Matt. "So, let's say tomorrow night, seven o'clock."

Tyler's grin slowly faded as he watched them.

"Seven sounds fine," said Matt, withdrawing his hand.

"See you then."

She and Tyler disappeared around the side of the house. Matt was about to close the door when he heard Veronica's door open upstairs. He stepped outside. Veronica was above him, sitting on the wooden swing, hugging herself in the cold night air.

"Look at that moon," he said, poking his head out from under his porch.

"It's going to be full this Christmas Eve," she said. "First full moon at Christmas in years."

"How's Angel doing?" said Matt, heading up to her porch.

She was clearly glad to see him. "Angel is upstairs resting. Do you feel like some coffee. It's pretty cold out here."

They went inside out of the chilly night, settling down in the living room, both of them quickly absorbed in each other. Neither of them noticed the partially-open door of the library, the eye pressed to the crack.

Matt and Veronica were together. Tyler and Bethany were together. Angel was alone.

7
Smoke

Veronica was clutching her pillow with both arms and just sliding into a deeply desired unconsciousness when she noticed the slightest hint of an odor in the bedroom. It was the faint, unmistakable scent of something burning.

She found herself suddenly wide awake. She stopped rustling the covers, held her breath, and waited to smell it again. Had the wiring in that ancient heirloom of a house finally turned lethal? She heard a muted thud from somewhere below. The sound was followed by another faint whiff of smoke. Something seemed to be going on downstairs.

She rose from the bed, tied her bathrobe around her, stepped into her slippers, and quietly opened the door. The short, third-floor hall was still. She could hear Angel softly snoring through the open library door. Veronica swiftly descended the staircase to the hushed living room. The smell was stronger. She stopped in the middle of the floor, and waited.

Another thud, followed by angry swearing directly under her feet.

Without hesitation, she darted into the kitchen and down the laundry room stairs. From the direction of Tyler's room there was only silence. Tyler and Bethany had left hours ago. The other door was outlined in bright cracks of light, just beyond the ironing board and the clothes washer. The door into Matt's apartment.

Halfway down the stairs, she heard several more thuds, then a metallic crash as though some heavy piece of furniture had fallen over, followed by a sudden whoosh of light. The brightness speared through the crack under the door, in a slice of yellow reaching all the way across the dark laundry room.

Veronica raised her knuckles hesitantly to knock, but couldn't make herself do it. She listened. Another sound, a sad human sound, on the other side of the door.

Slowly, carefully, she turned the doorknob enough to release the catch. She had never violated a tenant's privacy before, and was utterly shocked at her own behavior. She swung the door open a cautious inch.

Then the smell hit her full in the face, and she flung the door open wide.

The living room was murky with smoke that had nowhere to go. A smoldering fire struggled under heaped bundles of bound paper choking the fireplace. The damper was obviously closed. Smoke was churning back into the house.

Matt was crouched in front of the smoking fireplace like a human gargoyle. The grimace on his face was a firelit mask, swearing in frustration. He was barefoot, wearing only undershorts and an undershirt, reaching his bare arms into the fire, trying to tug and jerk burning objects back out again, cursing as he burned his fingers. Occasionally he tossed crackling, singed bundles of paper out of the fireplace into the black mess in the middle of the room.

She quickly crossed to the fireplace and yanked the handle of the hot damper chain.

"Next time open the damper when you decide to have a fire." A chilly gust of night air hissed in the flue, and the smoke was tugged back out of the room, sucked up and away. She turned from the singed, soot-blackened hearth. "Are you all right?"

"I'm so sorry." Matt stumbled backward to the end of the sofa, and slumped over onto it. A half-empty flask of Southern Comfort gleamed in the firelight on the coffee table. Beside him a metal file cabinet was overturned onto the floor and leaning on its side. Scattered around it were bulky mounds of paper, bound together.

"Matt, what in God's name happened?"

He couldn't talk at first.

"Please don't kick me out," he slurred. "I'm just cracking up. I was trying to spare the world an awful lot of crap, and instead I nearly set the house on fire."

"What do you mean, spare the world crap?" said Veronica, glancing toward the fireplace.

Before he could answer, she realized what was burning. She gave a cry, seized the poker, and began desperately prying away from the flames as many of the manuscripts as she could. For some it was too late.

"How could you be so insane?" she said, taking his stubbly cheeks between both her hands, smelling the whiskey on his breath, turning his blotchy red face to look directly into hers. "Tell me what's wrong."

"I'll tell you what's wrong," he said miserably. "I'm a failure, that's what's wrong. I've failed as a writer, and I hate my new job. I can't even cashier very well."

"Okay, okay, snap out of it," said Veronica. "I'm sure it's all true, and all very painful, but you've got to toughen up. We can all wallow in self-pity if we feel like it. Or we can be strong, and change things. Why this wave of self-doubt?"

"It's this *Daily* interview coming up tomorrow. I agreed to let a student reporter talk to me about my old shows. She'd seen *Wooden Boy*. She brought back the memories. Theatre!"

"You still love it, don't you?"

"I love it so much. I can't tell you what it's like, the excitement, the fun, working with all those crazy people, night after night, watching rehearsals, going out for drinks, creating a show together. It's like nothing else in the world. I could be so happy writing plays for the rest of my life. If I were only good enough!"

"Good enough?" she repeated. "I don't believe I heard that. Just because some of your plays had trouble—"

"No one hired me last season. Or this season."

"That doesn't mean you have to give up theatre. You can still write plays, can't you? Why don't you stop feeling sorry for yourself, Matthew Braddon, and write something worth writing. Write from your heart. With no deadlines, no pressures, write something you really care about, something that needs to be written. Something that matters to you."

She took his hand in both of hers.

"And next time you decide to make value judgments on the literary quality of your work, do it outside."

CHAPTER TEN
Friday, December 20

1
Unexpected Customers

That Friday was Matt's one day of the week to spend in the book department. He made the most of it. Working at the back of the bookstore by the windows, he unpacked boxes of newly-arrived books, shelved the titles that were waiting on bookcarts, checked his computer printouts on out-of-stock titles. He phoned in an order to the local book distributor.

He was shelving the new December paperback releases under the sign that said "Mysteries" when he looked up and saw Angel at the end of the aisle under the "Fantasy" sign. One knee was bent, her foot propped on a low bookshelf, her body in a spinal curve possible only for the young, her face half-concealed behind an open paperback held up close to her eyes.

He knelt beside her, placing a new mystery on the rack.

"Nice to see you," he said.

"Nice to see you, too," she whispered, without looking up from her book. "Professor Glass said you had a hard night."

"I did have a hard night," said Matt, "But I'm better now. What brings you to campus? Aren't your finals over?"

"I got tired of staying in that house alone."

"Of course, you did," he said. "Which one are you reading?"

She showed him the lurid cover of a popular fantasy. A magical psychic warrior princess sat mounted on the back of a rearing white unicorn, sword upraised.

"How is it?"

She grinned. "Great."

"People like that author a lot."

"I like books with women heroes," she blurted out. "I like women who make decisions and do things. I don't like books about women who are pretty and scream and get rescued."

The figure lunging up to them caught them both by surprise. Tyler stood before them, his athletic jacket hanging open on a dingy T-shirt. His unshaved cheeks were flushed red, his eyes bright with anger. He was scowling ferociously. His hair looked like trampled wheat, crushed down under his baseball cap jammed on his head slightly crooked.

"So, what do you think you're doing, stabbing me in the back?" he snarled.

"What are you talking about, Tyler?" said Matt. "I'm not stabbing anyone."

"Don't lie to me," he glowered. "You've got a date with her tonight. I asked her to go out with me. She can't. She's going out with you."

"You mean Bethany?" said Matt. "She's just interviewing me for *The Daily*."

"You expect me to believe that? Listen, how am I supposed to compete? All she talks about is Matthew Braddon, Matthew Braddon. Makes me feel about this tall. Nothing I did was good enough. And when I asked her out, you beat me to the punch. Which is what I ought to give you right now, a punch in the nose!"

He looked like he was seriously considering it, then became distracted by something behind Matt.

"Excuse me," said an ominous voice. Matt flinched, as though a sword had sliced between his shoulder-blades. "Were you helping these customers to find books, Matt?"

He turned around to face the grim features of Martha Ironwood. "They've both found what they were looking for."

"Good," said his boss. "It's always nice to know customers are happy." She did her best to smile in their general direction. Then she slowly turned a much colder, dangerous look straight into his eyes. "Matt, I'd like to see you in my office. Now."

2
Message

"What are you doing here?" said Clarice. "You've got no sane reason to be anywhere near Padelford Hall. Don't you know the concept of free time, woman?"

"Free *what*?" mugged Veronica. She smiled, shrugged, and sank down into the chair beside Clarice's desk. "I haven't been getting much done at home."

Clarice raised her reading-glasses onto her forehead, and regarded her candidly. "Your student house-guest? Teenagers are hard on the nerves."

"She's not alone," said Veronica. "She's getting help from my new tenant. Matt nearly burned the house down last night."

"Are you serious?"

"I wish I wasn't. He got depressed about his writing career, got drunk on Southern Comfort, and tried to burn all his manuscripts in the fireplace. At once. With the damper closed."

"Now, that is a man with something on his mind."

"I can't figure him out. He seems like he's got so much going for him, and yet—"

Bethany White suddenly appeared in the doorway. "There you are! Professor Glass, I'm so glad you're here."

"And how have I made you so glad?"

"I've been trying to leave a message for Matthew Braddon. He lives in your building."

"I'm aware of that."

"I made the mistake of asking his awful boss at the bookstore if I could talk to him. She told me to come back at four. Could you tell him that I can't be there tonight until nine o'clock?"

"You're coming over at nine?" repeated Veronica.

"I have to pick up the mail at my parents' house in Lake Hills," said Bethany. "Then drive back across the lake. So, I'll be over at nine. I've been calling him, but he doesn't have an answering machine or voice mail or anything. Could you just leave a message for him or something?"

"Or something," said Veronica.

"Thanks," said Bethany. "Nine." She vanished.

Clarice and Veronica regarded each other in silence.

An hour later, on her way to the Ave to meet Muriel for lunch, Veronica stopped at the bookstore in the HUB to deliver the message.

"Bethany White stopped by the English Department office."

"Who?"

"The one who's coming over at seven o'clock tonight."

"Oh," said Matt. "You mean the *Daily* interview." He kept looking nervously over his shoulder as he talked to her.

"Is that what it is? Well, she wanted you to know she can't get there till nine."

"Oh," he said. "Well, I guess it's nine, then. Thanks."

He seemed distant, cold. She decided against suggesting they get together for an early dinner.

3
Fortune Cookie

"What do I believe?" repeated Muriel Rose, looking down into her cup of steaming tea. What might have been the answer erupted in an explosion of Chinese from the kitchen in the back, but it remained untranslated and could just as well have been a comment on the weather or the sweet and sour pork.

"Are they real, or not?" Veronica had told her friend the whole story, from Matt moving in to Angel's most recent psychic encounter.

Muriel had listened intently, without interrupting, without missing a word. "Well, that's a tough question, Veronica. When you get to be my age, you've believed so many different things."

The old librarian cradled the teacup in her pale, fragile-looking hands, as though trying to warm herself from the cold wind sweeping down the Ave outside. Her white knitted sweater was draped over her shoulders to keep her warm. More and more lunchtime customers were crowding into China First, shivering in the doorway as they waited to be seated, letting in the icy air.

"What's your most recent theory?"

"Funny you should ask." The older woman smiled cryptically, and took a cautious sip of tea.

Veronica looked up from poking at the remains of her fried rice. She was too full to finish eating it, and had been idly picking out the colorful little good-parts. "Funny? What's funny about ghosts?"

"Absolutely nothing," said Muriel. "And I'm speaking from experience. I've just seen one."

"What?" Veronica's eyes betrayed their urgent interest. "You've seen a ghost?"

"Yes, dear, there's no way I can deny it." Muriel delicately sipped at her hot tea.

"Tell me at once," said Veronica, leaning closer across the table. "When did this happen?"

"Just last night. And it wasn't frightening at the time, just alarming. Of course, it gets more frightening the more I think about it. Especially the way it disappeared."

"You actually saw it vanish?" said Veronica. "Come on, Muriel, tell me what you saw."

"What I saw wasn't so interesting. Just a tall woman in a raincoat near the old stacks downstairs in Suzzallo. She wore her hair pulled back. She went behind a bookshelf just as the announcement came over the P.A. system that the library was closing.

124

"I was tired and grumpy and wanted to go home. I went after her to tell her she would have to leave. Every once in a while we get a homeless person who sets up camp in some corner of the library, hoping to spend the night there.

"I saw her on one of the last aisles, and walked right up to her. She turned around, but she didn't seem to notice me at all. She stared straight past me. I couldn't take my eyes off her. I suddenly realized I knew that face!"

"You knew her?"

"Her name was Carmen Brown. She worked in the library with me for at least a dozen years. She was a wonderful librarian, but when technology came to the library system and computers took over, Carmen was one of the losses. Computers were meaningless to her. When they threw out the card catalog, they threw out Carmen Brown.

"She changed overnight. She went to work at the post office on the Ave. She stopped wearing makeup, or nylons, or even stockings. She reduced her wardrobe to three dresses. She sold her house and her car, and moved into a one-room apartment in the O'Mally Building. Anyone who saw her in Safeway always said she was buying Ramen noodles and potatoes. And what did she do with her money? She set up an anonymous scholarship fund for students."

"Oh, my God!" said Veronica.

"She put every cent of her earnings into it. You could just see the woman losing weight. She still spent lots of time in the library, reading, researching, putting away books. She seemed very happy. And one day she was found at closing time in the Graduate Reading Room slumped over her book."

Veronica gasped, speechless.

"She left everything in her will to the scholarship fund."

"That gives me the chills," said Veronica. "It's too good for this world. And you saw her ghost?"

"Didn't look like a ghost. If I hadn't known she was dead, I would have thought it was Carmen. She walked right past me, and around the corner of the last row of shelves. I went after her. She was gone. No other way out."

Veronica shivered. "Sounds like one of my Victorian thrillers."

"Except that in Victorian thrillers, things get explained in the end," said Muriel. "In life we don't get the answers." She straightened her chopsticks into tidy parallel lines. "I'm not the only one who's seen her. Anita Fewgate saw her last year. So did Glenda Rickers. Always in the stacks. Always disappearing around the corner, with nowhere else she can possibly go. The library was her life. Clearly she doesn't intend to leave."

A red-uniformed young waitress swept efficiently by their table, snatching up their cold pot of tea and replacing it with a steaming duplicate. For a moment, Muriel and Veronica sat in silence, pouring themselves fresh cups. Faint strains of Chinese music surfaced over the mumbling and clinking of lunchtime diners. Two fortune cookies waited untouched between them, sitting on top of the bill, crisply folded around their secrets.

"And so?" said Veronica. "What does that leave you believing?"

"I can tell you one thing for sure," said Muriel. "I don't believe in calling anything supernatural. A very misleading term! The difference between what we call natural and what we call supernatural — dear, it's really just a matter of how often it happens and how much we understand it."

"So you believe ghosts are real?"

"As real as radio waves. As real as the wind. Simply not as frequent. Veronica, very few people believe in vampires or werewolves. But almost everyone knows someone who has had some kind of ghost experience."

"I suppose you're right."

"It's just that we've been trained not to talk about them." She reached past the soy sauce and put her almost translucent hand over Veronica's. "Ghosts are natural. Ghosts are real."

"But what does *real* mean?" said Veronica. "I've read hundreds of Victorian ghost stories, but they all seem to have different interpretations of ghosts."

"And you want to know my interpretation?" said Muriel. "Well, I think of it this way. When some kind of intense psychic event occurs, the vibrations can become recorded. It's like they're still there, waiting to be played back. Something triggers the recording, and it goes through its loop. It does the same thing every time. It doesn't interact with people, although it might seem to. It's a little home movie of the past. Ready to be re-experienced by the first sensitive who comes along."

"And so that's how you explain Carmen Brown in the library?"

"Don't expect explanations," she said, with a laugh. "This is life, Veronica, not a ghost story." Muriel reached past the teapot for one of the fortune cookies and broke it neatly in half. "Only in fiction do you get explanations."

Veronica took the other fortune cookie, and snapped it apart. Both women read their little slips of paper.

"Your dearest wish will come true," read Veronica. "Sounds promising. I wonder what my dearest wish is." They both chuckled. "And yours?"

"Ah, mine," said Muriel. "Mine is quite appropriate. *Your question will soon be answered.* And, of course, it will. When you're my age, my dear, the mystery of death will soon be solved. Won't be long, and I'll know the real truth about ghosts. If we're allowed to come back, I promise to tell you all about it."

Veronica smiled. "Please do."

They were stepping into the aisle and pulling on their overcoats when Muriel exclaimed, "Oh, I nearly forgot. Remember Stair #13 in the library? Well, the other day I had a thought and gave Stair #13 another try. Instead of going up, this time I went down." She paused, savoring the moment. "Can you guess where I ended up? Down in the stacks where Carmen Brown disappeared."

Veronica shuddered.

"It's starting to look like it might have been Carmen in the Graduate Reading Room."

"But what does it mean?"

"That I can't tell you." The old librarian smiled. "All I know is, two more pieces just fit together. We know a little more than we did before. We don't always get answers. Sometimes we just get a few more pieces."

4
Night Visitor

At the end of a long day, at the end of a long week, Veronica wanted nothing more than to forget campus, to forget the name of every overworked graduate student in her seminar, to forget homeless poets and depressed playwrights and troubled teens and take a long, hot bath at home and then curl up in bed with a good paperback.

Which was exactly what she did.

Angel had been reading in the library when she came home, and continued to do so while Veronica enjoyed her long, luxurious bath. The girl seemed withdrawn, inward.

"How did your day go, Angel?"

"Fine."

She left her that way. If the girl needed more time to herself, let her take it, because Veronica needed a little time for Veronica.

They both heard the footsteps coming up the stairs outside. They both glanced at the clock. They both knew who it was. Angel made no attempt to hide her curiosity. She jumped to her feet, hurried over to the French window, silently unlatched one glass shutter and swung it open, stepping stealthily out onto the balcony. She peered over the railing.

It was her. The one with the pretty blonde hair and the expensive, trendy clothes, half-hidden under an umbrella. Angel turned away from the window. The faint knock at the downstairs door was followed by a burst of phony, ultra-feminine laughter. They both pretended not to hear it.

Not too long after, Veronica looked up from her book to see Angel asleep in the armchair. She helped her to bed, covered her, turned out the library lights. She made sure the French windows were fastened shut. She closed the library door securely behind her. Angel would sleep undisturbed.

She tried to lie in bed reading, but within minutes she was yawning. A few more minutes, and the lights were out. Veronica snuggled under her electric blanket, her aching head beginning to soften into a painless lump. She drifted into a light, troubled slumber.

She dreamed that the bedroom door swung open. A figure stood in the doorway. The face was in darkness, but she knew it was her sister. Stephanie crossed through the shadows of the room toward the bed. She didn't seem to be walking exactly, but somehow getting closer and closer and—

Veronica opened her eyes abruptly, staring into the darkness of the room. One of the shadows moved. She froze, unable to breathe, scowling in fear at the spot, defying the shadow to move again.

The shadow moved closer.

"Who's there?" she whispered.

The shadow moved one step closer. Before Veronica could gasp enough air into her lungs to scream, she recognized the features emerging into the light sifting through the window curtains.

"Angel," she whispered. "You just scared me half to death!"

She might have been angry at the girl for invading her bedroom in the middle of the night, except that she could see Angel had wet cheeks and swollen red eyes from crying.

"What's wrong, Angel? What is it?"

"I'm so afraid," she managed to get out. "Please let me get in bed with you."

"In bed with me?" said Veronica. She drew her electric blanket up closer around her neck. "What's wrong with the library?"

"I'm scared in the library. Don't make me go back out there and be alone," she pleaded. "Please."

"Okay, okay," said Veronica. She pulled aside the covers, and Angel bounded onto the bed and under them. "Now, tell me. Did something happen?"

"No," she admitted. "But I feel like something is going to happen. So many things keep going wrong. All day I've been feeling it."

"Things like what?"

"Like the library door. It kept sticking today. Sometimes it jammed and wouldn't open. Sometimes it wouldn't stay closed. And the windows, too, the ones that go out on the balcony, sometimes they swung open for no reason, even when I knew I locked them. And all I know is, I keep thinking about your sister."

"My sister!" exclaimed Veronica.

"I think about her so much in there. Your library — that's where it happened, isn't it? That's where she died."

Veronica looked alarmed. "Did I tell you that?" She regarded the girl in quiet surprise. "You're amazing."

Angel grinned nervously. "I like to think so. I'm a little more afraid tonight, is all. I want to be with someone I can trust."

"I take that as a compliment. Just out of curiosity, why do you trust me?"

Angel clutched her pillow against her skinny body under the covers. "Because I like the way you talk. I like the way you say what you mean. I never missed one of your classes. I like your voice. It's soft and kind and smart. I like what you say about people. And you love books."

"All right," said Veronica. "Stay on that side. I'm not used to sharing my bed."

Suddenly Angel lunged at her, covers and all, and hugged her. The force of it nearly knocked Veronica off the bed's edge. Then the girl abruptly let go, turned away from her, clutched her pillow, curled up into a ball facing the other direction, and pulled the electric blanket over her head.

Veronica stared at her in touched bewilderment for a moment, then rolled over and followed her example. She made herself comfortable, closed her eyes, and tried to relax her way into unconsciousness. She tried not to think about her sister. She tried not to think about Matt downstairs being interviewed by that silly, gorgeous sorority girl.

5
Interview

Rain battered at her umbrella. The icy wind tugged at her heavy briefcase, which insisted on banging against her pretty, Spandex-coated thigh. The Italian briefcase was overstuffed, bulging with a handsome leather-bound interviewing portfolio and a new mini-recorder she'd purchased that afternoon with her father's Visa card for this very occasion. Her Adidas were soaked, her powder blue parka dark and streaming.

Bethany White didn't mind. In fact, she scarcely noticed. Fate was smiling on her. The night was hers. This interview was an opportunity waiting to happen. The poised, bright nineteen-year-old was pretty enough to have her pick of boys, and smart enough to grow tired of most of them. How amazing to think that a casual date with a cute nerd like Tyler could lead to meeting Matthew Braddon! This guy was in another league altogether. The handsome, moody fortyish playwright really appealed to her. He would not get away.

She had cancelled all plans for the evening and strategically moved the interview two hours later for no real reason, except that a business meeting became much more intimate and romantic at nine on a Friday night.

Which was exactly the time indicated on her gleaming Rolex watch. Time for the *Daily* interview of the year. An interview to launch a journalism career and possibly a romance with an older man. He was available. He wasn't gay. He had a sadder, wiser sexiness. Smart, but not a show-off. So casual and confident with his body. A body that looked more like thirty than forty, and was definitely her destiny.

She looked up the three flights of tipping cement stairs, through streaming curtains of rain, at the three-story monstrosity looking down at her, straight out of an old black-and-white classic thriller. It loomed up over the curving boulevard as though crouching ready to pounce, half-hidden by a huge, crooked maple tree. She watched her step. She didn't want any accidents. The last thing she intended to do tonight was make a fool of herself in front of such an attractive, classy man.

Matthew Braddon! Someone who had actually been there and done that. The guy who wrote *Wooden Boy!* Bethany had frequently considered theatre as a major. She had the looks for it. Daddy had made it clear that a theatre career would mean total severance from family funds. Bethany had majored in accounting.

Credits and debits had nothing to teach her when it came to dressing that night. Her attire was suggestively snug, provocatively skimpy, relentlessly tasteful. She looked like a fashion model arriving for a photo shoot on the soggy set of an old haunted house. She hugged her wet ski parka closer around her. She was freezing, but that was just another card to play later, especially if there was a fire. Maybe it was the relentless rain, or the combination of streetlamp and moonlight, or the moving shadows cast by the wind-tormented, wind-rattled branches of the maple tree, but the house awaiting her arrival was straight off the cover of a paperback Gothic romance.

Except that in her case, the heroine was sensible, smiling confidently, and armed with an umbrella, a college education, and a father on the Board of Regents. She was quick-witted, clever, and attractive. Exactly what a lonely, discouraged hunk of a playwright needed to help him lick his wounds, get back on his feet, and turn into Pulitzer Prize-winning material.

Enter Bethany White.

Regardless of the downpour, regardless of the forbidding flights of stairs, she dodged wet fern fronds, avoided patches of moss, and made her way up a hillside of rain-washed, gleaming ivy leaves. Toward a gloomy, brooding, triple-decker old house that was a psycho's dream. Bright cracks of light offered tempting glimpses through slightly open curtains.

Up on the third floor balcony, a dwarf-like shadow peered over the railing at her. Bethany froze, looked again. The small shadow was gone. The huge moon over Calvary Cemetery bathed the whole Montlake valley in blue-gray light. Bethany continued up the last flight, the highest curve of stairs, ducking under the camellia tree, umbrella raised over her head to ward off the downpour.

Three wet wooden stairs led up onto the small covered porch of the lower apartment. She knocked.

Curtains of rain streamed down over the porch's open sides. The clattering spill of rainwater muffled the opening of the front door. When Bethany turned around she found him standing before her.

"Hi there."

He certainly hadn't dressed up for the occasion. Sweatpants, T-shirt, cheeks dark with stubble. Definitely winding down for the weekend. She liked that. It excited her. A startled laugh was all that betrayed any loss of composure. "Well, here I am."

"Yes, I can see that." He smiled awkwardly, trying to ignore how appealing she was, taking a deep breath to anchor himself.

"And I'm full of questions," she warned him.

"As you should be. Come in."

He held open the springy screen door. She brushed against him sliding through. "Ready to get every word." She held up her mini-recorder. "Hope you don't mind this."

"I'm used to them," he said with a shrug. "They teach you to watch your mouth."

"Don't watch it *too* much." She pouted charmingly. "You've got to tell me some good stuff. There's a great story in you waiting to be written, and I'm the one to do it."

"Are you?"

She shivered. "If I don't get the chills and die first."

"Here, give me your coat. It's soaked."

"So is everything else, including me. It's so wet out tonight. Brrr!" While he set her umbrella to dry by the door and hung up her coat, she crept closer to the fireplace. "That feels good."

She crouched before the warmth of the flames. Something felt wrong. She glanced over her shoulder. Bethany had the unnerving sensation that someone else was in the room with them. She glanced behind her. A writing desk and computer. Farther back, a dark, empty kitchen. She looked the other way. An empty hall leading to bathroom and bedroom. Still, that sensation! As though there were an unseen watcher in the room.

"So you and Professor Glass and Tyler share this house? Just the three of you?" She tried to make her question sound casual.

"We've got a temporary fourth over the holiday break. A student from Veronica's class last quarter."

That explained it! "I know who you mean. The one who chopped off her hair." She reconsidered the shadowy dwarf she'd spotted on the balcony. More like a spying overly-bright kid with an identity problem.

She set up the mini-recorder on the coffee table. "This should help me get all the quotes exactly right." She pushed the buttons, getting no response. "Do you know how these things work? Do I need to plug it in somewhere?"

"There's an outlet right over here. Let's give it some juice."

"I knew I was forgetting something." They laughed together, acknowledging the limits of her technological skills.

"Looks like it's on now." He handed it back to her. Their hands touched in the passing, a lingering touch that he hesitated to break. "Just fire away, and I'm ready."

Bethany grinned. "I like that." She scowled in concentration. "Now, which button did you say it was?"

"This one. Just push it. Everything's set to go."

"But I *am* pushing it."

He took it from her hands, pushed buttons confidently, decisively, as though showing the mini-recorder who was boss. He scowled, and pushed the buttons again.

"Weird. Something's wrong with it. Doesn't want to work. Wonder why it's acting up?"

The lights flickered.

6

Phenomena

Veronica was sound asleep.

Angel stared at her from the other side of the bed, watched her breathing peacefully. She tried to breathe at exactly the same speed as Veronica, but it did no good. She couldn't fight down her rising sense of anxiety. She could hear faint voices downstairs in the stillness of the house. The girl stopped breathing, stopped rustling about, and listened. She recognized the voices.

She tried to stay in bed, but her eyes refused to close. She couldn't stop thinking about Matt down in his apartment with that sorority girl. Her sense of impending disaster continued to increase. Finally she couldn't stand it any more. She slipped out from under the blanket without disturbing Veronica. She padded across the cold bedroom floor and out into the upstairs hall, until she was standing at the top of the staircase. The living room below her was totally still. Except that from somewhere below that, muted by the intervening floor and ceiling, came the murmur of Bethany's laughter.

Such a warm, pretty, calculated laugh!

Angel descended the house's central staircase into the darkness of the living room. She slipped through the dining room to the kitchen, where she quietly opened the door leading down into the laundry room. She cautiously descended the crooked wooden staircase. Without reaching for the pull-cord to the overhead lightbulb, she felt her way through the darkness, past the washer and dryer, careful not to trip over the shovel.

A sudden whooshing roar!

Before she could bolt upstairs, she realized it was only the boiler automatically turning on. She crept farther into the darkness, around the water heater, toward the door to Matt's kitchen. She crept up to the keyhole, dropped to one knee, and peered inside.

Bethany was in full throttle, conducting her interview with all the charm and intimacy of a seduction. Poor Matt! His resistance was crumbling. She could see where his eyes were wandering, and no wonder.

Angel could feel the blood draining from her cheeks as she watched the pretty sorority girl weave her spell, as she watched Matt fall for it, coming up beside her, brushing up against her, taking the mini-recorder from her hands, pushing the right buttons confidently, decisively. He scowled, and pushed the buttons again.

The overhead lights flickered.

"Is something wrong with the electricity?" she asked.

"Not that I know of. Let's try the television." He rose and turned on the set. Speeding police cars, screeching tires, firing guns. "Seems to be working fine." His hand hovered over the control, ready to turn it off, as he squatted in front of the television, lit by the blue-gray glow.

The lights flickered.

"There they go, again!"

"Must be the rain," said Bethany. "Isn't that supposed to leave electricity in the air, or something?"

"Or something," said Matt. They both laughed.

A rumble of thunder.

The television screen started blipping, jumping.

Angel's lower lip began to tremble as she watched through the keyhole. She didn't want to see anymore. She was scared, filled with increasing dread, but she couldn't make herself go back upstairs where she belonged.

"Something's going haywire with the electricity in this house," said Matt. "Don't worry. It's nothing serious." He opened the television control panel and tried to adjust the skipping, shivering picture. "Well, so much for that!" He gave up and turned it off. "We don't need it, anyway. Unfortunately, if this keeps up, you won't be able to record the interview."

"Well, that just means I'll have to come back sometime when the power is working," she said. "No need for alarm. Come on back to the sofa. We might as well at least enjoy ourselves. What's the worst that can happen? The lights may go out. I'm not afraid of the dark. Are you?"

The lamp beside her began to flicker.

"We may be in the dark sooner than I thought," she said with a nervous laugh. "Must be electrical surges from the rain. Seems like it's been raining all month. This crazy city!"

Matt looked across the room, and scowled. "Wait a minute, that doesn't make sense. First the overhead lights blink, and now one lamp blinks — but not the other?" He strode across the living room toward the lamp by the armchair. He turned the knob. The lamp went off and on. "This one's fine."

"This one isn't," said Bethany. She peered under the lamp shade to see what was wrong. The lightbulb was shuddering underneath, jittering, blinking, as though not screwed in securely. "There's something wrong—"

The lightbulb exploded like a firecracker. Tiny bits of glass sliced and stabbed at her face and neck and arms. She flung herself away from the lamp with a shriek, knocking the coffee table clattering into the armchair. Her mini-recorder tumbled across the rug.

"Are you okay?" cried Matt, reaching toward her.

She tried to answer. No words came out. Her skin was suddenly crisscrossed by tiny, bright red lines. She started screaming.

By the time Veronica came rushing down through the darkened laundry room toward Matt's door, Angel was nowhere to be seen.

7
"It's Not My Fault!"

He helped Bethany down the hillside to Veronica's car, then drove her to the Acute Care wing of Hall Health Center on campus.

Veronica waited up for him to get home.

She offered him a glass of wine as he came inside. He downed it in a single motion. "She may be going into shock. The doctor on duty gave her some tranquilizers. I drove her back to her sorority. She should be better in the morning." He sank down into an armchair, and stared at the floor.

"Matt, I can't quite understand—"

"Don't ask me to tell you again what happened. I can tell you over and over, but it still won't make any more sense to you than it does to me." He rose from the armchair and began pacing the living room floor. "It was like there was some kind of very localized electrical interference." He shrugged. "Which makes no sense."

"And gives us no way to solve the problem." She sighed. "Too many strange things going on. Too many questions without answers." She seemed to consider a few. "Did you see Angel tonight after Bethany's accident?"

"No," he said. "Where is she?"

"That's what I want to know. She came into my bedroom tonight all worked up and scared, and I let her sleep with me. But when Bethany's scream woke me up, Angel was gone."

"How could Angel have anything to do with the lights?"

"I have no idea," said Veronica. "I'm not making sense anymore. Time to call it quits. I'm glad you're okay. Good night."

Veronica was so emotionally exhausted she could scarcely get into bed quickly enough. Before she could sink into the welcome forgetfulness of sleep, Angel was standing beside her.

"There you are!" said Veronica. "The invisible girl. Nice disappearing act. Where have you been?"

Instead of answering her, Angel said, "Tyler is freaking out down in the laundry room. I think he's crying."

"He's *what?*" Veronica got out of bed, summoned up her last reserves of strength, and went downstairs. She found him sitting on the laundry room stairs, shaking. She sat beside him. "Tyler, what is it?"

His face was a wet mess. "I'm fine, I'm fine."

"Are you upset about what happened tonight?"

He shrugged his shoulders.

"I've got some sleeping pills," she said gently.

"I don't take pills," said Tyler. He wiped his runny nose on the back of his arm. "I feel so guilty. Like I caused that. Like I wished it on them."

"Tyler, why would you even think it? Of course you didn't."

"I was jealous, wasn't I? I was angry! But I would never hurt her, never. How could something like that happen? It just exploded, for no reason at all. It's the work of Satan. I would never hurt Bethany."

"Of course, you wouldn't," said Veronica, trying to communicate her faith in him. "No one thought you would."

"I hated Matt. I hated Bethany. I wanted them to have a terrible time together."

"We all hate sometimes, Tyler, We hate when we feel helpless. That doesn't mean we're responsible for every—"

He turned his face toward her, to regard her straight in the eye. "Do you believe that Jesus Christ is your personal savior?"

She returned his look, answering him in a soft voice. "No, Tyler, I don't. Not the way that you mean."

"Do you think it's all crap, then?"

"Not at all. Not if it leads you to acts of goodness. Not if it teaches you about loving and telling the truth."

"But it can't explain exploding lightbulbs. Lightbulbs don't explode."

"Unfortunately, this one did," said Veronica. "There are times, Tyler, when there are no answers. You have to believe God has some kind of reason, because what happens isn't fair. We were just lucky it didn't happen to us. Listen, I've been meaning to ask you. What are you doing for Christmas?"

"I'm going to church," he said guardedly. "Why?"

"Besides church," said Veronica, with a smile. "You're not going back to Eastern Washington for the holidays? Tied up in some annual family event?"

"Not me," said Tyler, shaking his head, sadly smiling at something unspoken. "Not my family."

"What's all the noise out here?" Matt's door swung open into the laundry room. "Is there a party going on?" he asked, hair rumpled, bathrobe clutched around him. "Haven't you folks had enough excitement for one night?"

Tyler at once rose and stepped up to Matt's door. "I want to apologize for the way I acted in the bookstore today," he said, holding out his hand toward Matt. "I was out of line."

Matt took his hand. "Totally understandable. No hard feelings."

"You're just in time for an invitation," said Veronica. "I'd like both you and Tyler to join me. A Christmas Eve dinner for the members of this house without families. Which means all of us. Well?"

"Count me in," said Matt.

"I'm game," said Tyler.

Something moved at the corner of her vision. She looked up. Angel stood on the landing of the laundry room stairs, looking down the staircase at them, listening.

"How about you, Angel? Would you like to join us for Christmas Eve dinner?"

Angel stepped down one stair, another, then another, into the light. She nodded.

CHAPTER ELEVEN

Saturday, December 21

1
Devotion

The next morning Angel acted as though nothing had happened the night before. She asked no questions about Bethany's accident. She offered no explanations as to her own whereabouts. The terrors that had taken place in Matt's apartment appeared to have rolled off her without touching her.

Instead, she seemed strangely oblivious. She was up and about the house long before anyone else had crawled out of bed, wandering from room to room like an impatient, hungry cat, staring out the windows at the wet, gray morning, waiting for someone else to reveal they were awake.

That Saturday morning, both of her two new friends, Veronica and Matt, were entirely hers. Today they stayed home from work. Today they slept in. And they would continue to be hers throughout the rest of the weekend.

She had a brief moment of alarm when she saw Veronica putting on her overcoat. "I'm just walking up to Greek Row to check on Bethany," she said. "You're welcome to come along, if you like."

"Or," said Matt, "you can stay home with me, which will be much more fun, and we'll make a bachelor's breakfast together."

"What does that mean? Scrambled eggs?"

"Coming up," said Matt.

When Veronica got home, the three of them bundled up against the cold and drove down to University Village. The time had come to buy a Christmas tree. Angel was wild with excitement. She ran on ahead of them through the tree lot.

"This is the one!" she would cry. "No, this one is perfect!"

Veronica let her choose. Matt secured it to the top of the car with ropes through the windows. Angel bounced up and down in the back seat all the way home, chattering cheerfully, squirming with energy, silly with happiness.

Together the three of them managed to carry the tree up the zig-zagging hillside stairs and plant it securely in the stand in Veronica's living room.

Angel insisted on decorating it immediately. She helped Veronica lift down out of the closet all the boxes of bulbs and ornaments and lights stored from last year. She made sure every branch got its fair share of decorations, and draped tinsel everywhere, including liberal amounts on herself, Veronica and Matt. She even got Matt to lift her up so she could put the star on the very top.

"We've done it!" cried Veronica.

They stood back and admired their handiwork, thoroughly pleased. Then Veronica and Angel read the newspaper together, while Matt went on a run. When he'd rinsed off and thrown his running gear in the wash, the three of them talked over coffee in the library, in front of a crackling fire.

What a glorious day!

It was almost more than Angel could take. There was no longer any need to wander aimlessly through the empty house, trying to pass the hours until they returned home. She checked on one, visited the other, talked to one, helped the other, taking turns following first Matt around, then Veronica, both of them objects of intense fascination, pursuing them wherever they went, brimming over with sincere, unabashed devotion.

Only sometimes, when they murmured their adult things, private words between the two of them, when they drew close to each other or drifted into topics that excluded her or that she didn't understand, Angel became hurt and sullen.

Tyler was away from the house most of the day, which was fine with Angel. He spent the morning with Bethany. Angel was glad. She was more relaxed with him gone. The house belonged to just the three of them.

That afternoon she accidentally caught them talking in the kitchen. Neither of them saw her in the dining room, listening.

"She's so needy, she can get to you after a while," admitted Veronica. "But she's such a sweet kid, so bright."

Angel stiffened. Needy? What was that supposed to mean? She can get to you?

"She's a whiz, all right," said Matt. "That brain of hers is working ninety miles an hour. And so is her little heart."

"So full of life and good intentions."

Full of what? Angel wrinkled her nose. She wasn't full of any such things. She was full of mystery and anger and pain.

"But she needs so much attention," continued Veronica. The girl clenched her teeth, hating to hear herself criticized. "Emotionally she's so vulnerable. I haven't gotten up the courage yet to tell her I'm going to see a play tonight with Muriel. I've considered cancelling."

"Don't you dare," said Matt. "I can entertain her for one night. What have you got tickets for?"

"*The Unsinkable Molly Brown* at the Village Theatre."

"Good old Meredith Wilson. I can sing any song from *Music Man* by heart. *Molly Brown* isn't quite up to that. I mean, what do you do for a second act when you sink the Titanic in the first?"

"Good question. Is it worth going?"

"Plan on it." He turned and saw Angel. "Hey there, partner, feel like renting a video tonight and making a batch of popcorn?"

"Sounds great!"

"See?" he said to Veronica confidently. "We'll be fine." He turned to Angel. "Meet you around eight-thirty. We'll walk down to Blockbuster and find a movie we both want to see."

2
Broken Promise

That Saturday afternoon, while Veronica sat at her computer writing the conclusion of her book and Angel lay reading beside her, keeping her company up in the library, Matt retreated in needed solitude back down into his own apartment. There he wandered restlessly, unable to sit still, until he found himself staring at the mirror in his small bathroom.

He was tired. He'd been up most of the night, unable to sleep after driving Bethany to Hall Health Center, unable to forget the terror he'd seen in her eyes. He knew that terror. It was alive inside him too. He had no business being there. Except for Veronica. As he told his reflection in the bathroom mirror.

"She's everything I've ever wanted. I can't leave now."

"Get out," said his reflection. "Do you want it to happen all over again?"

"I won't let it happen again," he said to his reflection.

"Aren't you ever going to learn? Stay away from her, before it's too late."

In his confusion and distress, so preoccupied he hardly knew where he was or what he was doing, Matt inexplicably found himself talking to the mirror, thinking in dialogue.

Words started coming to him out of nowhere. He jotted down a line, a quick note here, an idea there. Then more lines. He turned on his computer, and sat down before the glowing monitor. Brief flurries of dialogue, thoughts, names, sudden flashes of concept and setting. Before he realized what he was doing, he was writing sketches, bits and pieces, patching them together into a musical which he found himself calling *Party House*. It was a seventies' nostalgia piece, centered on a college tragedy. Soon he was glued to the screen, passionately fingering the keys, talking to himself, mouthing the lines to a play that had decided to be written.

He finally got hungry after three hours of writing.

All it took was one sandwich and a bowl of soup, and he was sprawling asleep on the sofa, emotionally exhausted.

*

When he blinked open his eyes, the first thing he noticed was that the windows were black.

How long had he slept? He had no idea what time it was. Like an awakening slap, he remembered his promise, that he would entertain Angel while Veronica was gone, that they'd watch a video, make popcorn. He had stranded the poor girl, left her waiting for — how long?

He heard a floorboard creak directly above him.

He sat up abruptly on the sofa, stiff from his long nap, disoriented. He immediately doubted whether he had heard a footfall upstairs or not. He scratched his disordered thatch of hair. Had he imagined the sound? He owed it to Angel to go up and check, to apologize if she was still awake, to make sure everything was okay. He trotted into the kitchen, and opened the laundry room door, craning his neck toward the boiler and the stairs leading up to Veronica's floor, listening for anything unusual. Nothing.

He bounded up the laundry room stairs, and knocked softly at the door into Veronica's apartment. No answer. He quietly opened the door, and moved through the gray, moonlit kitchen and dining room into the night-dark living room.

No need to wake Angel, if she was already upstairs sleeping. Just a quick look-around, to make sure everything was in order.

Something moved in the corner. Matt spun to face it.

Angel emerged from behind an armchair and stepped out into the half-light. She wore a shapeless, extra-large T-shirt that glowed moon-white in the shadowy room, with a cartoon character from Dr

Seuss on her chest. Her face was a trembling battleground of emotions.

"It's just me," said Matt. "I thought I heard something up here. Don't be afraid."

"I'm not afraid," she sniffed.

"Good," he said. "Neither am I. We're two extraordinarily brave people, you and I. Sorry I missed watching a video with you tonight. I accidentally fell asleep."

"I didn't feel like watching a video, anyway," said Angel casually.

"Well, I just wanted to make sure you were all right. Guess we both need to get some sleep. Talk to you tomorrow." He turned toward the stairs leading back down to his unit.

Angel cried out in protest. "No, don't go!"

"I thought you weren't afraid?"

"I'm not," said Angel curtly. "I'm bored. I'm tired of being alone. I've been alone all night."

"You can come with me, then."

"Cool," she said. "We can play cards."

"Cards?" Matt was less enthusiastic. "I suppose. I'm not very good at card games."

"I'll teach you," she said. "You'll be great."

They were entering his kitchen when the ringing of the telephone interrupted them.

"Who in the world can that be, at this time of night?" He hurried into the living room and picked up the receiver.

"You're home?" cried a familiar voice. "Matthew Braddon, give me one good reason why an attractive, intelligent man like you isn't out on a beautiful Saturday night like this?"

"Beautiful?"

"It's not raining, is it?"

"Of course it's raining."

"Well, not very hard. You should be spending your precious, not-too-rainy Saturday night with someone who's attractive, intelligent, and fun — like me!"

Matt laughed. "You think that would help, huh, Tino?"

"I'll be by to pick you up in twenty minutes."

"Hey, wait a minute! I can't tonight. I've got plans. Angel and I are going to play cards."

"Who?" said Tino.

"Don't worry about me," interrupted Angel. "Go ahead and make plans with your friend. I didn't feel like playing cards, anyway."

"Are you sure?" said Matt.

Something Tino said distracted him, made him break into laughter. Momentarily forgotten, Angel backed sadly out of the kitchen into the shadows of the laundry room. He didn't notice her retreat up the stairs. He didn't hear the door close at the top.

3
The Bad Thing

As though being forgotten once that night were not enough! But, after all, he was talking to an adult on the phone. Adults were so much more important and interesting than kids. So he was going out with an adult friend that night. The same way Veronica had left with an adult friend. They had abandoned their guest. And why? Because she was just a kid. Kids didn't count.

She was in a foul mood and knew it. When her feelings were hurt, she didn't like anyone else to see how vulnerable she was. She wanted nothing to do with Matt, Veronica, or anyone. She just wanted to be by herself, brooding, pacing from one end of the library to the other, watching every few minutes from the French windows, waiting for the arrival of the car that would snatch Matt away.

He had no right to ruin their plans. Matt had been promised to her that night. They could have had so much fun together, just the two of them, with the whole house to themselves. But Matt's friend was interfering.

She could feel the bad thing crackling in the air.

The phone rang. At first she resolved not to answer it. She compromised with herself, picked up the receiver stealthily, without saying anything.

"Angel, this is Matt downstairs. Just wanted to let you know I'll be leaving in a few minutes. Veronica should be home soon."

"Thanks."

She hung up. She didn't dare try to talk. She might reveal how upset she was.

She unlocked one of the French windows and swung it open, stepping out onto the narrow, third-floor balcony. Down below, on the side of the stairs, Tyler's bicycle had been dragged up onto the brick-lined bulkhead.

She tried to pretend that the bad thing wasn't there in the room with her, trembling with power, but it was. She glared down into the darkness.

The bicycle on the edge of the embankment quivered.

Angel gripped the balcony railing with both hands. Her knuckles turned white.

The bicycle shuddered.

*

Tino Rodriguez could drive through anything.

Snow, hail, ice, no problem. Rain didn't daunt him in the least. Especially when a pal like Matt clearly needed to be pried out of his shell and reminded how to have a good time.

Backing in to the curb with a graceful purr, he stepped out of the car and splashed directly into an inch-deep stream of rainwater washing down the street. With a curse and one wet foot, Tino trotted across the gleaming wet sidewalk and up the brick-lined zigzag of stairs to Matt's apartment.

A wet fern leaf hanging over the embankment slapped him in the face. A stream of rainwater dribbled from an overhead camellia branch down the back of his collar. The light was on over Matt's front porch, but only one window was lit. Knowing Matt, he had probably planned on going to bed early on a Saturday night!

Trying not to get his clothes too wet, Tino didn't see the gleaming handlebars of Tyler's bicycle, leaning against the brick lining just out of sight around the zigzag.

His foot came down through the spokes of the rear wheel.

His other foot had nowhere to go. He lost his balance, managed a brief shout of alarm before the breath was knocked out of him in the impact of his chest against one of the handlebars. One arm crashed through the giant ferns lining the staircase. He slid off the landing. Bicycle and man tumbled shadow over shadow through the ivy, cracking through the rhododendron, colliding with the red-leafed Japanese maple, and snapping it in half. The spokes of the bicycle wheels gleamed wetly, spinning.

He found himself looking up into a night sky of falling rain, unable to move. He heard shouting from somewhere above him before he passed out.

145

CHAPTER TWELVE

Sunday, December 22

1
Casualty List

Matt awoke exhausted. Not even coffee could revive him. He was brooding, preoccupied. First Bethany. Now Tino. He had been up half the night, getting his injured friend out of the rain into the house, phoning a doctor, driving Tino to Swedish Hospital. He felt like he hadn't slept at all.

As planned, he and Veronica met outside that morning at nine-thirty. Together they descended the remaining flights of stairs to the sidewalk, and walked up the boulevard toward the off-campus streets lined with fraternities and sororities.

The pillared brick mansion had a prominent place on Greek Row. The pretty sorority girl sat enthroned in the immaculate living room of Sigma Sigma Nu. Bethany was reading the Sunday comics when she looked up and saw standing before her, like a vision, Matthew Braddon.

"Matt!" She tried to smile, in spite of the creams, pastes and medications hardened in daubs all over her face, neck and arms. What crooked, struggling smile she had mustered quickly faded when she saw her least-favorite professor walking down the entrance hall beside him.

"She's doing much better," said the house mother, arms folded across her chest, "but she's still very upset. Her parents get back from Europe tonight and will be taking her home."

"I can't tell you how sorry we all are," said Veronica.

"The doctor said there won't be any scars," said Bethany. She managed to make small talk until they ended their short visit and headed out the door.

"Well, at least she won't have any scars," said Veronica.

"Thank God," said Matt.

She elbowed him, appreciating his wry sense of humor. She needed humor that morning. Two guests injured in her house that

147

weekend had left her emotionally depleted. Having Matt beside her gave her an extra notch of strength.

They left Greek Row behind, walking back down through the fraternities and sororities to the house. Then they got into her Volvo and she drove out to Swedish Hospital to visit Tino.

He wasn't alone when they got there. His visitor rose in an awkward lurch out of a chair by the bed, turning around as they entered.

"Tyler!"

"I feel so responsible."

"Don't worry, he's safe," said Tino from his bed. "I never make passes at straight boys, no matter how attractive."

"At least he doesn't hate me," said Tyler, blushing. "For nearly killing him."

"Well, good to see you boys aren't fighting," said Veronica. "Although Tyler, I feel like I ought to throttle you. Every time I think—"

"Honest, I didn't leave it there," protested Tyler.

"How did it get there, then?"

"Look, you've got to believe me, Professor Glass. I would never leave my bike on the stairs again, not after what happened to Matt. Besides, it was raining. My bike was under the eaves, I swear it was. I just don't see how it could have slipped."

"Don't ever let it slip again," said Veronica sternly. "I mean it, Tyler. You endanger one more person, you're out of my house."

"I swear," said Tyler. He meant it.

"How did you get out here anyway, Tyler, since your bike is obviously out of commission?"

"Caught a bus." He glanced down at his transfer. "I probably should get going." He edged toward the door. "Hope you feel better soon, Tino. See you later." He turned to Veronica and Matt. "See you around the house." He escaped into the corridor.

She turned to Tino. "And how are you mending?"

"Breaking medical records," said Tino. "I'll be jogging up and down the hospital halls in no time. Matt, would you be polite enough to introduce me?"

Matt apologized and did so. The attractive man in the hospital bed siezed hold of Veronica's hand and didn't let go. "I hear you're very special. Matt probably hasn't told you yet, but he thinks the world of you."

His friend groaned. "Don't embarrass me, Tino."

"Straight guys don't talk about their feelings unless you beat it out of them," he said. "Though that can be fun."

They laughed together.

"How long are they going to keep you tied up here?" asked Matt, sitting on the bed beside his friend.

"One more day, at most. I'll be home by Christmas Eve. But while I'm here, I intend to have a good time. You should see how cute my doctor is. Oh, here he comes now!"

He turned a pained face toward the young man in a white medical jacket who entered the room. "Thank God you're here," said Tino. "I think you'd better have another look at my wrist." He winked at Veronica and Matt as they slipped out of the room, heading down the hall toward the elevator.

"Nice to see Tyler here, looking repentant," said Matt. "Good to see he's taking responsibility for his homicidal tendencies."

"Tyler!" She groaned. "That thick-headed, hormone-driven—! As if I haven't told him often enough about that cursed bicycle! If I ever see it on those stairs again, I'll— I'll— Your friend could have been killed."

A bright winter sun made the morning crisply clear. Churches seemed to be letting out their congregations on every side as they drove back down off Capitol Hill and made their way through the U. District toward home. For a moment it wasn't raining or blowing or freezing.

She reached across the front seat and took hold of his hand. She could tell at first touch. Something was wrong. The hand froze, did not respond. He looked straight out the windshield, avoiding her eyes.

2
Girl Talk

Angel was waiting for them, watching from the third floor balcony as soon as the car pulled up to the curb. She was wearing Tyler's baseball cap, brim facing backwards, exactly the way Tyler wore it.

"I like your headgear," called Matt from the stairs. "Does this mean you and Tyler are going steady?"

She made a sound of contempt, and hurled the baseball cap twirling into space. It soared down from the balcony, landing on the remains of the rhododendron. Veronica retrieved it as they came up the stairs.

Heavy clouds had closed in on the brightness of the morning, absorbing the light, dimming the sky to a helpless, darkening gray. Veronica walked slightly ahead of Matt, not wanting to see the look in his eyes, fearing the chill she felt edging between them. Angel opened the front door for them just as they stepped onto the porch.

"Well, they're both doing fine," said Veronica. "We've made our hospital calls for the morning."

"Let's hope we don't have to make any more," said Matt. "Two victims are enough for one weekend."

"Now, don't be scary." Veronica scowled at him. "Come on, Angel, let's go upstairs. You and I need some time for girl talk." She turned to Matt with a smile. "Sorry, no boys allowed."

"This boy will be writing downstairs," he said, reaching for the door to the laundry room. "You girls have a great time."

"How does hot cocoa sound?" she said to Angel, trying not to watch Matt's retreating back or wonder about his chilly behavior. The girl followed her into the kitchen where Veronica microwaved enough boiling water to fill two mugs with steaming chocolate. Angel had little to say. She followed Veronica up the staircase at her side, matching her stride for stride.

"He likes you a lot," blurted Angel unexpectedly.

"Are you still thinking about him?" Veronica smiled, making light of the girl's startling comment. "Oh, I think he might like me a little."

Angel smiled back, but it was a tight, guarded smile. "He likes you more than a little."

"You think so?" said Veronica. She could sense trouble ahead, and tried to steer clear of it. "Maybe a little more. But not much."

At the top of the staircase, they carried their hot mugs into the library, setting them down on the low coffee table in front of the fireplace. Veronica snapped on the lamp by the sofa. They accidentally looked up at exactly the same instant, straight into each other's eyes.

"Can you tell what people are thinking sometimes?" asked Veronica in a soft, soothing voice, a voice to induce trust.

Angel regarded her trustingly. She considered her answer. "Sometimes."

The girl's candor charmed her. Veronica smiled. "Can you tell what I'm thinking?"

"Sometimes." She giggled.

They both laughed together. Veronica's gaze was drawn to the framed photograph on her library wall. Abruptly, unintentionally, the humor dropped out of the situation. Veronica and Angel found themselves once again looking directly into each other's eyes, this time without the twinkle of humor, this time with a frightening urgency. "Can you tell what I'm thinking right now?"

The library darkened around them. Clouds blown across the winter sun diluted the window light into weak, dingy shafts. What light came through the glass made little headway against the encroaching shadows.

Angel didn't move. Her body stiffened in a disturbing way. "You think I'm like your sister."

Veronica acted as though the girl had slapped her. She stared in shock.

"You think I'm like the one who died." Angel looked back at her sadly. "I'm not Stephanie."

Veronica gasped. "No, Angel—"

Angel's eyes were big and wet. "Stephanie isn't happy."

"Stephanie is dead."

"Stephanie is angry with you."

"Angry? But why?" said Veronica. "Why should she be?"

"Stop lying to yourself."

"Lying?" said Veronica. "But I'm not."

"You threatened her."

"I never threatened Stephanie."

"You scared her."

"Scared her? Why would I? No, that's not true."

"You tried to force her."

"I didn't force her to do anything."

"You made her live up to your standards."

Veronica abruptly faltered. Now she was afraid. Had she not tried to manipulate her sister? Angel suddenly moaned loudly. Veronica wrapped her arms around the trembling girl, trying to comfort her.

"You betrayed her." Angel's dull, unearthly voice hardly seemed aware of what she was saying.

"No," said Veronica. "I didn't betray her."

"You cheated her."

"What a terrible thing to say! I didn't cheat her."

"You hurt her."

"I never — never — never—" But by then Veronica was crying and couldn't answer her.

3
Rough Draft

That night Matt couldn't stop staring out the window. He felt trapped. He was a prisoner of the past. He had an unbearable urge to leave the house immediately and forever, to set up camp somewhere else, in some other city, to head straight out into the darkness. The darkness seemed to offer someplace to hide.

Who would be next?

He couldn't get the ugly thought out of his head. What a weekend! If his nerves were a little jittery, who could blame him? An accident Friday night, an accident Saturday night. So, of course he might be a little nervous on Sunday night.

Headlights passed somewhere below on the boulevard. Wind tormented the maple branches scratching against the house.

He knew he should leave, then and there, for Veronica's sake as well as his own. He knew that. Instead, the words started coming to him again.

In a moment his computer was started up. He wrote for one hour, two hours, intended to call it quits around eight thirty, but by ten o'clock he had actually wrapped up a twenty-page rough sketch of the first act.

How exhilarating! He'd never be able to sleep without knowing how it sounded. He postponed his bedtime another hour. Time to give it a read-through, to hear and see what he had on his hands so far.

With a shiver at the coldness of his apartment, Matt grabbed the handful of pages and a red pen and retreated to the ugliest, warmest room of the house. The presence of the ancient boiler gave the laundry room a toasty warmth that went wasted. Some long-ago tenant had recognized this and dragged an old armchair over into the board-and-cement corner by the clothes dryer, rigging a lightbulb to dangle overhead.

Isolated and intimate, it was the perfect place to read a first draft. Turning off all the other lights, he settled into the one lit corner, thoughts focused on the script. Soon every page was covered with red scratch-outs and arrows and insertions.

"Matt—"

The whisper outside the laundry room's back door caused Matt to leap to his feet in a flurry of scattering sheets of dialogue. Someone on the other side of the door, someone outside, had quietly spoken his name.

"Who's there?" He tried to see out through the dark window glass. All he saw was his own reflection.

A voice outside the window whispered, "Matt—"

"Angel, is that you?"

No answer.

"Veronica?"

Though his dread almost crippled him, his need to know was greater. He forced his feet to approach the laundry room's back door. He forced his hand to slide back the latch. He stepped outside into the shadowy puddles of the stairwell.

Darkness. No one was there. Just an edgy stillness. Then one of the shadows moved. The figure of a woman. She stepped toward him.

"Matt—"

4
"Is Everything Okay?"

A cry outside woke Veronica from a deep sleep.

Her eyes snapped open. Rising quickly from her bed, she slipped into her bathrobe and slippers, grabbed a flashlight, and hurried downstairs to her front door. Flipping on the outside light, she unfastened the screen door and stepped onto her covered porch.

All the lights were out below in Matt's apartment.

Then she heard a moan around the side of the house. With dread and increasing fear, she crossed to the far end of her porch and peered over the rail.

A single light from inside the laundry room splashed a pool of illumination over the wet stairwell. Matt was standing outside the back door, propped up against the side of the house. He appeared to be staring into the rain. He wasn't moving.

Veronica hurried down the side stairs and around the front of the house to the stairwell on the other side. She rushed to him, wrapping her arms around him. "Matt? Matt, what is it?" He pulled free of her arms, hardly looking at her, completely disoriented, staring away from her as though he were trying to spot a particular star in the night sky. "Are you hurt? Did something happen?" Taking his arm, she guided him back through the door into the warmth of the laundry room.

"You're shaking. You're drenched."

"I thought I heard something—"

"What did you hear?"

"What I heard wasn't there," he said, leaning back against the cold white reality of the washing machine. "What I heard happened twenty years ago, so there's no way I could have heard it tonight."

"Why can't you forget that party?" Didn't she already hate that party enough, without hearing about it again and again? "Matt, it's in the past. The party's over. It can't be changed."

"The party's over, but I can't seem to get it out of my mind. Ever since I moved in here—" He pulled sharply away from her. "I don't belong in this house, that's the problem. And I don't belong with you. I'm the worst thing that could happen to you. I'll bring you nothing but misery, believe me."

"What in the world is that supposed to—?"

"Listen to me. I'm serious," he said. "I'm an invitation to disaster, just waiting to happen. I keep fooling myself, thinking you and I could have some kind of future. It's all lies! Get away from me while there's still time, and stay away. You're deceiving yourself if you think I'm going to bring you anything but unhappiness."

"Matt, that's not true!"

"Hello?" interrupted a voice, calling down the laundry room stairway. The person at the top was not visible.

"Is that you, Angel?"

"It's me. Is everything okay down there?"

"Everything's okay," said Veronica. "Go back to bed, Angel. I'll be right up."

The door closed.

Veronica took Matt's hand and led him into his apartment. They moved in silence. They couldn't speak. They didn't get any farther than the kitchen. Matt stopped in his tracks, turned her around, wrapped his rain-wet arms around her, and kissed her.

"Don't go back upstairs tonight," he whispered.

"But I just told Angel that—"

He kissed her neck, her throat. "Don't go back."

CHAPTER THIRTEEN

Monday, December 23

1
Stockroom Secret

"This is not the way a tax exempt sale is done."

He was bleary-eyed with lack of sleep, but he was smiling. Their night together! Veronica! The pulsing throb of a headache couldn't depress him. Not even the incessant orders of Dolly Wrangles could wipe the smile off his face.

"No, you press the other button first," said Dolly, looking over his shoulder. "Back up and cancel now, before you do that. No, no, no. Martha, would you come and look at this," called Dolly across the bookstore in exasperation. "Matt has done it completely wrong."

The bitter line of Martha Ironwood's features showed she had been waiting for this to happen. "The tax exempt form has to be imprinted, just like a check," she scolded. "How many times do I have to tell you that?"

Dolly Wrangles bumped past him toward the other cash register. "Let me help you over here, sir," she said to the next customer, "while he logs all those mistakes on his void sheet."

His world had changed overnight. She was incredible. She had suddenly stepped into the emptiness of his life and filled it perfectly. He knew he had no business in her arms, knew he could only bring her pain, and yet couldn't pull away from her.

With students and faculty gone until January, all Christmas merchandise in the HUB bookstore was already marked half-price and mounded on the clearance table. This pre-holiday sale managed to draw a few customers into the bookstore.

Matt stood by the cash register, suppressing a yawn. "I need more sleep," he told himself sensibly. He had seen the bags under his eyes that morning in the mirror. Maybe more sleep would provide a cure for the whispering voices and female phantoms and kisses in the night! If only he could blame them on drafts and creaks and echoes, on stray cats and prowling raccoons, on doves nesting under the eaves, on the scratching branches of the maple tree.

"Matt, you're not paying attention," said Dolly. "This isn't a cash transaction, it's a bank card sale."

"Of course," said Matt. "I wasn't thinking."

"You can't use the magnetic strip until you press total," said Dolly, breathing down his neck.

"Right, right," said Matt.

He accidentally pressed the button marked *Check Tendered.*

"Now, look what you've done!" cried Dolly. "Well, there's only one way to fix it now."

She nudged him out of the way, and punched the dozen different buttons that needed to be punched.

"There," said Dolly, stepping aside for him to regain control of his machine. "Think you can manage on your own now?" She watched him for a moment, then said scornfully, "Matt, you haven't even entered your employee number yet. Are you forgetting everything you ever learned?"

Dolly had scarcely returned to her station at the service counter, leaving him temporarily in peace, when he happened to notice someone who looked like Angel at the far end of a fixture piled high with spiralbound notebooks. When he turned to get a better look at her, she was gone. With a glance to make sure Dolly was occupied, he put up a *Closed* sign in front of his cash register and started toward the back of the store where he had seen her.

*

Angel hurried up the street toward campus.

It was the fault of that house. Maybe she just had to stay away from it. The upsetting seizure that had gripped her last night had frightened her so badly she couldn't even think about it. And her temper! She was always getting angry lately, flying into little emotional tantrums. It was people! People exhausted her. They caused trouble and hurt your feelings. What Angel needed was to be left alone. She had to keep people at a distance. For her own good, and for theirs too.

Besides, people didn't tell the truth. They said they liked you, and then left you alone. They said they'd spend time with you, and then forgot you. They don't need kids when they have adults around. Especially when the adults start sleeping together. Then kids are just in the way.

The Husky Union Building (HUB)

Veronica had lied. She said she was coming upstairs. Instead, she spent the night with Matt. Angel had lain awake half the night waiting for footsteps that never returned. She was too jealous to even begin to deal with her feelings yet. Only one thing was clear. She was on the outside again.

She was paying Matt a visit on her own.

The halls of the HUB were nearly empty. Scarcely a dozen customers were scattered throughout the bookstore. Matt stood behind one of the cash registers, waiting on a customer. He didn't see her slip past him. She drifted toward the back of the store, toward the candy bars and comic books, waiting to get his attention. She was glancing through the latest issue of *Fantastic Four* when she heard an odd sound. She heard it again, from the dark doorway of the stockroom, just beyond the chocolates.

Angel froze, and listened again.

At first she thought it was a frog. It repeated in wet gasps, in sucking gulps of air, a gagging sound. She approached the stockroom door. She could see shelves of boxes and packages of merchandise in the shadowy interior, the edge of a refrigerator, a drinking fountain, lockers, a broom handle, a feather duster. She stood in the doorway, staring, listening, peering into the cave-like darkness, discerning the edges of more racks, more boxes, more shelves.

Something moved behind one of the boxes.

*

He found the girl staring into the doorway of the stockroom with her mouth half-open, as though she'd temporarily lost her mind. He rushed up to her and took her by the shoulders. She seemed to snap awake, and let out a yelp of fear. Several nearby customers glanced uneasily in Matt's direction.

"Angel, it's just me."

"Oh." She was white in the face.

"Are you okay?"

She stared into the dark stockroom. "I thought I saw—"

That was all the farther she got before Martha Ironwood rushed up to them. "Surely you know, Matt, that no customers are allowed in the stockroom. It's a bookstore rule."

"Of course," he said. "She wasn't—"

"There are reasons for rules," said Martha. "That's why we have rules. For reasons."

"Sorry," mumbled Angel. "I didn't know."

She quickly slipped away from them, beelined for the bookstore doorway, and disappeared out into the HUB hall. Matt wasn't so lucky. Martha personally escorted him across the bookstore into the office, to the chair across from her desk.

With a swallow of cold coffee to wash down a peach-colored capsule from her prescription, Martha gave him a long, assessing look. "You probably don't believe in reasons."

"Reasons? You mean cause and effect?"

She sighed. "Let me tell you the reason why only employees are allowed in the stockroom. We had a very unpleasant incident — it must be seven years ago. You may have noticed, the Food Service here in the HUB sometimes hires people to clear the tables who — well, who aren't — you know." She tapped the side of her head knowingly.

He nodded. He had noticed.

"One of them, a little fellow, used to come up to the bookstore all the time. He was a sly one. When he thought no one was watching, he would fill his pockets. I always kept eye on him. Caught him too, more than once. Which is why I warned him. One more time, and I wouldn't let him back in the store. He couldn't resist. And then he must have thought I saw him, because he slipped into the stockroom with a big souvenir key-ring. No one saw him go in there. He must have gotten scared. The doctor said he tried to swallow it. The key-ring got stuck in his throat. We didn't find him until it was too late. I happened to notice something in the stockroom behind one of the boxes. It was his foot."

Matt shuddered.

"A very disturbing situation," she concluded, steering him back toward the sales floor. "Which is why we have rules now regarding the stockroom. Rules have reasons."

2
Changed Woman

"Why the big grin?" said Veronica, smiling irritably at her friend as she crossed the English Department office. "Is there some joke I don't know about?" Clarice rested her chin on her fist and regarded her analytically. "What do you think you're staring at?"

"Oh, nothing, nothing," said Clarice, her smirk growing larger. She seemed to be suppressing outright laughter. "My, oh my, don't you look like the fulfilled woman!"

Veronica turned to face Clarice in exasperated surprise. "Now, that's a very odd thing to say, even for you. What makes you say such a thing?"

"Oh, nothing," said Clarice, showing even more of her white teeth. "It's just that when a changed woman walks across the room, a person tends to notice."

"Changed woman?" Veronica laughed uneasily. "What in the world are you talking about?"

"Somebody in this room is looking extremely content and satisfied," said Clarice. "Is that plain enough for you?"

"I get it," said Veronica. "You're asking, did I spend the night with him?"

"I didn't ask any such thing."

"That's what you're really thinking, though, isn't it? You're so snoopy! Don't you think I've already got enough trouble with one tenant? Do you think I need trouble with another?"

"Now, give him a chance."

"A chance to muddle both our lives? I have no intention of getting involved again."

"Honey, we're all involved, whether we think we are or not. It's been seven years since you left Sam. Why isolate yourself? We don't live forever. Live now."

"I agree," said Veronica. "I'm glad you feel that way."

"Good," said Clarice, feeling confident she had made her point. "So, did you sleep with him?"

"Well, yes, I did, actually," said Veronica, faltering to find the right words. "And it was wonderful. It was incredible. He restored my faith in men."

"Am I hearing right?"

"He's such a special guy that it scares me. The whole thing is too Twilight Zone. He just comes out of nowhere and moves into my house and suddenly I'm in love. There's something strange going on here. I feel so familiar with him. So relaxed. Too relaxed. It's too good to be true. If only the rest of my life were going as well."

"What's that supposed to mean?"

"My teenage guest."

"That was asking for trouble."

"She keeps scaring me."

"Teenagers are scary. Ask me. I've got three."

"She's moody, insecure. All kinds of weird psychic stuff starts to happen when she's around. I mean, last night she started acting like she was channeling my sister's ghost."

160

"Doing *what?*"

"It's hard to explain. It's like she's having an epileptic seizure. I don't know what she's going to do next. And she's mine, all mine, till her parents come home!"

3
Spirits All Around Us

The spires of Suzzallo Library poked up into the sky, tearing at the ragged, darkening clouds.

At least there was always the library. She knew that she always belonged there. Denying that she had heard or seen anything in the stockroom, forcing all thought of the bookstore out of her mind, Angel clicked through the turnstile and proceeded into the heart of the old building. The line of yellow tape on the floor drew her, just as it always did, down the curving tile-lined staircase into the depths.

There ahead of her, at the other end of the reading room, was the wire-grid fencing with the "Staff Only" sign. She dropped into a study carrel, shrugged her backpack off her shoulders, and put her head down, buried in a pillow of her arms.

She hadn't intended to fall asleep. She woke to the sound of footsteps approaching. She lurched to her feet, seized with an irrational panic. Like an animal, she realized there was no other way out. She was trapped in a dead end. She had only one recourse. She hid.

A figure appeared in the doorway.

*

Closing time for Suzzallo Library during the Christmas interim was at five o'clock.

At five minutes to five, Muriel Rose began her nightly routine of bustling from room to room, glancing down every aisle of bookshelves, shooing everyone out. Tonight there weren't many to shoo. Right now she was in the lower levels of the library, trying to ignore that she was inspecting the very same stacks where she'd had her ghost experience. No one down there now. Though she felt a little creepy, Muriel was not an easily spooked woman. She was a cool-headed, sensible librarian. She methodically checked each aisle to make sure no one was left behind at closing.

Which was how she nearly stumbled over a short, half-hidden creature crouching behind the last shelves. The thing lurched to its feet in scrambling confusion, and became a teenage girl as scared as she was.

"I'm sorry."

"I'm sorry, too."

"I didn't mean to startle you," said the librarian, picking up the book the girl had dropped. "I thought everyone had gone home. I didn't notice you come in—" She paused, taking another look at the girl, imagining her with more hair. "I've seen you here before."

"I come here a lot."

Out of the corner of her eye, Muriel noticed that the girl wasn't the only lingering patron. She merely glimpsed the woman passing at the end of the stacks. Instead Muriel watched the girl's face. Her cheeks had drained of color.

"Is something wrong?"

"I'm scared."

She grabbed the girl's hand. It was cold. "Scared of what?"

"Didn't you see her?"

By the time Muriel realized what the girl meant, who she'd glimpsed passing by, the woman in the raincoat was gone, out of sight beyond the "Staff Only" sign.

Now the girl was studying Muriel. "You saw her too?"

"Of course I did." Muriel suppressed a shudder and crouched down before her, still clasping her hand, looking directly in her eye. "Have you seen her here before?"

Angel nodded. But her face had turned a pasty gray color. She was breathing with difficulty. "I've seen her, but I don't know who she is."

"Are you afraid of ghosts?" Before Angel could answer, Muriel added, "Because that's what she is."

"The tall woman in the raincoat?"

"Yes, a ghost," She could see that Angel was shivering. "I knew her when she was alive. Incidentally, I believe you know my dear friend, Veronica."

Angel practically jumped. "How do you know that?"

"Veronica told me about you. You're one of her students. She cares about you very much. My name is Muriel."

"I'm Angel."

They shook hands solemnly.

"Have you seen other ghosts, Angel?"

The girl hesitated, then said, "Sometimes lately, I feel like — like all of a sudden I'm not alone anymore."

"At Veronica's house?"

"Other places, too." She considered mentioning the bookstore stockroom, but was clearly in no condition to talk about it.

"If you feel someone's there, someone probably is," said Muriel. "Many, many are. There are spirits all around us. The surface of the earth must be teeming with ghosts. And so many of them are unhappy. So many are filled with confusion and regret. They're calling out to us every day, begging for our help. Sometimes, if you're quiet, if you listen carefully, you know they're there."

Angel looked up at her, and solemnly nodded. Then she grabbed her backpack and fled.

4
Whispers

Matt was exhausted by the time he got home. A long day at the bookstore, after almost no sleep the night before, after a weekend with even less sleep, had left him punchy and humorless. He had a long, hot bath, then microwaved a frozen dinner into some semblance of a meal, ate it quickly without tasting a bite, and was aiming for bed when a knock at the door stopped him. He opened it at once.

Veronica stood in the laundry room doorway, looking more beautiful than ever. Her eyes, though they also betrayed exhaustion, glowed with a rich, vibrant life.

"Hello there," she said. He became aware, from the movement of her eyes, that he was wearing only his sweatpants. "Did you manage to make it through the day without snoozing on your feet?

He grinned. "Just barely."

"You haven't seen Angel, have you?"

"She stopped by the bookstore today. Why? She's not around?"

"Haven't seen her since I got home."

The girl's absense clearly made her nervous, and Matt had his own reasons for being disturbed. He couldn't forget the way he'd found Angel staring into the stockroom. Almost as though she knew what had once happened there.

"She'll show up soon. I'll talk to you tomorrow."

He closed the door behind her, pulled off his sweatpants, turned off the lights, and dropped into bed. He slept briefly, fitfully. Then once again he plunged into nightmares.

He was there again twenty years ago, and the shadows of the house were packed with dark, faceless people. He was struggling in vain to extricate himself from the crowd. They were all shouting and screaming as they fought to get past him, pushing and shoving, while revolving blue police lights cut through the night-darkened windows like laser beams. He was trying to find someone. He was fighting his way up the staircase, but everyone else was hurtling desperately in the other direction, and he could make no progress, no progress at all—

Matt half-woke, struggling up out of his dream but unable to make it all the way. He found himself stuck in a restless, in-between state, terrified of sinking back into the nightmare.

A floorboard creaked at the other end of the bedroom.

He awoke completely, wet with sweat. He raised himself up onto his elbow and peered through the darkness in the direction of the sound. Then he jerked into a sitting position, his heart hammering.

The figure of a woman—

But nothing was there. What had looked like a spectral apparition was really only a bathrobe on a hook.

He listened.

What was that? Whispering? Snickering, smothered laughter. Where was it coming from? Or was he only hearing it in his head?

A figure was standing at the foot of the bed.

It stepped forward. It was Angel.

Matt sighed with relief. "Congratulations. You nearly gave me a heart attack." He quickly tried to regain his composure. "Angel, what are you doing here?"

The girl approached the bed, but she wasn't looking at him. Instead she was looking from one wall to the other, as though the walls were suddenly speaking to her in voices only she could hear.

"Whispering," said Angel. "Didn't you hear it?" She cocked her head slightly to one side, listening intently, waiting for confirmation. "Somebody was whispering."

Matt stared at the girl, trying to read her inscrutable face, trying to keep his own face a mask. He did not want to contaminate her with his own soaring fears.

"I didn't hear any whispering," he lied. "I don't know what you're talking about. You've had Veronica worried about you tonight. She didn't know where you were."

She heard what he said, but her attention was definitely elsewhere. "I was at the library."

He decided to be straightforwardly blunt. "Angel, when you were at the bookstore today, what did you see in the stockroom?"

She took a long time answering. She looked directly into his eyes. "Nothing."

He concealed his frustration. "Next time leave a note for Veronica, so she won't worry. Now, get back upstairs where you belong. And stop spooking yourself — and me. Nobody's whispering."

5
What Child Is This?

Veronica tried to sleep.

The entire house was tight with tension. It seemed unusually cold. She reached down to the luminous control beside her bed and turned up her electric blanket. Then she wrapped the covers closer around her. The room itself seemed almost frosty. Angel must have accidentally bumped the thermostat downstairs.

It was so unpleasantly chilly she dreaded sliding out from under the covers, but the thermostat would not correct itself. With a groan of resolution, Veronica forced herself to throw back the covers and jump out. She darted over to the closet where she immediately wrapped herself in her robe and slid into her slippers. The temperature in the house felt like it had dropped below freezing.

She descended the staircase to the dining room. There was the thermostat, clinging to the dark wall in the corner like a gleaming beetle. She stared at the dial in disbelief.

Sixty-five degrees. Right where it was supposed to be. Could it possibly be broken?

Slowly she climbed back up the stairs through the hushed house. It wasn't as cold downstairs. She hesitated on the landing. She could feel it getting colder. The door into the library was open. A cold slab of moonlight stretched out from the open door. As Veronica stepped closer, a shadow crossed through the moonlight.

The girl must be awake.

Veronica walked up to the library door to announce her presence, trying not to startle her by a sudden appearance. She looked inside. The makeshift bed, moonlit, squeezed between walls of books, was empty.

"Angel?"

No response.

If it wasn't Angel, then who was skulking about in the dark through the library? "Who's in here?" The edge of something moved out of the moonlight on the other side of the room, retreating. "Angel, is that you?

No response.

165

Veronica clicked on the library lights. No one there. Just a palpable sense of not being alone. She turned the lights back off and was about to return to bed when she heard a far away voice singing a Christmas carol.

> *What child is this*
> *Who laid to rest*
> *On Mary's lap is sleeping*

She shivered. That voice. Where was it coming from? Slightly louder now. Not from a recording downstairs in Matt's unit. Not from anywhere in the house.

> *Whom angels greet*
> *With anthems sweet*
> *While shepherds watch are keeping*

Impulsively she unlatched one of the French windows and swung it open. The room was suddenly engulfed by a blast of cold. Veronica hardly felt it. Who was that singing?

> *This, this is Christ the King*
> *Whom shepherds guard*
> *And angels sing*

She stepped outside onto the narrow third-floor balcony. Down below her, the house dropped away three floors to the staircase of stone slabs winding down the hillside.

Her hand lightly touched the wooden railing. That voice! She looked out across Montlake valley toward the dark hillside of Calvary Cemetery. She knew that voice. The clear, lovely voice singing that Christmas carol belonged to her sister. Her sister singing. On the night her sister died — the night before Christmas Eve.

She spun around. Angel stood framed by moonlight in the doorway. "Angel! Where were you?"

"Downstairs talking to Matt." The girl took a step toward her, regarding her anxiously. "I thought I heard something. Was that you? I heard someone singing."

CHAPTER FOURTEEN
Tuesday, December 24

1
God's Downpour

That Christmas Eve it never stopped raining.

Within an hour of dawn, the early morning drizzle started coming down in sheets. It got rapidly worse, until Ravenna Boulevard below the house was streaming with water, rushing in a current along the curb. The weather shifted from classic Seattle wetness to drenched unpleasant nastiness. From accustomed inconvenience to pounding persistence to outright nightmare.

Veronica lay in bed, staring out the window into the dark, wet, troubled morning.

> *What child is this*
> *Who laid to rest*
> *On Mary's lap is sleeping*

She forced the tune out of her mind. She forced herself to forget the disturbing voice she'd heard singing. She did not want to think about last night. She especially did not want to think about her sister.

Angel had heard it, too.

No! She thought about clearing her office desk today before the holidays. Most of her fellow faculty members were long gone by now. Padelford Hall would be half-deserted. She would be among the last to abandon ship.

One last session in her office ought to do it.

She flung back the covers, forced herself out of bed, and headed for the bathroom to prepare herself for the day. Twenty minutes later she was heading out the front door when she came to an abrupt stop.

Tuesday was garbage morning. Once a week, the two plastic garbage cans were carried down to the first landing of the stairs, where they were emptied by the garbage man. Matt and Tyler had both forgotten to set out the cans. She was going to get drenched, but there was no way around it if she wanted room for next week's trash.

Leaving her books, briefcase and umbrella on the porch, buttoning up her overcoat to the neck, Veronica hurried down the side stairs toward the black plastic cans nestled in the hollow below the staircase. Rain streamed down in curtains from the roof, dribbling in cold drops from overhead branches.

She had grabbed a wet handle and was hauling the awkward, garbage-filled plastic tub out into the rain when she noticed a mound of rags huddled behind the cans, a human-sized bundle of rubbish curled up into a wide-eyed crouch of terror.

She stumbled back away from him, out into the rain, tripping on the edge of the concrete walkway. "What are you doing here?"

"Please," said the homeless man, "please don't be angry. Please don't make me go back out in all that. Please please please."

"But you can't just camp under people's stairs!" she objected. "You can't just decide to burrow under somebody's house."

"I need someplace dry where I can write my poems. I won't bother you. Please. See, here's a poem I wrote for you." He thrust it toward her.

A love from the past
How long can it last?
No cure for a heart
Thats broken apart

Memory burns
The wheel turns
Endure the pain
Love is sane

"What do you think of that?" She tried to give the poem back to him, but he took hold of her hand in his weathered fingers and looked her straight in the eye. "Please, can I stay here?"

Veronica pulled away from him, lugging the garbage can after her. She dragged it down the stairs and propped it on the landing. The poem had thoroughly upset her. His poems always seemed to be hovering on the edge of things he couldn't possibly know. She hurried back up the stairway through the rain.

She rushed right past him as though she didn't see him, and on up the stairs leading to the dry shelter of her porch.

He sighed, and turned to gather together his belongings.

A moment later Veronica came back out into the rain with her arms full of spare blankets, an overcoat, and a plastic bowl half-full of microwaved pasta leftovers.

She didn't leave for campus until the homeless poet was wearing the overcoat and wrapped in the blankets and stowed beneath the porch like an Egyptian mummy in his tomb, hunched forward over the plastic container, eagerly gobbling the steaming leftovers. She hardly noticed how wet she was.

"I have to go to work now."

He paused in his eating, his lips smeared red with pasta sauce. "Have a good day. My name is John."

2
Bookstore Bedlam

"Have you forgotten everything I've ever told you?" snapped Martha Ironwood, her patience exhausted. That bookstore was going to be the death of her! "How many times do we have to go over this, Matt? It's not that complicated. Surely you remember how to do a credit return on a bank card."

The new employee was the worst the Personnel Department had stuck her with in years. Shirttail half-untucked as usual, glasses slid halfway down his nose, a fortyish loser who always looked like he needed a shave, was always mentally off in la-la land — and who always found the wrong way of entering a transaction on the cash register.

Martha glanced toward the clock. Only a few minutes remained before the daily lunchtime surge of staff personnel converged from all over campus at the HUB. One of the bookstore's busiest times of the day.

"Look," said Martha, in the reasonable voice she reserved for dealing with idiots, "there's a button especially designed to do that one thing. The name of that button is *Bank Card Return*. Clearly this is the button you need."

Thoroughly embarrassed, the broad-shouldered woman from Plant Services looked down at the counter, eying the bottle of aspirin she so desperately needed, waiting anxiously to get her credit card back so she could flee. The Asian woman in a black leather jacket behind her, waiting to buy a book on judo, looked up alertly. She wasn't the only one watching. Martha realized that her voice was carrying.

"Dolly," she snapped in a harsh croak of an undertone, "make sure he does it right."

Her assistant was leaning over the service counter, resting her heavy bosom on the glass case, telephone receiver propped against her ear, tracking the wanderings of some long lost purchase order. Dolly lurched up off the counter at the sound of her voice, ended the phone conversation in a sentence, and bounded toward her boss.

"I'm leaving you in charge here," said Martha. She didn't wait around to see the gleam in Dolly's eyes. The woman loved taking charge. Instead, Martha took a deep breath and strode across the bookstore.

Just outside her office she paused. There was that irritating girl again with the horrible haircut, the one who had tried to go into the stockroom yesterday. Half the morning, as usual, she had seen the girl at the back of the store reading one of those trashy paperbacks with dwarfs and dragons on the cover. Lost in time and space, dirty foot propped up on the shelf, blocking the New Releases from anyone who might want to really buy one.

But that wasn't where she was now, which was what bothered Martha. This time the kid wasn't reading at all, but standing just inside the bookstore entrance, staring at the front cash register in a very odd, suspicious way. She had trouble written all over her. Possibly shoplifting. Possibly drugs. Kids these days!

Martha intended to keep an eye on that one, but she had something else to do first. She ducked off the sales floor into the stockroom, and straight to the employee drinking fountain. Fumbling down a brown bottle from the rack overhead, she shook out two huge blue capsules of her new prescription.

*

Always happy to take charge, Dolly Wrangles pushed her way into the cashier cage. Matt steeled himself to receive a torrent of orders. He needn't have worried.

"It's simpler if I just take over!" she said. Impatiently bumping him aside, she swiped the plastic card through the slot and began punching all the right buttons. "You've really got to learn how to listen better," she grumbled in his direction, swiftly slipping duplicate forms this way and that way into the cash register, causing a variety of buzzes and dings. The machine clearly approved of what she was doing. "You don't pay attention. That's your biggest problem, Matt. You seem smart enough. But you always forget the most important thing. Rules! It's so simple and — Matt, you're not listening. This is a perfect example! Once again your mind is elsewhere."

Matt was staring at the open till of money in front of Dolly. For some reason, the black metal till was trembling slightly.

"You've got to concentrate more," said Dolly, straightening the checks and the charge slips, tapping them into neat piles. "And always remember the rules. They make everything so simple. You don't have to waste time thinking. It's hard for intellectuals like you to understand, but in some situations, too much thinking works against you. You just do what the rule tells you to do."

The quarters, dimes, nickels, and pennies, all neatly segregated in a row, were very softly tinkling in their compartments, shivering together.

Matt started feeling uncomfortable, and glanced back over his shoulder. He stiffened in alarm. Angel was standing just inside the bookstore entrance, staring blindly straight ahead, her face drained to an unhealthy white. She didn't seem to see him, or much of anything else.

"Rules aren't just for dumb people," said Dolly. "Rules are how civilization works. You need to know the rules for a customer who wants to return a book. The rules are the same for everybody."

A sound came from Angel's mouth like a very soft moan.

"Matt, you haven't heard a word I said. Do you think you're too important to be a good cashier? Honestly, I look at you and talk to you, and it's like I'm talking to the moon—"

The cash register till slammed shut on Dolly's hands.

Dolly screeched. With a wail, she tugged her hands free, whimpering over fingers curled up into claws. "Oh, my poor fingers! Matt, get on the other register."

He hurried to the other machine, punched in his employee number. Nothing happened. The cash register buttons refused to respond. "It's stuck."

"What's going on here?" hissed Martha Ironwood, appearing in the stockroom doorway in response to Dolly's wail. She came striding toward the stalled registers. Not until then did she see what had happened to Dolly's hands.

Two customers were waiting in line, now three.

"Oh, my fingers!" said Dolly. "Did you see that? It shut on me. It actually slammed shut on me."

"Something's wrong with the power system." Martha picked up the telephone to file a complaint with the switchboard. She jabbed the number into the telephone buttons, then scowled at the receiver. "What's wrong with the phone?"

Squeezing around the whimpering hulk of Dolly, Matt worked his way out of the register cage over to the service counter and lifted the telephone receiver. "This one is dead, too." He glanced nervously back toward the bookstore doorway. Angel was leaning against the centerpost, braced, her mouth open, her eyes wide and staring.

Five customers were waiting in line, now six.

The lights overhead flashed. One of the long fluorescent tubes blazed, sparked, and exploded. Two customers screamed. Several others abandoned the merchandise they'd been intending to buy and hurried nervously toward the doors.

"My God, what's happening?" whispered Dolly.

As though in answer, the magnetic locks on the bookstore doors suddenly lost their power. The doors slammed clattering shut. Somewhere in the building a buzzer began to wail.

Matt looked back at the bookstore doorway. The girl's face was contorted and red, as though she were holding her breath. The moment she noticed he had seen her, she banged open the door and fled, colliding outside in the hall with the Doctor's Choice cosmetics sign and sending it reeling with a crash to the floor.

"Angel—!" He abandoned his post at the cash register, hurrying toward the bookstore doorway.

"Matthew Braddon, where do you think you're going?" demanded Martha Ironwood. "Don't you dare run off now, in the middle of all this. You're needed here. Do you hear me? Stop!"

3
Echoes and Footsteps

He didn't see exactly where she went.

He saw someone who might have been Angel, the same size, build, who ran when she saw him approaching.

"Angel?" Matt lunged down the main hall of the Husky Union Building. He looked wildly this way, that way. He thought he saw her heading toward the stairs. "Angel—!"

His footsteps clattered down the stairs after her. As he rounded the first flight, he heard a door thud shut somewhere below. He continued down the next flight, into the basement of the HUB.

The echoing clatter of bowling pins brought him to a halt in front of the bowling alley. He almost missed her. Then he looked behind him and noticed a door down the long tiled hallway at the other end. It was closing. He hurried after her, past the restrooms, past the employee locker rooms and the student rental lockers.

Up ahead he saw doors marked *Danger Restricted Area*.

The doors clattered shut behind him. He found himself standing on a service ramp leading down the side of the storage room into a caged area below. Inside the mesh wiring were dozens of bundles of colorful feed tubes leading to various upstairs carbonated drink dispensers.

"Angel?"

He had given up on ever finding her when he heard an echo of running footfalls ahead.

"Angel, is that you?"

The only answer was the closing thud of a door somewhere just out of sight. He turned the next corner, flung open the door. He hurried past the coolers and salad kitchens of the Food Service. Past skids of piled pop cans. When he saw no other direction to go, he noticed a door wedged open. Rust-red pipes lined the high ceiling, leading into a narrow hallway. An isolated cement tunnel in the depths of nowhere.

"Angel?"

His voice echoed. No answer. Halfway down the hall, he heard the echoing sound of a door closing.

"Angel, is that you?"

Footsteps. Approaching quicker. Abruptly stopping.

He froze, silently listening.

Nothing.

Where had she gone? Could she have run upstairs to the street? Had she darted down behind the bowling alley, and gotten out the back way? She wasn't there now.

When he got back upstairs to the bookstore, he found a "Closed" sign posted in the HUB hallway. Four black-suited University of Washington police officers were inside, inspecting the scene. One was trying to explain something into a walkie-talkie. One was examining the cash register. A nurse from Hall Health Center, who had been shopping in the store during the electrical malfunction, was bandaging Dolly Wrangles' hands, while Dolly explained in great detail about her painful experience.

Martha Ironwood was waiting for him. The pills in her prescription bottle were rattling in her fist.

"Here's the other employee, officer," said Martha, "The one who ran off when it happened." One of the campus police nodded in her direction. She turned back to Matt in a cold fury. "They'll be wanting to ask you a few questions. And I have a question, too. What made you think you could run out of the bookstore just when our entire system broke down?"

Matt opened his mouth to reply.

She didn't wait to hear his lame excuse. "That's the last straw. I've had enough. You'll be paid for the hours you've worked. Gather up your personal belongings. As of this moment, Matthew Braddon, consider your employment at University Book Store terminated."

"You can't be serious!" cried Matt. "That poor kid looked like she might have been in serious—"

"Have I been unclear?" Martha Ironwood could barely contain herself. In a bookstore where every cash register, telephone, and lock had dared to defy her, she would not allow a mere employee to do so. "Let me put it to you in plainer language. You're fired!"

In the angry thrust of her arm, the cap popped off the prescription bottle. Blue capsules burst out splattering in all directions.

4
What Librarians Want

The downpour showed no sign of letting up. She had promised to meet Muriel in the library. Veronica could no longer avoid getting another taste of the day. Umbrella popped open, overcoat buttoned to the neck, she hesitated in the Padelford doorway, looking out.

"If you're foolish enough to want to experience that awful mess," said Clarice from the door of the English Department office, "would you mind dropping off these envelopes for me at Miller Hall?"

Not even Veronica's umbrella was able to protect her from the driving sheets of rain. She was soaked completely down one side by the time she reached Miller Hall and the In Basket for the College of Education. From there, Veronica crossed the rain-drenched Quad toward Suzzallo Library. The sky was already so dark it seemed like evening. The Gothic spires of the library poked into the lowering thunderclouds. Curtains of rain blurred Red Square, covering the bricks with puddles of rainwater.

She hurried into the library. Her footsteps echoed hollowly inside. A last few eccentric faculty members prowled the shelves. Local homeless people warmed themselves over magazines. Here and there

Suzzallo Library on Red Square

harried graduate students nodded in their study carrels, struggling to stay awake.

"She's up in one of the collections," said the woman at the Information Desk. "You know Muriel. If she's trying to find the answer to something, she doesn't stop until she does."

Veronica listened to elaborate directions on how to find her friend, then lost her patience and trotted up the curving stone staircase.

The third floor of Suzzallo Library was deserted. The air was thick with the stuffy, suffocating silence of row after row of books. She tugged open the thick, wooden door of a reading room she'd never noticed before. The heavy door thudded shut behind her with a hollow boom.

"Muriel?"

No answer. The thick, old books seemed to absorb the sound of her voice.

"Muriel?"

Several tables were spread with open volumes in mid-research, but with no sign of her librarian friend. Somewhere she thought she heard someone clear their throat. She headed toward the sound.

"Is that you, Muriel?"

She peered around the tall bookshelves, one dark, skinny aisle after another.

"Over here."

Veronica flinched backward. The voice came from above her. The old librarian was on the other side of the bookshelf, standing on a small ladder propped against the books, examining volumes high on the topmost shelf.

"There you are!"

"Don't worry," said Muriel. "I didn't forget."

"Forget what?" said Veronica.

"The book I was telling you about. It might be able to help you." The small, thick volume was clutched in one hand. "It's by Colin Wilson — his study of poltergeist phenomena. The author taught here in the late sixties. I remember hearing him speak. I even sat in on a few of his classes. A brilliant thinker. He became obsessed with the paranormal."

"His book is about what?" Veronica stopped at the bottom of the ladder. "Poltergeist phenomena?"

Muriel descended, rung by rung. "You'll see. Poor thing, you've been very distressed lately, haven't you? I don't blame you. But the pieces are starting to fit together. Too soon to come to any conclusions, but I've got some ideas. And, of course, now that I've actually met her—"

"You've what?"

"That's when I realized what the problem might be. The girl has an incredible gift."

"What are you talking about? You've met Angel?"

"You read this book, and it will all become clear. With a little luck, your ghost problem is about to be solved."

Veronica put her arm around her friend. "You dear thing! And what do you think is the answer?"

"As for the answer," said the old librarian with a smile, brushing back a wild wisp of hair as though it were a bothersome cobweb, "we all come to different answers, my dear, especially in spiritual matters. If we could only know for sure what to expect when we crossed over, it would change everything, shape the whole course of our lives. That one fact — the one all-important thing we don't know. What happens on the other side?"

"Do you believe?"

"Of course, I believe," said the old woman. "But that's not what I'm after. I want to *know*. Nuns believe. Librarians want answers."

Veronica's smile was brief. "I just wish I knew how to help the poor girl."

"Take this Colin Wilson book and see if it sheds any light. If you can just somehow help her understand her own powers—"

"And if I can't?"

"That's what I'm afraid of." Muriel tapped her lightly on the hand. "Let's be optimistic, and trust that you *can* help her."

"Muriel, you're such a dear friend!"

She squeezed Veronica's hand affectionately. "I want you to know, dear, that every Christmas Eve I get down on my knees and thank God for the friends of my life. I consider my friends God's greatest gifts. And I always say your name first."

Veronica was so touched that she couldn't speak. By the time that she could, she asked, "What are you doing tonight, Muriel?"

The old woman immediately looked evasive. "Oh, family plans, the same as everyone else."

"I didn't know you had family here in Seattle."

"Oh, I don't," said Muriel. "Out of town."

She clearly didn't want to discuss it, so Veronica went on. "I've invited a couple of the other tenants to join me tonight for dinner. If you should happen to be free?"

"Oh, no, dear. But thank you."

"You'd be more than welcome."

"Thanks, anyway." Muriel kissed her on the cheek. "You're a sweetheart to ask me. You'll be in my thoughts. And make sure you read that book. The answer is right in front of us somewhere, so close we could trip over it. If we just knew where to look!"

5
Scaring People

The afternoon finally ground to a halt. It was over. Her office desk was clean and clear. Her courses for next quarter were planned. The textbooks were ordered. The winter holidays had begun.

Veronica locked her office door with a giddy rush of exhilaration. The elevator promptly swallowed her. She felt the doors whoosh closed around her with a sense of relief. As she was heading toward the exit ramp, going past the English office, she noticed Clarice still sitting before her word processor. Veronica poked her head into the doorway.

"Merry Christmas."

"Two Inkjet printer cartridges," droned Clarice into the receiver, "three boxes of No. 10 staples, two dozen legal-size manila folders." She was dictating a last order for office supplies into the telephone, but managed to rise to her feet, receiver clenched between shoulder and ear, and wave. "You have a great holiday, honey," she called. "And be nice to Mister Santa. You give him a great big kiss."

Popping open her umbrella, Veronica headed out into the downpour toward home. The campus streetlamps were brightening all around her. The dormitories were lifeless and empty. Traffic on 45th was an urgent river of streaming headlights and faceless drivers. The rain was relentless.

As she came up the stairs toward her front door, Veronica glanced nervously around the side of the house, into the depths of the trash can shelter beneath the stairs. The blankets were folded into a neat pile, the overcoat laid across the top. No sign of John. In spite of the rain, he had gone about his business. Just as well.

She didn't see the poem pinned to the overcoat until she had gathered the whole bundle into her arms. She set the blankets and coat back down, unpinned the poem, and was so intent on reading it that she wasn't careful enough with the pin.

Broken hearted
No escape
Pieces bound
With string and tape

Lovers love
And turn to dust
Come tomorrow
Learn to trust

As she finished reading the last line, a tiny drop of blood fell on the paper.

Another frustrating, enigmatic little doggerel!

Angry with herself for letting the poem upset her, Veronica crumpled the poem in her fist, popped the finger into her mouth, and hurried up the side stairs.

Angel was inside. She could hear the girl singing to herself. Dropping the wadded-up poem into the waste basket behind the front door, she hurried up the central staircase. She found the girl in the bathroom, wearing one of Veronica's T-shirts, combing her chopped-off hair as though it were still long and pretty.

"Angel."

She jumped. "You scared me." She resumed brushing. "You shouldn't scare people. I was just looking at my hair. The person who cut it didn't know what he was doing. Maybe you could touch it up for me sometime? Straighten the back, you know, make it even." When Veronica didn't reply, the girl glanced at her warily. "Why are you staring at me?"

"You didn't tell me you'd met Muriel."

The statement caused the girl to stiffen guardedly. "I don't know what you're talking about."

"The librarian."

"Oh, her." Angel shrugged, and went back to looking in the mirror. "Yes, I met her. She said she was your friend. She said you talked about me."

They both flinched at a sudden knocking. Angel watched from the bathroom as Veronica descended the staircase and swung open the front door.

Matt was drenched, but that wasn't the problem. He looked like he was in shock. He didn't seem to realize that the front door had opened, that she was standing there.

"Matt, come in. Are you all right?"

"No," he said sadly. "Unfortunately, I'm not all right. I just got fired."

"You've got to be kidding!"

"You're looking at an unemployed man."

"Fired on Christmas Eve? That's horrible. I thought that only happened in Dickens. I'm so sorry, Matt. Did something happen?"

"All hell broke loose in the bookstore today. And I think Angel had something to do with it."

"Angel?"

"She was in the bookstore when it happened." He looked up the staircase toward Angel as he said it.

"We'll be right up, Angel," called Veronica, before Matt could say anything more. She turned to him. "I don't know what she did, but whatever it was, try not to be too angry with her. Kids do stupid things. That's how they learn."

"Don't worry," said Matt, "I can remember being a kid once. I did a few stupid things myself. This wasn't a stupid thing. This was a scary thing."

"Oh, no," she said. "Well, you talk with Angel while I make sure the pork roast is doing all right in the oven. You and I can talk later. Try not to be too upset. We're going to have a wonderful Christmas Eve dinner. Real mashed potatoes. Homemade applesauce."

She disappeared toward the kitchen.

He started up the stairs. Even before the girl was in sight, he could hear her tearful desperation. The moment he appeared in the doorway, she rose out of the corner of the bathroom where she was cowering and hurtled toward him.

"Please don't be mad at me," cried Angel, clinging to him as though his denim jacket weren't drenched with rain.

"Angel, calm down," said Matt. "You know I'm not mad at you. How could I be? I owe you big-time. When I fell in the park, remember how you helped me get home?"

Angel looked up at him, eyes wet with emotion. "Yeah," she said. "I did, didn't I?"

"If you ever need me, I'll be there. Believe me."

"I believe you."

"So, tell me what happened back there in the bookstore. Did you have something to do with all that?"

Her features went slack. She was immediately on the defensive. Her eyes studied his face, intently scrutinizing every facial expression to be sure he wasn't leading her into a trap.

"It wasn't on purpose," she said. "I don't know why it happens. Lately it's been happening more. When I get upset. Things fall. Things break. And it always has something to do with — with me being there."

"Thanks for telling me the truth."

"It scares me."

"Of course, it scares you," said Matt. "It scares me, too, and it's not even happening to me. There's nothing so scary as having something happen to you that you can't explain."

"But you believe me?"

"I was there. I saw it happen."

"Then, what should I do?" she asked urgently.

"There's only one thing you can do. You've got to stay as calm as possible. If you can understand it, you can learn to control it. In the meantime, you've got to be careful. Very, very careful. You can hurt someone. Hurt them very seriously, without meaning to at all."

6
Interrupted Dinner

As planned, with the approach of evening, Matt and Tyler came up through the laundry room and joined Veronica in her apartment. Wonderful smells filled the kitchen, seeping through the rest of the house. Both men had attempted to look a little neater and nicer than usual. Matt wore a long-sleeved plaid flannel shirt, with the sleeves rolled up to the elbow. Tyler wore a trim, preppie sky-blue polo shirt. He had even submitted to Veronica's request and left his baseball cap in his room.

"God rest ye, merry gentlemen!" said Veronica, welcoming them both into the living room. A delicate silver necklace highlighted her olive skin above the low neckline of her red silk dress. Red stones sparkled in her ear-rings. "Let me offer you some cheer."

She guided them toward the bright, twinkling lights of the Christmas tree. Candles, red ribbons, and classic antique decorations adorned the mantelpiece. The tinsel-draped boughs engulfed the room in a heady pine scent. They gathered around the carved crystal punch bowl, centered on the glass coffee table in front of the fireplace.

"Hot cider!" said Matt with a forced smile, trying to sound happier than he was. "Exactly what's called for on Christmas Eve."

"Employed or unemployed, you're among friends," said Veronica, "which is the important thing. Now, I'm warning you, this is pretty potent."

"Just the way I like it," said Tyler. "Fill 'er up."

"Not quite yet," she replied. "All the guests haven't arrived. Wait — here she comes."

They all turned to look.

Angel came down the central staircase. It was a calculated entrance. She was very aware that she had all of their attention, and she wanted it. She and Veronica had secretly contrived her outfit. It was a simple white silk dress, too short for Veronica, perfect for Angel. Her short hair was crowned by a wreath of delicate, white baby roses that Veronica had surprised her with an hour before. Angel wore the baby roses like a crown.

Everyone gasped appropriately at her pure, unaffected loveliness. She struggled to suppress a grin of delight, but it finally forced its way onto her mouth.

"You're as pretty as a real angel," said Veronica. "The loveliest Christmas ornament in the house."

"Allow me to do the honors." Matt took over the punch bowl.

"I get some too, don't I?" said Angel.

"Of course, you do," said Matt. "Special permission on Christmas Eve. Tonight you're one of the adults." He poured steaming cider into her glass cup first, then served his housemates and himself in quick succession.

"A Christmas toast," said Tyler, raising his dripping cup toward the other three. "A merry holiday to the members of this fine house."

Cups clinked. The hot tangy liquid gave them all a warm rush as it spilled down their throats.

"Now, that's Christmas cheer," said Tyler.

Angel made a funny face, wrinkling her nose at the taste.

"Well, if *you're* ready, dinner is ready," said Veronica.

Her three guests sat down at the large, old-fashioned table. It filled most of the dining room. She brought in the steaming roast pork and began carving it. Tyler was already serving himself another cup of cider when an unusual rustling caught their attention outside the house, a bumping and jostling of garbage cans.

Veronica's heart sank. "Oh, dear," she said. "I'm afraid that sound means only one thing. The homeless poet has come back. I found him under the stairs this morning."

"You found a what?" said Tyler.

"Are you talking about the same man we saw on Candy Cane Lane?" asked Matt.

"The same. It sounds like he plans to hide under the stairs for Christmas Eve." She didn't seem to notice the changing expression on Angel's face. She regarded Matt and Tyler. "Well, what do you think? Do we keep to ourselves or invite in our homeless neighbor?"

"The more, the merrier," said Tyler, raising his punch cup in good cheer, tipping back his chair, tipping back his head, teetering precariously as he drained the cup. "After all, he's our brother in Jesus Christ."

"Remember you said that, because he may have a bit of an odor," warned Veronica. She stood by the front door as she put on her overcoat. "And conversation may be difficult. He probably doesn't talk to people very often."

She closed the door securely behind her, and went down the rain-drenched stairs to the trash can shelter below.

"John, is that you?" she said, in the general direction of the cavity beneath the stairs.

"It's me," replied a meek voice. "And you're here at exactly the right time. I've just finished a poem for you."

The lanky poet unfolded himself from behind the trash cans and handed her a sheet of paper. On it was written:

For the dead
You grieve
In the living
Believe

No more lies
Seek the light
Only love
Can make it right

"That's beautiful," she said quite sincerely, carefully rolling it up to protect it from the rain. "John, please come inside. We want you to have Christmas Eve dinner with us."

"Are you making fun of me?"

"Come on."

John crouched down to emerge from the garbage shelter and plodded hesitantly after her up the stairs to the porch, squinting as he stepped inside into the light.

"I should wash," said John, looking down at his hands with some misgivings.

"Of course," she said. "The bathroom's right up here." She led him upstairs. He followed slowly in her footsteps, looking in every direction as though entering an alien spacecraft. She turned on the bathroom light. "Don't worry about getting it dirty. Come downstairs when you're through."

He didn't close the bathroom door. He didn't flush the toilet. When he came back down, she escorted him into the dining room where the others were gathered waiting.

"John, I want you to meet Tyler. And this is Matt. And this is Angel. All of you, this is John. We're going to have a wonderful Christmas Eve dinner together."

Anxiety gleamed in John's wide eyes. He was staring at Angel, and she was glaring back at him.

"What are you doing here?" said Angel aggressively.

"Angel, what's wrong with you? Do you know John?"

Angel didn't answer. She and John exchanged looks, guarded and cautionary, like two wary animals sheltering in the same cave.

"You look different," said John, confused by the garland of tiny white roses.

"I am different," said Angel, with confidence.

"You're not a boy anymore."

"I never was a boy."

"Would you like to see my new poem?"

"I don't like poems," she said.

"Oh." He stared at her in horror.

Veronica had no idea what to make of their curious exchange, but could see it wasn't having a good effect. "Come on, all of you, let's enjoy our dinner. John, let me serve you some roast pork."

The dinner awkwardly resumed. She and Matt struggled to keep a light conversation afloat. Rain lashed the windows. Tyler had another cup of punch, and began to think everything everyone said was funny. The lights in the apartment blinked.

"Oh, no," said Veronica, "not on Christmas Eve."

The windows flashed with lightning, followed by a thundercrack and a redoubled downpour. The lights steadied. There was a collective sigh of relief around the table.

Then the telephone rang.

7
Long Distance

Veronica didn't recognize the voice at the other end of the line. She could tell the call was long distance.

"This is Raymond Harrow. I'm calling from the Big Island. My wife and I want to wish Angela a, a — what is it, dear?" He conferred in a mumble. "Mele Kalikimaka."

"How wonderful," said Veronica. "Just a moment, Mr Harrow." She looked up with a smile. "Angel, it's your father calling."

But Angel was no longer sitting at her place at the table. She had bolted out of her chair and was already halfway across the dining room, her face a grimace.

"Angel, what's wrong with you? He's just wishing you a Merry Christmas."

She gave a hardened stare of resistance. "I'd rather not."

"There's no need to be upset," said Veronica. "Your parents just want to hear how you're doing."

Angel only became more agitated. "I'm not upset. I just don't want them to lie to me anymore. I hate it when they lie to me. Please don't make me talk to them. Please, please, please."

"But Angel, if you were my daughter," said Veronica, "I'd be so happy to hear your voice."

"But I'm not your daughter," cried Angel. "That's why you don't understand. I'm *their* daughter. Ask them if they're going to get a divorce, if you want to help. Or ask them if I still have a home. Or you can ask them if either one of them has given me one single thought."

"Parents aren't perfect," said Veronica. "They're just people. They can get caught up in their own troubles, the same as anyone else. That doesn't mean they don't care."

"But mine don't," said Angel. "They're nice and they mean well, but they really don't care. I'm just in the way."

"Angel, he's not too busy to be on the telephone right now, asking for you," said Veronica. "You need to talk to him. Loving your family is part of Christmas."

"You're my family," said Angel. "They don't need me. I belong here with you."

"Please, Angel—"

"No."

She was so surprised by Angel's repeated refusal to take the telephone that Veronica was doubly surprised when Tyler suddenly finished his drink at a gulp and snatched the receiver out of her hand.

"Hello there," he said boldly. "Mr Harrow, I've got something to say to you." Tyler cleared his throat. "You don't know me, but I just want to tell you what an incredible daughter you've got. She is beautiful and kind and smart and funny and fun to be with, and we all love her here. You've got a treasure on your hands. I just hope you realize that before it's too late."

He then handed the telephone back to Veronica, while she and the others stared at him speechlessly. He crumpled back down into his place at the table.

"Mr Harrow?" said Veronica into the telephone. "Mr Harrow?" The line had been disconnected. She set the phone aside and sat down next to Tyler. "Well, looks like you scared him away. Would you like to explain?"

"What's to explain?" muttered Tyler. He put both of his elbows on the table, and buried his face in his hands. He spoke through his fingers, without looking at her. "Wasn't everything I said true?"

"Admittedly true," said Veronica. "But what possessed you to be so rude to someone you don't know?"

"I'll tell you what possessed me," said Tyler, taking away his hands, showing his eyes. "I never got a chance to say those words to my own parents. They got a divorce five years ago. They made me feel like it was my fault. Like I made their lives so difficult. Like I took away the romance, made them feel trapped. So I know what it's like. Hope he heard what I said. Might do him some good."

He felt the girl's arms around his neck before he realized she was coming. By the time he sputtered her name, Angel had squeezed him briefly and slipped out of reach, returning to her place at the table as though the phone had never rung.

8
Under the Floorboards

Veronica and Matt continued to do most of the talking. Tyler did most of the drinking. Angel and John stared at each other distrustfully. By the end of dinner, the five of them were so stuffed they could hardly move.

One by one, they rose from the table, and stretched. Tyler was visibly wobbling from the punch and had started slurring his words, but had maintained his dignity and been cheerful company.

Veronica gathered Angel and the three men around the Christmas tree and passed out brightly colored gifts to each of them, including a quickly improvised gift for John. They took turns unwrapping their presents with great drama and laughter. A candle shaped like an angel. A jigsaw puzzle of beer labels. An Iris Murdoch novel. A set of new pens. Then the five of them had more hot apple cider and sang Christmas carols. John joined in the singing enthusiastically, even when he had no idea of the tune or words.

Their laughter was interrupted by sounds of scuffling and scratching.

"What is that?" said Matt. "Is that coming from my apartment?"

"It's coming from down there somewhere," said Veronica. "But it sounds like it's coming from underneath the house." She listened, and groaned. "Those raccoons again!"

"Is that what that sound is?" said Matt. "I've been hearing some odd noises lately. If it's raccoons, then I think they were at it last night, too."

"If you look at the front of the house," said Veronica, "you can see right where they get in. They've pried loose the lower board under the front window, enough so they can squeeze through. They think they're going to live under the house."

"We shoot raccoons where I come from," said Tyler.

Veronica groaned. "No one will be shooting any raccoons, thank you. I like raccoons. They're fun to watch. But raccoons have been known to kill cats. We don't want raccoons living down there."

"Raccoons are good for one thing only," said Tyler, with a grin. "Target practice."

That's when they heard the first scream. It sounded almost human.

"Oh, God," said Matt.

Together they hurried down the laundry room stairs into Matt's apartment. Another scream. It was coming from directly under the floorboards. "Those raccoons have got a cat under there." A horrible thought occurred to him. "I sure hope it's not that friendly cat, the black one—"

"Oh, no!" cried Angel. "Not the black cat!"

Another scream. And another.

"No telling what cat it is."

"Sounds like it's getting ripped apart."

Veronica stamped her feet on the floor above the noise, trying to drive it away. Her stompings had no effect. The hair-raising screeches continued.

"Can't we do something?" wailed Angel. She was so upset she started to cry. "It's so awful!"

"It's not awful at all," said John. He was the only one unmoved by the death-cries. "It's natural. It's just animals acting the way animals act. The cat was probably snooping around where it didn't belong. You've got to be careful when you're snooping. God's creatures do what God made them to do."

The sound abruptly stopped. They waited, listening.

"Maybe it got away," said Veronica lamely.

"Maybe," said Matt.

"Right, maybe," said Angel. "You don't have to lie, just because there's a kid present."

"Well, we can't let it ruin our Christmas Eve," said Veronica, decisively taking Angel's hand. She tried to look happier and more hopeful than she was. "Come on, all of you. Let's go back upstairs and enjoy the Christmas tree."

9
Wet Departures

Not until they started climbing the laundry room stairs toward Veronica's apartment did it become clear what kind of condition Tyler was in. Halfway up the stairs, just at the turn around, he seemed to lose his balance, forget which way he was going and topple backward. Matt caught him and nearly went down with him.

"Whoa, that last stair was a doozie!" chuckled Tyler. His knees kept buckling out from under him. He was looking worse. "I think I'm going to be sick."

Veronica turned to Matt. "Help me get him to his room."

With one on either side of him, they steered Tyler back down the stairs and around the boiler and into his studio.

"I should never have let him drink so much," said Veronica.

Together she and Matt toppled him into bed.

*

John was stranded alone with the girl. He regarded her warily from across the room, on the other side of the Christmas tree. He started busily writing. She sat on the sofa in front of the fire. They ignored each other. Then he walked over to her chair, and handed her a sheet of paper. On it, he had written:

In the jungle
In the city
Flowers in her hair
So pretty

Baby roses
Deadly white
Frozen hearts
Tonight

She solemnly ripped the poem in half, then into quarters, then into a shower of tiny bits. She didn't say a word. Neither did he.

He sat back down and was afraid to budge. He tried not to attract her attention. Not to make her angry. Not to turn her against him.

"What are you looking at?" she snapped.

"Nothing," he said at once. "Nothing nothing nothing."

"Do you think I'm weird, or something?" she asked defiantly.

John's features became troubled. "You *are* weird," he answered honestly. "I saw what happened in the park.. I saw what you can do."

"Well, I can do a lot more than that," said Angel. "And I'm going to, because I hate you. You gave me this awful haircut. You made me look ugly. You made my parents mad at me. You made me run away. You ruined my life. I wish I'd never met you!"

One of the ornaments on the tree fell off and shattered. Both John and Angel stared at the jagged bits of ornament on the carpet next to the shredded remains of the poem.

He twiddled his thumbs nervously in his lap. "You'd better calm down, or you're going to hurt someone." He looked down at his hands intently, scowling with concentration.

"If you're smart," she said, "you'll get out of here. Or the one I hurt will be you."

"I was thinking that," said John. "I'm smart. I don't want to get hurt. I'm leaving. Houses aren't my thing, anyway."

*

When Matt and Veronica came back upstairs from Tyler's room, they found John had put on his tattered parka and was standing by the front door.

"John, you're welcome to spend the night," said Veronica. "After all, it's Christmas Eve."

"No, no," said John. "I couldn't." He glanced in Angel's direction, and then quickly away. "It's the house," he said awkwardly. "I could never sleep in this house. It's too disturbing."

"Disturbing?" echoed Veronica, with a short, nervous laugh.

"I don't like houses much," he said. "Sorry sorry sorry. Don't mean to offend."

"Not at all," she said, "but you'd better be careful with those raccoons out there."

"Oh, I'm not worried about raccoons," said John. "Raccoons are easy to figure out. Raccoons are God's creatures. They just act the way they're supposed to act. I'm not snoopy, like some cats I know. I don't go poking my nose where it doesn't belong."

"Don't go out in all that rain. Really, you're welcome—"

"Thanks for everything," said John, opening the door. "Don't worry about me. I'm safer out in the rain than I am in this house. I'm too nervous here. I don't like sleeping inside much. That's just who I am. Thanks for dinner. Here, I wrote a poem for you."

He handed her a sheet of paper. She read it.

Memories knocking
At your door
Hungry sorrow
Hurt no more

Hungry hurting
Stay away
Learn to love again
Today

When she looked up from reading the poem, he had already descended the side stairs. He was standing below her, looking up at the house, at the covered porch where she was reading his poem, oblivious to the downpouring rain beating on his upturned face.

"I tried to help you," he said. "Poems can help, you know. The best medicine, that's what poems are. But if you fight them, they're useless. If you ignore them, they can't do a thing. A poem can give you all the help in the world, if you like poems. But you don't like

190

poems. Oh, well. It's not my job to make you like them. I'm a poet, not a policeman. You can't make people like poems. All you can do is write poems. Write them and hope."

He disappeared down the stairs into the rain.

10
"It's Her"

Angel sat in the living room, stiffly alone in the exact center of the sofa, staring into the fireplace as though Matt and Veronica had gone down the stairs with John and weren't coming back.

"Are you feeling okay, Angel?"

At first she didn't answer, but the muscles of her lips moved, as though she were fighting back the words. Finally the words came out. "I suppose you want me to go to bed."

"Go to bed?" echoed Veronica. "Of course not! Why would I want you to go to bed early on Christmas Eve?"

"So you two can be alone."

Veronica blushed. "Not at all, Angel. We'd much rather have your company. I can be with this guy anytime. Your visit is special."

Angel laughed scornfully. "Right. I can believe that. That's why I've been sitting here all by myself." She rose impulsively from the depths of the armchair. "Well, I feel like sleeping, anyway. I feel like being alone. So there. Don't worry. I won't ruin your Christmas."

"But, Angel—"

"Guess the party's over." In one quick snatch, she tugged off the crown of baby white roses and hurled it into the fireplace. Before Matt and Veronica had time to do more than gasp, she trotted quickly up the stairs to the third floor. The library door slammed behind her. The two of them sat together in stunned silence, watching the rose buds blacken and shrivel, hissing in the fire.

"Well, what do you make of that?"

Matt shrugged. "She's emotionally exhausted."

"It's us," said Veronica. "We make her feel left out."

"Do you want to go talk to her?"

"No," said Veronica decisively. "Not this time I don't. I have other concerns that are more pressing. Like, for instance, I would very much like to spend some time talking with *you.*"

They found themselves alone on the sofa before the fireplace with the twinkling lights of the Christmas tree, the crackling, snapping fire, the pattering of the rain.

"Actually, this worked out rather nicely," said Matt, stretching his arm along the back of the sofa, his hand around Veronica's far shoulder. "Our little Christmas Eve party has naturally whittled itself down to a very manageable size."

"A perfect size." Veronica squeezed his hand. "I must admit, I can't think of anyone I'd rather be spending Christmas Eve with than you."

They drew closer.

"Thanks to you it's turned into a pretty wonderful night. I could have been very depressed over losing my job."

"You'll find another job," she said confidently. "There are worse things to lose."

Their talk became softer, intimate. One hesitant kiss led to another, not quite so hesitant.

He pulled away from her. His cheek had become wet from brushing against hers. "You're crying!"

She smiled, sniffed. "I suppose I am."

"But why?"

"Oh, don't mind me." Veronica wiped at her eyes. "It's just that I never expected all this to happen. I thought part of my life was over forever. The part about loving and finding someone special. I never thought there'd be anyone in my life again."

"And then I come along," said Matt, giving her a kiss on each of her wet cheeks. "And move right into your house!"

They laughed softly together.

"Do you realize *that* was the biggest thing against you, at first?" she said. "The simple fact that you had just moved in."

"Is that so?" said Matt. "What was the biggest thing *for* me?"

They giggled as their hands broke free of the last shreds of restraint. They were eagerly unfastening each other's clothes when they heard the voice.

"Ronny—"

They froze. At first they thought it was Angel. They were quickly re-buttoning and re-fastening when they heard it again.

"Ronny—"

Veronica's high school nickname.

She quickly forgot about everything except that voice. As though Matt were no longer there, she scanned every direction, every corner, desperate for some kind of explanation. "Angel, is that you?" No answer. But it wasn't Angel. She already knew that. She recognized the voice. Her eyes filled with tears. It was the familiar, heartbreaking voice of her sister.

"Ronny—"

Her sister's voice, beyond a doubt. Yet the voice she remembered had been warm and eager with love. This voice was not happy.

Veronica couldn't budge. Something was happening to Matt's face. "Matt, what is it?"

He turned away from her, with a shudder.

"I know that voice." He could hardly talk. "I don't believe it. I'm not imagining things. I know that voice. My God, it was just like — it was exactly like—" He closed his eyes, trying to wall out the memory. He was trembling.

"Ronny—"

Veronica held him. "What are you talking about, Matt?"

"It's her. It's always been her. I should have known as soon as I saw this house."

"Who, Matt?" she asked, gripping his shoulders, unable to conceal her mounting terror.

"I never knew her name."

The library door opened at the top of the staircase. Angel cautiously stepped out on the upper landing, her eyes wide, looking nervously in all directions.

The doorbell rang.

11
Ghosthunter

Through the window of the front door she saw a short, skinny old witch with a cane standing on the front porch, in the middle of the doormat, like a life-size Halloween leftover on the wrong holiday. Not until Veronica looked again did she recognize Muriel Rose. What she had mistaken for a pointed cap was a big Russian helmet of fur. What she had seen as leaning on her cane was really an old-fashioned wooden umbrella.

"Muriel!" she cried, swinging open the door at once, her whole body still trembling from the sound of her sister's voice. "Come in, come in!"

"Forgive me for just showing up unannounced on Christmas Eve," she said.

"I'm so glad you're here. Muriel, this is my downstairs tenant, Matt. Matt, this is one of my dearest friends." They exchanged civilities.

"I tried to call, but your telephone isn't working."

"Not working? Why, of course it is," said Veronica in confusion. "We just got a call from Hawaii." She picked up the receiver, listened, pushed the disconnect several times, listened again. "Of all the—" She sighed. "Oh, well. Not much we can do about it now."

"Anyway," said Muriel, "I felt I should come at once."

"I'm glad you did," said Veronica. "Here, give me your coat, it's soaked. Are you all wet?"

"I'm fine, dear." She surrendered her dripping overcoat, following Veronica to the closet and back. "Now, listen to me. I've been reading the library's other copy of Colin Wilson. It was just as I suspected. I got here as soon as I could."

"Well, I'm grateful to Colin Wilson!" said Veronica. "But what about the out-of-town family you were having for Christmas dinner?"

Her wrinkled cheeks were already rosy from the chill of the night, but they reddened even more. "I'm afraid that was a fib, my dear," confessed Muriel. "I usually spend Christmas alone. No need for sympathy, it's fine with me. It's easier that way, believe me. I've got my own special diet and a bathroom always handy. And I've got my collection of pictures, my collection of memories. I was looking at the little framed photograph I have of you on my mantelpiece tonight when I realized you needed a warning."

"Warning?" said Veronica uneasily.

"Not just a warning, but more information."

"Any information you can give us will be welcome," said Veronica. "But first, Muriel, what you need is something hot to drink." She noticed Angel standing at the top of the staircase. "Angel, this is my very dear friend, Muriel."

The girl cautiously descended halfway down the stairs. "The lady in the library."

"A pleasure to see you again, Angel," said Muriel. "Well, I might as well tell you all at once, since I have your attention. Please, I must be frank. I believe this house to be in a state of grave psychic disturbance. You're all in danger."

"This has become a very frightening and dangerous house," said Veronica.

"I think I finally know why," said Muriel. "You say your sister died in the house. Is it possible she committed suicide?"

Veronica repressed painful memories. "Yes, actually, it is possible. Stephanie fell off the balcony on the third floor. Although she's officially listed as having slipped, we've always known the possibility that she jumped. No witnesses. We'll never know for sure."

Angel was the only one who seemed to notice Matt's face. It was drained of color, as though he had suddenly become very ill.

"The poor child!" said Muriel. "Cut off from the sweetest part of life, so suddenly. Well, that makes sense, you see. Suicides can have a very difficult time after death. They can become stranded on the earth plane. They can't find the Light. They're forced to remain where they died, all caught up in the same fears and angers and desires that tormented them while they were alive. If your sister was terribly unhappy when she killed herself—?"

Veronica smiled grimly, and nodded. "The last time I saw her that night she was terribly unhappy. But I've lived in the house for years, Muriel, and it's never been a problem before. None of my tenants have ever complained about a ghost."

"So, what's different?" urged Muriel. "What's the new factor that's triggered this haunting? Something has changed. Think, dear! Only you can know."

"Yes, of course," said Veronica. "The new factor. The new tenant." She indicated Matt. He looked uncomfortable. "Or it could just as easily be Angel." The girl backed up against the wall of the staircase, looking like she was ready to run back upstairs. "Those are the only new factors."

"Well, one of them, it seems, has somehow disturbed the spirit of your sister," said the old woman. "Interacted with her in some way. And I suspect it may be more than that. Tell me, are you familiar with the idea of poltergeist phenomena."

"I saw the movie *Poltergeist.*"

"Oh, isn't it great!" said Muriel. "But really, *Carrie* is the ultimate poltergeist movie. Poltergeist phenomena are almost always triggered by the presence of a troubled girl. A girl just entering puberty."

Veronica didn't look at Angel. "Muriel, you're not suggesting I take that seriously? I've always written it off as an old wives' tale."

"No one understands it," said Muriel. "But think about it. A young teenage girl, especially from a disturbed home, just as she's becoming a woman, just as her body is confusing her, chemically in flux, a storehouse of troubled emotions. A girl like that might be able to activate psychic powers beyond anyone's understanding."

"Powers?" repeated Angel. She came the rest of the way down the stairs, frightened, wanting to know more. "What kind of powers?"

"I suspect you know," said Muriel. "Plates go flying. Silverware bends. Tables float. Bottles leap off the shelf. Horrible poundings shake the house."

Angel stared, her eyes large with terror.

195

"Things fall and break," she said quietly. "But why me? I didn't do anything."

"Of course, you didn't," said Muriel. "You didn't have to. Sometimes inside a young girl's body a chemical-electrical change takes place that acts as a kind of battery for all kinds of alarming things."

"Why just girls? Why doesn't it happen to boys?" asked Angel, irked at the injustice.

"Once in a while boys. Mostly adolescent girls. Maybe because they've got so much bottled-up emotion."

"I'm afraid," whimpered Angel.

"If what you're saying is true," said Veronica, "we have a teenage girl here who fits the description. What can we do to protect her?"

Muriel smiled, and shook her head sadly. "She's not the one who will need protecting."

"I don't want to hurt anybody!" cried Angel. "Honest, I would never hurt you."

"Not on purpose, dear. Of course not. What I suspect is — this house is already troubled, and that deep disturbance is being activated, accelerated, by Angel's presence. The girl is generating a current of power straight into the unhappy spirit trapped in this house."

"I am not!" cried the girl.

Matt put his hand on her shoulder. "It isn't just you, Angel," said Matt quietly. "Believe me, I know that for a fact. You're not the only one upsetting this house."

They all turned to regard him.

"There's something I have to tell you," he said.

12
Blow-Out

The fire in the hearth had become jerky and uncertain, but none of them noticed. Matt sat at one end of the sofa, draining another cup of cider, staring into the flames as though hoping to find an easier story to tell there. Reflections of firelight leaped and shuddered in the lenses of his glasses. Muriel shared the sofa with him, turned sideways to face him, her pale, slender hands folded in her lap. Veronica sat on the other side of him, perched forward on the edge of the armchair.

Angel alone wasn't sitting down. She couldn't. She was too nervous. She flitted from spot to spot, her body angular and tense, her arms hugged tightly across her chest.

"I was such a rebel in college," said Matt. "Doing everything I wasn't supposed to do. You get the idea. I was in *that* phase.

Muriel chuckled. "We've all been there."

Angel scowled. "Some of us still are."

"That Christmas I decided not to spend the whole holiday break with my family, but just to show up in time for Christmas Eve. Right now I'd give anything to have my folks alive again, to spend a whole Christmas break with them, but back then I'd had all the family I could stand. Besides, my dormitory roommate had invited me to an incredible U. District party on the night before Christmas Eve. A party in this house."

Veronica didn't realize how tightly her fingers were digging into the armchair until Angel's hand unexpectedly came down on hers. The girl had appeared beside her, hovering, half-sitting against the armrest.

"Somehow I misunderstood you over the phone when you told me where this house was," said Matt. "I didn't recognize the address, then went into shock when I saw the place. Remember?"

Angel pulled away from Veronica and began pacing in front of the fireplace, whimpering without realizing that she was making an audible sound.

"I guess I knew it would come to this." Matt sadly shook his head. "Sooner or later I'd have to tell you. I just didn't expect to tell you on Christmas Eve."

"Tell me what?" Veronica wasn't sure she wanted to know.

"Tell you about the party," he said. "That incredible party! Dancing, making out, getting high, getting drunk, everybody doing it all at once. It was amazing just to witness. I was on the outside, not quite part of it. I didn't know many people. Then I met this girl.

"Afterward I could never remember her name. Maybe she never told me. She was a knockout, younger than me but much more experienced, full of life, full of fun. Obviously interested in me. I was a miserable college virgin, clumsy and scared and so turned-on I could hardly think straight. Well, she couldn't keep her hands off me. I thought I'd died and gone to heaven.

"We were crazier in those days. She said she knew a place in the house where nobody would bother us. I didn't put up any resistance. She took me up those stairs right there." He pointed at the staircase leading up to the third floor. "Up to the room at the top, and then into a closet so huge there was a bed inside it, and a window, and she took me into the closet and introduced me to a whole new world. But then—"

His voice cracked, faltered. For a moment he didn't think he could go on. Muriel took his hand in both of hers. But he wasn't looking at Muriel. He was watching Veronica's face. It was a battle-ground of emotions.

"There was some pretty crazy partying going on — in particular by my dorm roommate, this flipped-out airhead named Brad. He had a stereo turned up blasting, competing with two other stereos just as loud. The party was way out of hand. We were asking for trouble. Somebody had to deal with Brad, before the men in blue uniforms paid us a visit. Somebody had to turn down the music.

"'I'll be right back,' I told her. 'That's about two stereos too many. It's that roommate of mine. Stay here.' I pulled on my pants.

"'No, don't go,' she said. 'Please don't leave. Is that all you wanted? I believed you. I thought you were special.'

"'I'll be right back,' I told her.

"'Now, there's a good line!' she said. 'Am I supposed to believe that? You're just like all the others.'

"'I'm not. Trust me. Just give me a second to talk some sense into that idiot who's turning the music up so loud. I'll meet you right here. Don't leave.'

"And with that, I went downstairs. By the time I got there, Brad was on the phone with the police. Before I could knock the phone out of his hand, he was complaining about the stereo on the second floor being too loud.

"So we got into this fight. It was mostly hot air and pushing and shoving and threatening. And then somebody heard the sirens coming and the blue lights started flashing and the whole party went ballistic. Somebody turned the lights out. People were shouting, screaming, knocking each other down in the dark. And all anybody could think was — get out!

"That's what I was up against getting back to that girl who was waiting for me. When I finally did, she wasn't there. I waited for her. That's how I ended up being one of the bad-luck eleven who spent the night in the Wallingford Police Station."

He hesitated uncomfortably. "The next day, once we were all out of jail, I heard that some girl at the party had died. I was always afraid that maybe — maybe it was her—"

Veronica hit him. The blow across the face was unexpected, and it left Matt staring in shock. He was even more shocked when she struck him again.

And again.

Angel screamed.

Muriel hurried around the coffee table and grabbed Veronica's wrist, pulling her away from him. He hadn't tried to avoid her blows. He didn't try to defend himself or pull away. He simply looked at her sadly. She was shouting and crying at the same time. She repeated one word.

"—sister."

13
Notice

A hush gripped the living room. Veronica had stopped crying. The crumpled wads of brightly-colored wrapping paper, discarded from their Christmas presents, seemed like happy relics from a lost and distant time. The merry twinkle and blink of the tiny lights infesting the Christmas tree were suddenly meaningless.

Veronica was so upset she didn't realize what she was doing until Muriel pulled her away from hitting him. Even now, being comforted by Muriel, she couldn't stop staring at him in shock, trying to keep her body from shaking. He stood by the fireplace, his arm along the mantelpiece propping him up as he studied what was left of the fire.

"Why didn't you tell me?"

He turned to regard her, surprised she could ask such a question. "I was afraid I'd lose you."

She felt so unhappy she could hardly speak. How could she not see what was right in front of her eyes? She had read hundreds of ghost stories. Why couldn't she figure out the secret of her own? That the man who had won his way into Veronica's newly-awakened heart was the one man she could never love.

"It was too good to be true," she said sadly.

"Every love has obstacles," said Muriel, with a reassuring arm around her.

"Yes," said Veronica, "and sometimes they're insurmountable."

"Veronica, we can deal with this," said Matt.

"How?" she replied, a stinging edge to the word, trying to sound angry so she wouldn't start crying. "I see absolutely no way to deal with it. There's no changing the past. What happened between my sister and you can't be improved or forgotten. She died in misery over you. Period. Her spirit has been terrorizing this house ever since you arrived. How do I deal with knowing I'm making my sister miserable beyond the grave every time I kiss you? Takes the fun out, don't you think?"

Matt stepped away from the fire and crossed to the coffee table, directly in front of her. "We have much more than fun between us."

"We have nothing between us," she said quietly. "It's all over, Matt."

"It doesn't have to be."

"Yes, it does," she said, with strained, painful insistence, not daring to look at him. It was so horribly simple and clear to her. "You broke my sister's heart. You pushed her over the edge. You may not have meant to, but you did. Nothing can ever change that. Nothing can ever make me forget that."

"But I hardly knew your sister," said Matt. "We only spent a few hours of our lives together. She and I were just being crazy kids. The rest was a freak of fate. It's not like you and me. Veronica, I love you."

"But I can't love you," she said. "Because when I love you, I cause my sister agony. Am I supposed to pretend I don't notice? Can't you see how it's upsetting her? She was cheated by an early death, and now I'm taking what she wants most. Our being together, Matt, is what's troubling this house. It's us. We're the villains, not her."

He knelt on the other side of the coffee table. "Please, Veronica, we deserve a chance—"

"Matt," she said with difficulty, pulling away from Muriel and rising to her feet, forcing the tremble out of her voice, knowing she had only one choice and trying to say it as quickly as possible, "I'm giving you notice to move out."

"Oh, Veronica!" said Muriel, "you're being hasty."

"Please, don't!" cried Angel.

"Stop it, both of you," said Veronica, sternly enough to make them believe her. "I'm an adult making a decision. It's my house. I know what's best. I cannot torment my sister, living or dead, by loving the man she couldn't have. Leave, Matt. You can't stay here. You don't belong in this house."

"Don't I?" he said sadly. He wasn't doubting her word. "I wanted to belong here so badly. I was really starting to believe I did belong. I'll leave if you want me to leave." He rose to his feet.

"I want you to leave."

Angel was quietly crying. Muriel took the girl into her arms on the sofa and held her.

"I'll always feel responsible for what happened to your sister." Matt turned away and started past the Christmas tree, across the living room toward the door in the kitchen that led downstairs.

"You *should* feel responsible," she said coldly to his back. "You are responsible."

"Maybe I am." Her words hurt him, antagonized him, forced him to retaliate. He faced her, his eyes dangerously bright with emotion. "But, I tell you, I went back for her. Your sister gave up too soon, because I was where we agreed to meet. That's why I was still in the house when the police started arresting people. I tried to meet her there. She left before I got back. She was the one who lost faith!"

14
The Other Side of the Story

"Oh, God!" she said.

The other three stared at Veronica in confusion.

"It was me!" she said in sad amazement. "After all this time, after all the hating and judging, it was me. I'm the reason she wasn't there. I made her leave. I told her she was a fool to wait around for some jerk who used her and left her. I'm the reason she wasn't waiting for you."

Her shoulders shook from emotions she could no longer hold inside. She looked like she was about to lose her balance. Muriel hurried over to give her support, and led her back to the sofa. Veronica hardly knew what she was doing. Suddenly all those memories she had taken as facts had a different perspective.

"There really was an arrangement between you?"

"A promise," said Matt. "A promise I kept."

"She seemed so sure, but she'd been so sure before—"

"It's too hard to understand you, dear," said Muriel. "Tell it from the beginning."

"Poor Steph," said Veronica. "It was her first quarter at the U. She was commuting from home. She'd had two bad relationships in a row — good-looking talkers who did their thing and dropped her. She was feeling blue. That's why I invited her.

"I remember that night so vividly. I'd gone home to my parents' house for dinner. We were all four together, Mom, Dad, Steph and I, just like we had been all our lives growing up. It was our last happy meal together — and we didn't know it.

"The party was three days away. I invited her in the upstairs hall, out of hearing of my parents. 'This is going to be your first real adult party, you realize.' I was always acting older and wiser.

"She hated the Big Sister act. 'Of course, I realize. I'm an adult.'

"'Almost an adult,' I teased her. 'What I mean is, there will probably be some pretty wild stuff.'

"'Neat. I like wild.'

"'Watch it, kid.' I tried another approach. 'I mean, some people always end up going too far and making fools of themselves.'" She grinned just to irritate me. I pretended to box her in the nose. 'Just don't go being impulsive, Steph.'

"'I am impulsive.'

"'Think twice.'

"'I never think twice.'

"Well, you saw what it was like. Refrigerator packed with beer and champagne. Joints passing everywhere. Someone added psychedelic mushrooms to the spaghetti sauce. My dear husband-to-be, supposedly our host, decided to drop two hits of blotter acid. He was stretched out on the bed upstairs, entering Seventh Heaven. He didn't believe me when I tried to tell him the police were coming.

"I'd never been at a party that was busted before. When I heard the sirens, I panicked. Everyone was going crazy, trying to get out of the house the quickest way they could. Suddenly I realized it had been a long time since I'd seen my sister.

"Well, it wasn't easy, but I found her. She was upstairs in the library, half-undressed in the closet. I grabbed her. I yelled at her. I forced her to get dressed immediately, which she was willing to do, but then she totally amazed me.

"She refused to leave.

"She kept begging to wait around for some guy. She'd been on a real loser's streak, so I figured she was just being desperate, throwing herself at some jerk. I knew what was best. I dragged her with me. No matter how much I tried to talk sense into her while I was getting her out of the house, she fought me all the way. She refused to listen to me. I refused to listen to her.

"'Ronny, you don't understand!' she kept saying. 'You don't understand, Ronny.' Well, I was sure I understood. She'd made a fool of herself again. When was she going to learn that guys would say anything to get what they wanted? I dragged her out the back way, so we wouldn't be caught by the police. I knew what was best for my sister, all right. I wouldn't let her wait around for you."

They stared at each other helplessly, as though a chasm had opened between them.

"She spent the night at my place. I put her in bed myself. She was there when I got the call from the police. She must have come back here right after I left. She must have been waiting for you. When I got back to the house after picking up Sam at the police station, we started to walk up the stairs and — that's where we found her." She

202

started crying. "Maybe she lost her balance. Maybe she fell. Oh God, I'll never forget— Did I scold her too much? Did I make her ashamed? Were my words too harsh? I'll always wonder if I pushed her too hard. If I made her think my love was conditional. That she wasn't living up to my standards." Matt reached for her hand. She pulled away from him. "And now the man she was waiting for finally comes back, and she has to watch her sister in his arms."

"And then," said Muriel quietly, "your sister finds a power source that allows her to release her anger."

"It wasn't me," said Angel in an outburst. "I didn't want to feel those bad things. I didn't want anyone to be hurt!"

"We know you didn't," said Muriel, but the girl didn't seem to hear her. Angel pulled away from her, scrambled awkwardly to her feet, wringing her hands.

"Angel, is something wrong?"

Angel stood before the fire, rigid with panic. Her eyes grew wider, larger. The lips of her open mouth trembled. She began to wobble. Veronica rushed forward to support her. The girl was wet with sweat. She was shivering like someone with a fever.

"Angel, are you feeling sick?"

"I'm okay."

"What happened?"

"I'm so cold—"

"Come on, Angel, put your arm around me," said Veronica decisively. The girl did as she was told. "What you need is a nice, relaxing hot bath. Come on, Muriel, help me." She turned to Matt. "You and I need to talk. Don't leave."

"I'll be waiting for you," said Matt.

15
"What I'm Afraid Of"

"Professor Glass!" The cry rang through the third floor of the house. "Professor Glass—!" Her name was being shouted on the other side of the closed bathroom door.

Veronica cautiously opened the door halfway. "Angel? Are you all right? Are you hurt?"

"Please come in."

She stepped into the hot, steamy room. Muriel appeared behind her in the doorway, where she hovered. The girl's wet, skinny shoulders protruded from the water.

203

"Don't leave me alone in here."

She awkwardly approached the bath. "How do you feel?" She knelt in the thick white weave of the bathmat beside the old-fashioned porcelain tub.

"Better."

"At least," said Muriel, "she's not shivering anymore."

"I'm so scared," said Angel.

"You don't have to be scared," said Veronica. "Nothing can hurt you here."

Angel avoided looking at her. "Yes, it can. What I'm afraid of, it's *inside* me. It's what I am. That's what I'm afraid of."

"You don't have to be afraid of yourself, Angel," said Muriel. "You're not responsible for what you can't control. It's important to believe in yourself."

"But how can I?" wailed Angel. "Bad things happen when I'm around. I'm not stupid. I can put two and two together. It's me. There's something wrong with me."

Veronica didn't lie to her. She told her what was more important for Angel to know. "Whatever it is you have to face, Angel, you won't be facing it alone. That's one thing you can be sure of. You're not alone."

"Count me in, too, dear," said Muriel. "And there's Matt, as well. You see, you've got a team of helpers who love you." Angel surged up onto her feet without splashing too badly, and grabbed a towel off the rack. Muriel hesitated a moment, considering her words. "But don't be fooled. You *are* more involved than you realize. That's what you've been learning about yourself, isn't it?"

Angel nodded fearfully.

"That's what makes you afraid," said Muriel. "You have the power to do things that other people can't do, things you don't understand. Isn't that right?"

Angel stepped out of the tub. "I don't have any power. Things just happen."

"I think you do have power, Angel," said Veronica. "I don't think you can control it. But we know that your power is real. You are the key here."

"I don't want to be," said Angel uneasily.

"We don't mean you're responsible, dear," said Muriel. "The haunting of this house has nothing to do with you. There's no doubt who walks in this house."

Veronica nodded sadly. "It's her, all right. It's my sister. But she's never done anything like this before."

"Because she's never been this strong before," said Muriel. "She never had the power. Why now? She's drawing energy from this girl."

Angel didn't want to know anything else about it. She regarded her lovely white dress in a heap on the floor, dirty and stinky with the sweat of fear, then pulled on a sweatshirt and sweatpants.

"I know how upsetting this must be," said Muriel, with a reassuring touch. "But you're smart. You may not be able to stop it, but you might be able to control it. There's one main thing to remember. Try not to let it frighten you when it happens. Fear is natural. But fear weakens you. Fear is the only weapon the dead have left."

"You need to be brave right now, Angel," said Veronica. "Because it seems like my sister is somehow in contact with you."

"If anyone found out," said Angel, "they'd put me in a nut house, wouldn't they?"

"I'd never let them," said Veronica.

"But if I ever told anyone, they'd think I was crazy."

"People with special gifts are often called crazy," said Muriel. "It's just ignorance."

"My father isn't ignorant," said Angel confidently, looking at herself in the steamed bathroom mirror. "And my father would definitely say I was crazy."

16
Revenant

Alone in the living room, waiting for Veronica's return, Matt found himself growing comfortably sluggish in front of the fire. At last, a pause in all the intensity. He was emotionally exhausted. He needed to relax. He kicked off his shoes and stretched out full-length.

They'd all be better now. He'd finally told Veronica. The secret agony he'd endured was finally over. It was out in the open, at last. Most of it, at least. As much as he could tell her.

He punched the pillow behind his head, plumping it out comfortably. Hard to believe that the unthinkable had almost happened. He'd nearly lost her. He'd almost had his happiness snatched forever out of his reach. And he wasn't out of the forest yet, by a long shot. He still had to be careful. But at least he had something to hope for. She had given him notice, but still wanted to talk. It wasn't over yet.

He closed his eyes.

Soon Veronica would be coming down the staircase. Soon the two of them would be alone together before the fire.

A kiss woke him.

"Veronica?"

Another tender, lingering kiss—

He opened his eyes. He felt her move past him just as he looked, slipping around to the other side of him before he caught a glimpse of her, leaving him shivering in front of the fireplace. He turned to see where she was, to see if the fire had gone out.

Something was blocking the heat from reaching him. Something gray and transparent and cold was interfering between him and the fire. He could see flames leaping on the other side, but the other side of what? A dim, human figure, the consistency of smoke, but consistent enough to recognize.

That beautiful, unforgettable face!

Matt tried to understand what was happening to him. His brain was moving too slowly. His comprehension was so sluggish that he couldn't quite reach any kind of conclusion. He couldn't be seeing her! He tried to sit up. He was unable to move.

The pale hands of that lovely girl from so long ago reached down toward him, gently touching him the way she had touched him on that unforgotten night, the way she had excited him.

He forced the words out. "No, please—"

She ran her fingers slowly over his trembling body.

"I tried to come back," said Matt.

A cold hand stroked his cheek.

"You weren't here. You weren't waiting for me."

Cold fingers trailed down his chest.

"It wasn't what you think. I came back the next morning, but you — you—" He opened his mouth to scream, but he could feel himself getting dizzy, the sofa shifting beneath him, the floor tipping.

*

Halfway down the staircase, Veronica could see him sprawled across the sofa, his arms extended as though trying to protect himself, his face in a grimace of terror. As she watched, he slid off the side of the sofa, tumbling to the floor, overturning the punch bowl on the coffee table in a splashing, shattering mess across the hearthstone.

"Matt!"

She hurried the rest of the way down the staircase.

"Be careful, don't move," she said, stepping carefully to his side. "There's broken glass all around you." She helped him to his feet, amid the gleaming bits and pieces.

Angel appeared at the top of the stairs, freshly bathed, in her clean sweats. "What happened?" she called nervously. Muriel appeared beside her, putting her arm around the girl.

"Nobody's hurt," called Veronica, carefully picking up the biggest pieces of glass. "Nothing to worry about, as soon as I get this mess cleaned up." She turned to Matt. "Are you all right?"

He was clearly shaken. "It was her."

That had been her worst fear. He arranged himself in one corner of the sofa. She shared the sofa, far enough away. "It's my sister," she said to Angel. "She's using you to hurt us."

"Why is she trying to hurt you?" The girl was now standing beside her.

"Because Matt and I hurt her once," said Veronica.

"We hurt her very badly without meaning to," said Matt. "And now — now we're hurting her again."

"And she can't forgive us." Veronica hugged the girl sadly. "If only my sister could forgive us!"

"How can we stop her?" asked Angel.

"There's nothing we can do," said Veronica.

"But there must be!" said Angel, with a fierce exasperation. "If she can reach out to us, why can't we reach out to her? There must be some way to communicate."

"Once there was." Muriel put her arm around Angel. "The ancient Greeks had underground temples for that very purpose. If we were in ancient Greece right now, and Veronica needed to contact her sister, she would go to the psychomanteum in Ephyra."

"The what?" Angel grinned in spite of herself. She liked the old librarian. "What would she do there?"

"She would be taken down into the underground tunnels," said Muriel. "She would be kept there for a month, without once seeing the sun. Then she'd be escorted by priests into a torchlit hall to look down into the reflecting bottom of a huge water-filled cauldron, where she would see whoever had died."

"Wow," said Angel. She shuddered nervously. "How could people believe something so crazy?"

"They went there in droves" said Muriel. "And do you know why? Because it worked. We no longer have psychomanteums. Today we turn to experts instead, to priests and mediums and channelers. Back then people weren't so afraid of contacting the other side themselves. People approached their own dead relatives, to come to peace with them. For you, my dear, that would be natural and easy. In case you don't know it, you're a sensitive."

"A what?"

"A person who is more highly tuned to psychic phenomena. You don't mean to be. You just are. You feel the presence of Veronica's sister. You give her more power than she's ever had before."

"Oh," said Angel. "I see." Her features trembled with half-concealed surges of emotion. "Well, then there's a simple solution. All you have to do is take away her power." Angel kept her voice steady, but only barely. "She's getting her power from me. None of you are safe here, because of me."

"No, Angel, you've misunder—"

"Nobody can help me," she said in a flat, logical voice. "There's no cure. No defense. Only one solution."

"Angel, that's not at all—"

A terrible scream tore out of her throat. A glass candlestick-holder toppled off the mantelpiece, shattering on the floor.

"No, Angel!" cried Muriel. "Fight it. Control it!"

Angel was crying. "I can't control it," she said, backing away from them. The other candlestick-holder tumbled to the floor and smashed. "I love you all so much. I could hurt you so badly."

She ran upstairs.

17
Psychomanteum

Angel darted into the library and slammed the door behind her. Back pressed against the door, she took a deep breath to calm herself. No more accidents, no more breaking things, no more anger flashes. Just pack and get out.

She didn't want any interference. She knew what had to be done. She grabbed a chair and stuck the back of it under the doorknob to keep everyone else out. She didn't want to talk about it. She was smart enough to understand the situation. She was dangerous.

She dragged her small suitcase out from under the bed. She could take care of herself in her own home on Park Road. Without her parents there, life would be easy. She didn't need to stay here and be miserable and a hazard to everyone. She was leaving immediately, as a Christmas gift to them all!

She hadn't brought many things. Packing was easy. Most of her few clothes were on the floor by the bed. Her sweater, her sweatpants, the other sweatshirt. As she picked up her blue jeans, something flashed out of the corner of her eye.

208

It startled her. She looked again. It came from across the library. Nothing was there. She moved her head slightly, and a reflection of lamplight from the street below caught and sparkled on the tip of the framed photograph on the library wall.

The face of that smiling girl! Remembering the photograph now made Angel want to see the face again. She left her clothes half packed, and crossed the library for a last look at the picture of Veronica's sister. Such a pretty girl! Yet she could see something unhappy in those eyes, even though the lips were smiling.

She never knew how long she stood there looking at the photograph before a soft creak startled her out of the trance. It seemed to come from the other side of the library. She turned quickly, peering into the shadowy corners, listening.

It came from the direction of the closet. A step closer, and she could see what was making the sound. The closet door was slowly swinging open. All by itself.

Explainable! There was a small window at one end of the closet. It provided light and probably a slight draft.

Seeing the closet reminded her that her overcoat was still hanging inside. She felt a flutter of dread at the thought, but chose to disregard it. She'd been trapped in that closet once, but she'd been so upset and vulnerable at the time that she'd panicked. She had been her own worst enemy. She was certainly brave enough now to get her coat. She walked boldly up to the closet doorway.

Reaching inside, she pulled the cord for the lightbulb overhead. Nothing happened. She yanked the string a few times, but no light flickered. She batted the string out of her way. The little window provided enough light. She could see right where her coat was hanging.

She reached into the closet, grabbed it by the sleeve and pulled. It was caught on something. She hesitated, then she propped open the door with a small waste basket, and took two steps deeper into the closet toward her coat. The walls were crowded with books, the floor with boxes. An old oval mirror at the end of the closet flashed shifting reflections at her as she tugged her coat down from the rack.

The closet door slammed behind her, sending the waste basket clattering.

The sound was so startling that it knocked Angel forward onto her knees, taking the overcoat down with her. She'd been sealed up inside the closet again! This time, however, she wouldn't panic and scream. She would stay calm, spring the latch, and the door would swing open. Then she saw what was happening in the surface of the oval mirror.

Something was forming in the black glass. A shape that resembled a human figure.

The figure in the glass was not a reflection.

It was the girl in the picture.

That confident, alluring smile. Angel knew who she was the moment she saw her. She didn't feel fear at first. What she felt was awe, sheer amazement, as the beautiful girl in the mirror reached out of the glass, pushing through the shiny surface as though it were a thick, black liquid.

Reaching toward her.

*

They heard the library door slam upstairs.

"Let's leave her alone for a few minutes," said Veronica, handing Muriel a roll of paper towels. "We've got plenty to keep us busy, cleaning up all this spilled cider."

Matt reached out to right the coffee table.

"Leave this to us," said Veronica, setting him safely aside in one corner of the room. "You've just had a very upsetting experience, Matt. Sit down. We'll take care of it."

"Sorry I'm such a clumsy—"

"Seeing ghosts can be hard on the nervous system."

"It's that girl I'm concerned about," said Muriel. She delicately picked up a jagged shard of glass, and looked up toward the library. "All my talk about poltergeist phenomena must have been terribly upsetting for her. How inconsiderate of me!"

"She's very sensitive," said Veronica. "But she's also very smart. She sometimes just needs a little space to think things through on her own."

When Veronica felt the girl had had time to compose herself, she went up and knocked on the library door.

"Angel?"

No answer.

"Angel, I don't want to disturb you. We're all just concerned about you. Please answer me, and I promise we'll leave you alone as long as you like."

No answer.

Veronica knocked again. Then she turned the doorknob and tried to open the door. Something was blocking the way. She banged her shoulder against the door. She hurt her shoulder.

"Angel, what have you done to the door?"

No answer.

"What's blocking the door, Angel?" cried Veronica, her voice quavering. "Answer me."

A terrible silence in the library. Matt could remain seated no longer. He rose reluctantly to his feet, staring up the staircase toward the darkness at the top. Wanting nothing to do with that room up there, he stepped over the sopping mess he'd created, over the broken glass and cider stains darkening the rug. He went up the staircase and joined her outside the library door. Muriel, at her own speed, was halfway up the stairs behind him, still clutching the roll of paper towels she'd been using to soak up the spilled cider.

"Angel," said Matt, his cheek pressed to the door. "Angel, are you all right in there?"

No answer. He tried the doorknob. The door was stuck.

"Don't make us break down this door, Angel," said Matt. "Let's not damage Veronica's house. Please don't scare us. Please say something."

He looked at Veronica. She nodded. He battered his shoulder against the door. Battered again. The obstructing chair clattered out of the way, and the door banged open.

"Angel?"

All three of them rushed into the library, eager to help the girl, ready to do whatever was called for.

The library was empty.

The first thing Matt saw was the open closet. He forced himself to go directly across the library and step inside it. The only one in the closet was his own reflection staring back at him. He closed the closet door behind him, and took another look at the library. Just beyond Angel's half-packed suitcase, spread out across her bed, one French window was swinging open. The glass panes of the shutter glittered wetly. The gauzy white curtain flapped in the rain.

Veronica stepped out onto the small third-floor balcony. It was deserted. Peering over the railing, down on the drenched stairs below, she saw no sign of the girl.

"Angel—?" She went back into the library, her face dark with concern. "No sign of her."

"But she has to be up here somewhere," said Matt. "How can she have gotten past us?"

"Are you sure she didn't go into the bathroom?" said Veronica. "You can climb out the bathroom window onto the back porch roof. The bathroom — she must have!   Because there's no way out of the library. The roof out there—" She gestured toward the French windows. "—is too steep, too dangerous. And the branches of that maple tree aren't strong enough for anything heavier than a cat."

"In other words," said Muriel, "she could be anywhere."

"Let's start eliminating the possibilities," said Matt.

Together the three of them went from room to room, calling her name throughout the house. She had to be there somewhere. Thirteen-year-olds didn't just disappear. "Angel!" Their voices echoed and overlapped from floor to floor. "Angel!"

"The poor thing's so upset," said Veronica. "Did you see that suitcase? And now she's run off all alone."

"She won't be alone," said Matt, walking straight out of the library. "I'm going downstairs to get my jacket."

"I'm going, too," said Veronica, starting down the staircase after him. "I can't stand the thought of her out there in this downpour."

"We don't know that she's out there," said Matt. "No need for you to get drenched, too."

"I'm the one who's responsible for her," said Veronica. "I'm the one her parents trusted to take care of her."

"That's why you should be here, when she shows up." Before she could object, Matt trotted down the last of the stairs. "I'll be right back."

He bolted down the laundry room stairs. A moment later, she heard his front door slam below, as Matt ran out into the rain. She heard his footfalls crashing and crunching through the ivy around the sides of the house, his voice calling. Then footsteps and voice died away down the wet hillside into the darkness.

18
Eternal Sister

Veronica and Muriel were suddenly alone together in the house. "I'll get a fire started upstairs," said Veronica, turning to her friend. "It'll be nice and warm in the library."

Together they walked up the staircase. Veronica clutched the bannister as she mounted from stair to stair, as though trying to steady herself, to get a grip on the shambles of her life. Her entire world had shifted and broken. She quickly made a fire in the library, then began pacing in front of the fireplace, chewing at the tip of a fingernail. "Where can the poor kid have gone?"

"She won't go far," said Muriel, drawing aside one of the long, lace curtains and staring out into the downpour.

Veronica was about to break the brief silence when she experienced an odd sensation. It began as uneasiness, an uncomfortable tension that made her nervously fuss with the first book that came to hand, fluttering aimlessly through its pages. She felt the muscles in the back of her neck tighten. She glanced over her shoulder. She found herself listening for sounds. She became convinced that she and Muriel were no longer alone in the library. An icy chill flashed through her body, even though she was standing in front of the fireplace. She tried to dismiss it, to disregard the intuition, to reason her way out of it. Instead, she found herself becoming terrified. She fought for some scrap of control. She peered in every direction.

"Angel, are you in here with us?" she asked abruptly into the silence, hoping to calm her fears. "Angel, answer me."

A hush, but not an empty one.

"We're not alone," said Veronica.

"I feel it, too," said Muriel. Without exchanging another word, they looked into each other's eyes.

"Stephanie?" said Veronica. The single word seemed to resonate in the stillness. "Steph, is that you?" She slowly turned around in a circle, scrutinizing every shadow in every direction, peering behind every familiar bookshelf and end-table. "Are you here, Steph?"

She waited, tense, expectant.

A radiant smile spread over her lips in spite of her cheeks being wet with tears. It *was* her. She knew. Some part of her sister was really there in the room with them, some intangible, invisible part that Veronica could recognize.

"Steph, I can feel you," she whispered. She pulled away from Muriel and slowly rose, peering anxiously in all directions. "You're so close. Oh, Steph, let me see you. I miss you so much. It is you, isn't it? Where are you, Steph? Can you hear me?" A presence seemed to stir in the house. "Can you see me, Steph? Can you touch me?"

She hesitated, waiting for the touch out of nowhere.

What came back at her out of the walls was an ear-splitting howl that shook the house's foundations. The sheer deafening volume of the sound slammed Veronica back against the fireplace, her hands clapped defensively over her ears.

"You don't understand."

Books lurched up off a shelf on her right and were flung flapping and smashing to the floor.

"No, Steph, please—!"

"Where's Angel?" said Muriel, looking wildly around her. "She must be nearby. This couldn't be happening otherwise."

Treasured first-edition novels tumbled at their feet. They both dropped to their knees, picking up and straightening the fallen volumes, smoothing back the smashed and creased pages, easing the broken bindings back together.

"You don't understand!"

A shelf of books on their left came clattering down beside them, thudding into a smashed heap on the carpet. While Veronica and Muriel tried to preserve the fallen books, the plaintive wail rang through the library.

"Ronny, you don't understand!"

She didn't. How little she understood! There she was, facing her dead sister's rage, helpless to solve or heal her pain. Such a tangled web of love! It would destroy them all. An Edith Wharton ending. No one would live happily ever after.

19
Discarnate

A gargoyle crouched on the roof overlooking the third-floor balcony. As Matt looked up from the sidewalk, the misshapen shadow came to life. It scrambled and clawed its way down the side of the windowframe.

Matt rubbed his eyes in disbelief, squinting up at the house through streaming curtains of rain.

"What in God's name is that?"

The gargoyle was gone. In its place he could see the silhouette of Angel high above him on the rain-drenched balcony.

"So that's where she was!"

She had been hiding on the roof, crouching above the French windows — no wonder they hadn't seen her. He watched her now, and for one terrifying moment, he thought she was going to jump.

He was soaked, breathless. He had run all the way down Ravenna Boulevard to the park and shouted her name. Then he had run from one end of Candy Cane Lane to the other. He had called up into the trees on the hillside, peered between parked cars, searched every porch, every stairway, every corner and window-well. His running shoes were sopping from the rainwater rippling in black currents down the street. His denim jacket hung soggy and heavy on his back.

Returning to the house in defeat, from where he stood on the sidewalk below he could see her up above him. Her hands were gripping the balcony rail in front of her.

"Angel!" he cried.

The figure flinched, fumbled back away from the railing, seemed to stumble. He lost sight of her.

Matt bounded up the streaming hillside, up the rain-drenched wooden side stairs. He lunged across the porch and pushed open Veronica's front door. The living room was deserted, half-lit from a dying crackle in the fireplace. He leaped up the central staircase to the third floor. He flung open the door at the top of the stairs, startling the two women in the library who were already wide-eyed with fear.

He looked blankly at Veronica, trying to frame the words of a question that was never asked. The tension in the room seemed to be literally alive, to pulse with a living presence.

"Matt—"

Neither of the two women had spoken. The word was only whispered, and yet it rumbled through the house. It stopped him in his tracks, dripping wet from outside, one hand on either side of the doorway, all thought of Veronica standing before him, of Angel out on the balcony, forgotten. He knew that voice. His face went white.

"Matt—"

The word seemed to hum in the very walls, to throb in the floorboards. He stepped into the library he had done his best to avoid.

Halfway across the floor, his attention was drawn toward a picture on the wall, a photograph he'd never noticed before on his brief ventures into the room. He caught a glimpse of the face in the frame, and stopped in his tracks. All other thoughts were at once forgotten. He recognized the girl in the portrait.

The library door slammed behind him like a gunshot. He stiffened, stopped moving.

"Matt—"

Years of disappointment and betrayal resonated in the unhappy sound as it shuddered through the house.

"I kept my promise," said Matt, in the hush of the library. "I came back for you. And now that's over, and I love your sister. I truly love her, and I want you not to hurt us. I'm begging you."

An ear-splitting howl.

Matt's features grew slack with dread. Sweat broke out along his forehead. He seemed to hear a voice no one else could hear. "I can't talk about it. Not yet," he mumbled. He tugged free of his soaked denim jacket, dropping it in a sopping pile on the edge of the hearthstone. "I'm not ready yet. I don't want to. I've never told anyone." But it was becoming more and more apparent that it was the one

215

thing Matt most needed to do, perhaps the very reason the restless ghost had waited for him to return. To confess that one thing. To tell Stephanie's sister once and for all what he alone could tell her.

"I left out part of what happened," he mumbled. He knelt, wet and cold, before the fire, not looking at either of the women, staring sadly into the ashes. "I didn't feel that you had to know. I told you what I thought was enough. It wasn't enough."

He ran his fingers back through his sweat-drenched hair.

"I was released from Wallingford Police Station at four in the morning. The first thing I did was run for a Yellow Cab to get me back to the U. District. I had to see her again! That was all I could think about. How would I ever find her? All I knew was our plan to meet back at the closet on the third floor.

"Maybe it wasn't love. She was my first. She opened new doors for me. I was ready for more. The taxi skidded to a stop down at the bottom of the stairs. I paid the guy and turned around and there she was, up on the balcony above me!

"I think I shouted something. I can't remember. I waved. She waved back. I remember her waving. Then I started running up the stairs. I was taking them two at a time, so I was looking down at the staircase. I didn't see anything, not until the very end when she actually hit the stairs.

"That's all I know. If you ask me, she didn't jump. She lost her balance. She fell. Possibly after too much to drink. Possibly when she waved. It was horrible, the sight of her. More awful than I can say. I took one look, I almost threw up, I almost started sobbing. And then I ran. I never looked back. I never told anyone. I was afraid someone might accuse me of something. I think I've been running ever since."

Matt's shirt was dark with rain and sweat, his face shadowed by the fire. His fingers knotted together, clasped in front of his lips. His forehead sank down onto his hands. For a moment, it almost looked like he was praying.

"Always running. In every relationship. Especially running from myself. Because I always had this small, dreadful suspicion in the back of my mind that my arrival had something to do with her fall. Maybe my running up the stairs. Maybe the wave. That I might have caused her to lose her balance. So I've always lied about that night. Until tonight."

The library was still, numbed by the constant pounding of the rain. Veronica trembled. She didn't know what to think. Everything she thought she knew had suddenly changed forever. And Angel? The brilliant, disturbed teenager, her former student, her Christmas holiday guest, had disappeared into the night. "What about the girl?" she faltered. "Did you find her?"

"Angel!" Without taking the time to explain, he lunged across the library, and pushed open the French windows.

A drenched figure sat on the balcony railing in the downpour.

20
Balcony's Edge

"Angel!" cried Veronica.

"Don't move," said Matt. "Just stay right where you are, and I'll come and get you."

She had turned to look at them over her soaked shoulder. Her legs, in the drooping wet folds of her sweatpants, dangled over the edge of the balcony into empty space. Her hair was plastered to her skull by the streaming rain. The features of her face looked like they were melting.

"Don't come one step closer," said Angel. She was smiling, but the smile had hardened. "Unless you feel like cleaning up a mess down below."

"Oh, Angel, please!" said Veronica, coming up behind him, watching helplessly.

An icy blast of night wind blew spatterings of rain at them standing in the open window. Muriel stood beside them, staring in dismay out at the dripping, miserable girl on the balcony.

"This is no joking matter, Angel," said Matt. "Please, no clowning around."

"Okay, no more clowning," she said with a sad grin. "You can come out here and join me, if you want to. It's a beautiful night, if you don't mind the rain."

"Please, Angel, stay still," said Matt uneasily.

"Staying still is for sissies," said Angel, "like you."

He made himself step out the French window into the night. He took hold of the rain-drenched balcony railing, clenched his teeth, did not look down, and swung one leg over the side. The moment he did, Angel scrambled recklessly away from him along the edge of the railing. "It's hard to stay still when you're having fun."

"Slow down!" Veronica called out angrily.

"Be careful, dear!" cried Muriel.

Angel climbed over the edge of the railing, sat down on the glistening shingles, and began edging out toward the gutter.

"Please, Angel," he said, one leg on either side, clinging to the rail. "Don't—"

She scurried out closer to the edge, acting as if the wet roof was no more dangerous than the kitchen floor.

Matt scolded her from the balcony's edge. "Watch where you're going!" She refused to obey him. She rose to her feet defiantly, raising her arms as though they were wings and she were about to take flight.

"There's something you ought to know." She laughed, wobbled, righted herself. "It wasn't the sight of you that made her fall. You'd like to think it was you. So dramatic. Well, no such luck!" Matt stared at her, rainwater dribbling down the lenses of his glasses. Angel laughed again, a sadder laugh, with a sob tucked away in it. "You didn't kill her. Neither of you killed her." A peal of laughter.

Veronica wasn't laughing. "What are you talking about?"

"It was the cat," said Angel. "The black cat who lived here. Your sister was holding it. She must have squeezed it or crowded it or petted it the wrong way. You know how cats can be. It scratched her and jumped out of her arms. She lost her balance. That's why she fell." Angel's face grew sad. "Maybe it was even the same cat. They get nine lives, don't they? I wonder if it has any lives left. Especially after tonight."

That was when Muriel realized what must have happened. Suddenly the girl knew too much. Suddenly she was so sure of herself. It wasn't the same girl.

The old woman stepped out onto the balcony, looking utterly frail and inconsequential. "Stephanie," she said quietly and with authority, scarcely noticing the rain at all. Her voice had a gentle power. "Stephanie, we're your friends. We're here for your own good."

"Muriel, stop it!" demanded Veronica, horrified. "Why are you calling her my sister's name?"

"Because that is your sister," said Muriel. "The spirit of your sister is inside that girl. She's invaded her. We've got to get her out, before she does any damage." She turned to Angel. "We can help you, Steph."

Angel glared back at her. "Stop calling me that!"

"You don't fool me," said the old librarian. "I can see exactly what you're doing. You're clinging to this house, because it was here you suddenly found yourself no longer alive. You're clinging to your sister, because you want her love. You're clinging to this poor girl, because you can steal her energy. You're hurting her. Get out of her. Now!"

218

Angel laughed, a hollow, humorless sound with a nervous edge. "You crazy old bag!"

Muriel went on, undaunted. "You have only to ask for help, Steph, and it will come." She spoke directly into the cold sheets of rain, straight at Angel. "Ask for help! There are spirits in your dimension who will be there, if you just ask. They can take you where you're supposed to go. You've got to move on, dear. It's not good for you to stay here and it's not good for us, either."

"Shut up!" cried Angel angrily. "Stop talking to me like I was dead. You're just trying to freak me out!"

"Enough, Muriel! You're frightening her," said Veronica. But she knew her old friend was right. That was no longer just Angel on the edge of the roof. The phrasing, the tone of voice, the attitudes and gestures, something about them was achingly familiar. She spoke to the girl wavering in the blue light of the streetlamp.

"Angel," she said, "I think my sister's spirit is sharing your body right now. I don't know how, but she is. And I want my sister to know something. No matter what, Steph, always remember that I love you. I love you like I will never love another human being the rest of my life. You're my one precious sister. I love you, no matter what. I know now what you wanted Matt to tell me. That you didn't take your own life. But Steph, I love you just as much. I always will."

"Let go, my dear," said Muriel. "Go into the Light now. Let your sister be happy. Don't deny her the happiness that you were denied. Love your sister, Steph. Let go."

A rush of cold air, as though an invisible window in the night sky had been flung open. The house trembled. Angel stared out into the rainy night. She clenched her teeth. Then the features of her face slowly relaxed, softened. After twenty years, the unhappy spirit of Stephanie Cella was finally at rest.

With the coming of peace to Veronica's sister, the last of Angel's crazy confidence dropped out of her. The girl sagged forward, then shook her head foggily, as though coming out of a dream. She didn't seem to know where she was. She stiffened, her eyes widening, as she stared around her at the dizzying rain-slickened rooftop. When she saw Matt standing on the balcony, she reached out an urgent hand to him.

"What am I doing out here?" she managed to wail, but in her fear, in the twisting of her body, she threw herself slightly off-balance. With a twist of her ankle, she slipped, then skidded clawing and scraping to the edge of the shingles. One of her legs slid over the side.

"Angel!" Matt cried out. "Hang on, hang on!"

There was only one way he'd be able to help her. He swung his other leg over the railing.

"Matt, be careful!" urged Veronica.

"Give me your hand," he said. Veronica clasped hold of his outstretched hand with both of her own.

He took a step away from the balcony out onto the shingles of the roof. Another step. He tried not to look down. He tried not to think about Stephanie's fall. He tried to believe that Veronica would not let go of him. He focused all of his thoughts on the wet girl in front of him, clinging to the roof's edge, like a drowning rat about to be washed into the gutter by the rain.

"I'm here, Angel," he said. He took another step toward her. His foot skidded on a slippery shingle. He slipped with a jerk, hauling Veronica up against the railing. Muriel wrapped her arms around Veronica's waist.

He recovered his balance. He closed his eyes, forced himself not to think about it, not to remember where he was, not to imagine how far he would fall. "I'm ready for you, Angel. Now — very carefully — let go of the roof and take hold of my hand."

He reached out to her through the rain. She stared up at his wet hand, her eyes wide with fear. Behind him she could see Veronica and Muriel, a human chain to haul her back to safety.

But would there ever be safety for her friends with her around? Wouldn't it be easier on everyone if she just stopped fighting it?

Veronica sensed what she was considering. "Angel, I lost my sister here — I don't want to lose you!"

But the girl had already let go.

Matt lunged out in a last straining reach to grab hold of her hand. His rainwet fingers locked around her wrist. Her weight knocked him off-kilter. Veronica tightened her grip on his hand. Angel scrambled up the shingles, scraping her knees, up into the enfolding clasp of his free arm, which clutched her to him. Muriel reached out for the girl, helping her back over the railing. He had almost succeeded in following the girl to safety when the dizziness hit. He fell to one knee.

But by then Veronica's arms were around him.

CHAPTER FIFTEEN

Wednesday, December 25

1
Friends

Backed-up rainwater dripped noisily from the leaf-choked gutter as morning touched the library window. The plunking and splashing woke Angel. It sounded far too loud in the stillness. Then it became clear why the morning seemed so quiet.

It had stopped raining.

That was the first thing she realized when she opened her eyes. The second was that it was Christmas Day.

For a moment she just lay there under the goosefeather comforter. She had bandages on her knee and elbow from last night's rooftop madness, and was sore all over. She didn't mind. It was her body and hers alone, and it ached, and that in itself was comforting. What mattered was that she was herself again, alone inside herself at last. She glanced nervously across the library at the closet door. She was in no rush to go anywhere near it.

Flopping aside the comforter, she scrambled out of her makeshift bed and pulled on a T-shirt and jeans. On her way across the room she stopped in front of the framed picture of Stephanie. In the early morning light, the smiling girl in the photograph looked radiantly happy.

Angel was happy, too. She was no longer afraid. Well, not much — just a little nervous about the closet. She looked across the library, then made up her mind and walked straight up to the closet door, opened it, and stepped inside. There was her overcoat, crumpled on the floor where it had fallen. She brushed it off and hung it up again.

Padding barefoot over the cold floor, she trotted out of the library and down the short third-floor hall to Veronica's bedroom. After a cautious listen, she swung open the door. But it wasn't Veronica she found sitting up in bed, reading. It was Muriel.

"Good morning, dear," said the little librarian. She was bundled up in one of Veronica's bathrobes, with an electric blanket drawn up

221

warmly all around her. "I was too tired to drive home last night. Why, just look at that smile! I can tell you feel better already."

"I do feel better."

"And you should!" said Muriel. "I'll tell you what else you should do, dear. Use the telephone."

Angel looked at her quizzically.

"I traced the call from your parents last night," said Muriel. "I've written the number down for you here. Now, promise me you'll give them a call after breakfast."

Angel's features collapsed into gloom. "Do I have to?"

"Dear, just look at all the new friends you've made. You're far from alone any more. Parents are just people who make mistakes. Some of them should never have had children in the first place. But there's no use hating them for it. Might as well be pleasant about it. Now, will you?"

"I'll call them," said Angel.

"Good," said Muriel briskly. "One other thing. This has all worked out quite nicely, but you're far from cured. There's no proof that you won't have another incident, maybe several. But I want you to know that young people who trigger poltergeist phenomena always lose that power, sooner or later. It isn't permanent. It weakens and goes away. Remember that, when you're afraid. Nothing triggers those unhappy powers more than fear."

"I'll try not to be afraid," said Angel bravely.

"Good," said Muriel. "Well then, I'm just going to read a few more pages to the end of this chapter, and then I'll get dressed and go downstairs and put on some tea. Why don't you go see if the others are awake?"

Angel started toward the door.

"But before you go downstairs," said Muriel, stopping her in her tracks, "go put on some shoes. Don't be running around barefoot after that broken punch bowl. There could be splinters anywhere."

Angel bounded back into the library. Her shoes were there somewhere. She had just found them under the bed and put them on when one of the French windows clattered open.

She leaped to her feet in fear.

Nothing happened. She relaxed. She was about to latch it shut again, but the fresh, chilly air seemed to call her out onto the waterlogged balcony. The morning was bright and clear. The crows across the street were already in fine vocal form and complaining furiously.

In fact, the crows seemed especially unhappy about something, and were expressing themselves in no uncertain terms. Curious, Angel leaned over the railing, trying to see what was annoying them so. When she saw it, she gave a cry. Then she ran out of the library and down the staircase and out the front door and down the side stairs. Halfway down, she stopped running, so that she wouldn't scare it away from Matt's porch.

"So the raccoons didn't get you, after all!" she cried, scooping it into her arms. The black cat allowed itself to be scooped. "Or the possums. Or whatever you were fighting. You're too smart for them, aren't you?"

The cat purred.

She looked steadily down into the cat's eyes. She tried to guess how old it might be. "You couldn't possibly be the same cat who made her fall, are you?"

The cat looked back up at her and purred louder.

But it wasn't just the cat purring, it was also the little red sportscar purring up the street. It stopped abruptly in front of the house, and then backed up in a smooth, graceful loop to the curb. The red door swung open, and a trim, muscular Santa Claus climbed out and started up the stairs. He wore a tight red jumpsuit with tanktop straps showing his shoulder muscles. Puffy white fur cuffs circled his wrists. With a friendly smile at Angel and the cat, he gave a confident tat-a-tat on Matt's door.

A moment later, a scruffy, sleepy Matt in a bathrobe fumbled open the door, blinking in bewilderment. Santa pulled down his bushy white whiskers and fluffy beard to reveal the grinning face beneath.

"Merry Christmas," said Tino Rodriguez. "And a ho-ho-ho! I had to show you this costume from a party I went to last night. What do you think?"

"Christmas will never be the same," said Matt.

"Hey, but that's not the real reason I'm here. I've got good news. A.C.T. wants you to give them a call. They're interested in your new musical for next season."

"A.C.T.!" cried Matt, suddenly very awake. "My new *what?* And just how did A.C.T. hear about my new musical?"

"I was having a drink last night with friends. Mentioned you were back in town. Do you really have a new musical? I just made that part up."

Matt gave Tino a hug.

"You're too good to be true!" said Matt. "But what I don't get is why you're up so early? Especially after a party. You never open your eyes before noon."

As though in answer to his question, Tyler came around the side of the house, baseball cap on backwards, suited up in his jogging sweats, a dripping ice-pack clutched to his head, his forehead wrinkled in the pain of a serious hangover.

"I didn't hear you honk," said Tyler.

"Good morning!" said Tino. "I didn't honk. I wanted to show Matt my costume. Don't worry, my running gear's in the car. Didn't you tell them?"

"Uh, no," said Tyler. "I forgot."

Tino turned to Matt. "Tyler and I are going on a Christmas morning jog around Green Lake." He grinned at the sheer disbelief in Matt's eyes. "So, what have you got against exercise? We're both athletic guys. You're welcome to come along — if you think you can keep up."

2
Family

Veronica was no ghost. She was very real, and very beautiful, and still lying in his bed when he got back from answering the door. What a happy sight to see her there, smiling in thought, remembering last night, remembering long ago. He shrugged out of his bathrobe and let it drop. He took off his glasses and set them on the bedstand, on top of the folded piece of paper he'd found tucked under the front doormat.

He resumed his former position.

"It was very kind of you," he said, "to give up your bed last night to a tired old woman."

"It was the least I could do for my dearest friend." She kissed him on the nose. "Besides, I figured there might be compensations."

"And how do you feel this morning?"

"Compensated." They laughed together. Her face grew serious, and she looked up at him from the pillow into his eyes. "I feel like my sister is at peace, really at peace," she said. "And I feel like I'm standing on the edge of something pretty wonderful with you."

He kissed her.

"Speaking of wonderful—" He reached for the piece of paper on the bedstand. "Look what I found on the porch."

"What is it?" she said, rising up on one elbow to see better. One glance and she knew.

Eyes not seeing
Hearts not wise
Truth is hidden
Love the prize

Learn to love
What hearts are for
Live the truth
And love some more

"Do you get the feeling he's trying to tell us something?"

He kissed her again. Neither of them felt like talking much, especially about last night. They simply lay in each other's arms. They had endured so much in the last twenty-four hours that they were still trying to assess what had happened to them.

They were exhausted and confused. And happy.

*

By the time Matt and Veronica had bathed and dressed and come up to start preparing a Christmas morning breakfast, Muriel and Angel were already in the living room, huddling before a lively, crackling fire, sipping mugs of hot cranberry tea. Soon all four of them were gathered around the Christmas tree and the fireplace with steaming mugs, warm and dry and rested, in their bathrobes and sweats, together in Veronica's toasty, spice-scented living room.

The telephone rang.

"What a pleasant surprise!" said Veronica. "It's working again."

Angel jumped to her feet, and ran to get it. She talked into the phone briefly, and hung up. "I've invited someone over. Do you mind?"

"Not at all," said Veronica. "Who was that?"

"Her name's Ellen Wu. She's older than me, but shorter than me. She's an EEPer, too. She wants to be friends."

"How did she know to call you here?"

"I called her this morning, before you woke up. She asked me to call and she's nice, so I figured, why not?" She hesitated. "I called her right after I called my Mom and Dad to wish them Merry Christmas."

"Good for you!" said Veronica.

"I woke them up, but they didn't seem to mind too much."

"I'm sure they didn't," said Muriel. The girl became suddenly awkward. Muriel noticed. "Unless I'm imagining things, young lady, you appear to be keeping both hands behind your back for some mysterious reason."

Angel approached Matt and Veronica, grinning. "You two stay right where you are." She moved her hand until it was just over their heads. "Mistletoe."

"Where did you get that?"

"From Santa," she said. "And he told me that both of you would know what people are supposed to do under mistletoe."

"Mistletoe!" said Veronica. "Ah, yes. I seem to remember vaguely what to do."

"I think I even remember how to do it," said Matt.

"Then do it," said Angel. "That's what mistletoe is for!"

They did it.

Photo by Ron Rabin

Nick DiMartino is a Seattle native and U. District resident. He is the author of two ghost thrillers set in the Pacific Northwest, *Christmas Ghost Story* and *University Ghost Story*.

He's had 18 plays in full-run productions. His *Dracula* premiered at Seattle Children's Theatre in 1982, followed by his adaptations of *Pinocchio* and Hans Christian Andersen's *The Snow Queen*. His *Frankenstein* sold out in Honolulu, Nashville, Louisville, Dallas and Milwaukee. His plays include *Raven*, inspired by Pacific Northwest Indian legends; an authentic Arabic version of *Aladdin*, and a Grimms Brothers version of *Snow White*. He wrote three musicals for Bellevue Children's Theatre, including *Ozma of Oz*.

His four-woman Victorian vampire thriller, *The Red Forest*, won 2nd Place at the 1987 Pacific Northwest Writers Conference. His Italian farce, *Stop the Wedding!*, was a finalist in the 1988 New City Theater Playwrights Festival. His new version of *Babes in Toyland*, with the original music of Victor Herbert, was the 1994 opening production of the new Village Theatre in Issaquah, Washington.

Charles Nitti is an internationally-published illustrator and a national award-winner for restaurant design. He created theatre sets for a presentation of Tennessee Williams' short stories for the Chicago Art Institute. He painted the Chicago Film Festival poster for 1985. A native Chicagoan, Nitti relocated to Seattle in 1995.

Recently he designed and painted trompe l'oeil and faux finishes in La Trinidad Church in San Fernando, California, as well as an outdoor mural in a drive-through museum in Venezuela and billboard art on the outsides of three 747 jets.